TWISTED
RETRIBUTION

DONNA ARP WEITZMAN

To all the women who suffer abuse
and resulting mental health struggles.
I pray your journey brings safety and peace.

Other books by Donna Arp Weitzman

Cinderella Has Cellulite and Other Musings of a Last Wife

Sex & the Siren: Tales of a Later Dater

The Wind Blew Innocent: A Memoir

Dear Melania: Love Advice from a Relationship Expert

I grew up on a farm in Montague County, Texas, near the Red River. The dirty river derived its name from the red mud that stuck to everything that came into contact with it. Montague County was the northern border, a 1930s iconic bridge separating the states of Texas and Oklahoma.

In 1979 cell phones didn't exist in Montague County, but the gossip that ensued on the party line phones served as the information source for most of its residents. I moved to the Dallas area for work, but being a Southern girl, I made sure to call my mother every week. She kept up with the local news through the thin weekly paper, the three available television stations, and of course, the hotline: her white wall phone.

One day she answered my call saying, "Donna, you'll never guess what happened!" I was mildly curious, thinking one of my mother's elderly friends had baked a festival-winning cake or a grandchild had helped win a local basketball tournament.

"Mrs. Rich was found murdered!" she breathed into the line. Murder in Montague County was rare, typically saved for dysfunctional families.

I couldn't believe what I was hearing. What? Who? And why would anyone kill Mrs. Rich?

My mother went on to tell me that a drifter had stayed with Mrs. Rich for several days working as her handyman. Mrs. Rich was a widow and would sometimes take in borders to help her meager social security check stretch farther.

"His name is Henry Lee Lucas," my mom said. "They say he chopped up her body and put it in a pot-bellied stove! Now he's on the run."

I was horrified by the thought of the elderly and frail Mrs. Rich dying in such a grizzly manner. The name Henry Lee Lucas has haunted me for four decades through the memories of a tiny town, a lonely old woman trying to survive, a knife sharp enough to cut bone, and a nasty, black potbellied stove serving as the corpse's coffin.

Later when I heard Lucas was caught, we learned he had likely killed other people. Rumors around Texas were that he was a cannibal, he had killed more than 500 people, and was a necrophiliac. Henry Lee became an informant with the state agencies and served as a consultant on murders committed throughout the US. He often admitted guilt to unlikely homicides so he could stay out of federal prison in Huntsville, Texas—a maximum security facility housing only the hardest of criminals. Henry Lee would live there until he died. Rumors again said he was a model inmate and even found religion, as many of the incarcerated do.

I hated this man although, thankfully, I never met him. My mother was not a close friend to Kate Rich but had known her most of her life. If Mrs. Rich could die at the hands of a deranged maniac, no one was safe.

Since 1979, every television show and news outlet

reporting on serial killers always revived the image of Lucas in my mind. When considering writing a crime thriller, he was my natural interest.

Twisted Retribution is not based on real life characters, nor are the names of any persons in the book accurate except the public names of Henry Lee Lucas and Ottis Toole. The book's characters are fictional accounts based on actual people who may or may not have committed any crimes in their lifetimes and are composites of some people I have known.

These characters, as all of us do, have periodically twisted thoughts, bizarre fantasies, and unmet needs. The difference between normal people and the characters in *Twisted Retribution* is a healthy psyche and loving heart. I'm not sure the people I dreamed up in this book possess either.

I hope you enjoy *Twisted Retribution* and momentarily put yourself in some of the situations the characters face. What would you do?

Donna Arp Weitzman

1

"Dear God, my face hurts."

Sarah prayed silently as she wiped the cuts across her cheek. Her mind raced, and she dabbed at the fresh blood stains covering previous scars made by her husband's right hand.

Sarah had made a promise to God that for better or worse, she'd stay with Pete forever. She told herself that God would reward her in Heaven for staying with her husband.

Blood erased and makeup applied, Sarah went downstairs to start dinner. "I'll make Pete's favorite tonight, pan-fried steak and potatoes," she told herself and then added, "I promise, God, to be a better wife."

Sarah was a fast and efficient cook because Pete had no patience for slow or messy. He wanted everything on the kitchen cleaned up by the time he sat down to eat.

"Put a lid on that meat," she scolded herself, knowing that any spattering grease spots from the frying pan might cause Pete to administer another blow to her body anywhere he could reach first.

"Stop the tears," she commanded. "God is with me! I'm a good wife." She prayed that her punishments from Pete remained the secrets of the Sears family. No one could ever know. He'd beat her to death if word ever got out.

"Honey, come to supper," she called up the staircase to her husband. Pete had worked as a telemarketer for many years, a new and growing trend in sales that allowed employees to work from home. The job required only a phone, and working at home proved ideal for Pete. He had free time to hunt and take on handy man projects as he chose. Money was much looser when Pete was officially employed. He was on the phone most of the day talking to customers in stilted, pseudo-friendly conversation. Pete hated most everyone he spoke to.

Sarah learned quickly never to interrupt his conversations. Any disturbance by her could set Pete off in a rampage. Someone would pay, either a sudden blow to the little black rescue dog they had early in their marriage or Sarah with some form of punishment.

"Honey, come to supper," she called softly again outside the door of an upstairs bedroom that Pete used as an office.

His steak and potatoes were half-finished when the house phone rang. Sarah picked up the receiver and greeted her daughter Olivia.

"Mom, I'm at church and won't be home until late," the teen informed her mother. Olivia was a church regular, unlike most fifteen-year-olds. Sarah's deep faith had penetrated Olivia's soul early in her life. For this, Sarah was grateful to God and especially to Reverend Thomas who headed their local congregation.

"Okay, baby. Say a prayer to God for me," Sarah said and hung up.

Pete, who had made his way downstairs to the kitchen by then, scowled at Sarah. "That kid just uses the church as an excuse to get out of housework. Can't you see that?"

Sarah nodded, afraid to disagree. She was thankful that Pete never lost his temper with Olivia. A loving mother will willingly take the abuse to save her children. Sarah accepted her fate alone, happy she could withstand the situation.

Sarah never gave up hope that Pete's temper would soften and he'd take Jesus in his heart. Jesus was the only way to salvation in Sarah's eyes.

Pete had nasty manners, never waiting for Sarah to join the meal. He was silent other than making chewing sounds with the meat. He peered at Sarah, finally barking, "Cover up your face. It's ugly and bruised."

Sarah immediately hurried up the stairs to do a better makeup job.

After his meal, her husband went back upstairs to watch his favorite Westerns on a small, black and white television in his office. Sarah cleaned the kitchen and later silently slid between the bed covers hoping he wouldn't demand sex. Sometimes after a beating, Pete was sexually aroused and forced Sarah to relent.

The clock seemed to tick faster as Sarah listened for Olivia walking down the upstairs hall to her bedroom. Finally, around 11:00, the familiar screech of the kitchen screen door announced Olivia had returned. Sarah, who was still alone in the bed, half-smiled and hoped to remain undisturbed the rest of the night. Maybe Pete would fall asleep on his office couch and not enter their bed tonight.

Saturday mornings were dangerous, as Pete didn't work. It was highly likely he would have a temper flare-up over something, with only God knowing the reason. Sarah busied herself, staying out of his line of sight. Olivia slept until after noon on many Saturdays.

Pete paid all the household and family expenses. Inflation was biting into the Sears household, especially with Pete's company spending less and less on their telemarketing division.

Pete's hours were dwindling, and the strain showed on the Sears family budget. "Goddammit!" Pete yelled one Saturday morning, throwing the family checkbook across the kitchen table. "Why in the hell do you spend so much?"

Sarah was silent.

She prayed that she might find outside work and Pete might agree for her to take a job. She knew this scenario could cause him to punish her, but maybe God could convince him it would help the family. Sarah glanced at Pete and barely made a sound when she spoke.

"Maybe I could find a job," she offered. Pete glared at her without responding and walked out the back door.

Sarah thought about the Sears' neighbor Johnny Campbell who worked for the Montague County sheriff's department as a deputy. He often chatted with Pete across the wire fence between their two properties, telling him the goings on in the little rural county. Sarah was fascinated by law enforcement. She believed wholeheartedly in the Old Testament principle of "an eye for an eye and a tooth for a tooth." This summed up Sarah's beliefs, except when it came to marriage. The woman must take a backseat only to her husband, not other men. Sarah had schooled Olivia early about never letting a man hit or abuse her.

"I promise, Mom. Nobody will hit me and get away with it," her daughter had assured her.

Today Johnny was cutting his grass close to the Sears' fence line. Olivia was out visiting friends. He waved at Pete, who started to walk his way. Sarah could hear the two men laughing and hoped Johnny's local stories would put Pete in a good mood.

She went out on the front porch and waved at Johnny, who called out, "Hey, Sarah, come here a minute." Sarah had a habit of doing what she was commanded, so she walked over to the men.

"Didn't you go to college?" Johnny asked, looking at her intently.

"Just for two years," Sarah answered apologetically, wary of Pete's demeanor. Pete never liked Sarah having any power over him, and Sarah never mentioned her two years at community college since she got her degree before Pete did.

"What did you study?" Johnny persisted.

Sarah hoped his conversation would end quickly. "Psychology," she murmured.

"Wow," Johnny smiled and continued. "We're gonna have an opening in the county sheriff's office. Having a little college might give you a leg up. Shoot, having a little extra money around the house is never bad. Right, Pete?"

Sarah was acutely aware of the danger lurking in this conversation. Pete was hiding his fury from Johnny but would unleash it when he and Sarah were alone later. His manhood had been threatened by his wife's discussing her uppity education with another man. Sarah would pay for this.

She hurried back in the house, leaving Pete silently fuming and Johnny unaware of the harm he'd done. She started rattling pans, making it obvious she was cooking supper and prayed Pete would collapse on the couch and let this one go.

She was opening the refrigerator just as Pete came charging through the back door. Stunned, she couldn't deflect Pete's fist jammed into her face and reeled from the blow. Pete wasn't finished with one hit. He grabbed her hair and pulled her head inside the cold ice box, its contents spilling on top of her head and falling on the floor.

Demeaned and injured, Sarah began to cry.

"Yeah, cry you stupid bitch. Call your mama," Pete taunted. "Pray, pray. That's all you do. How did I get stuck with such a bitch?" He stomped into the living room.

Sarah's head pounded and hands shook as she cleaned splashes of milk on the shelf where he had jammed her head. Pete would use any handy prop to get across his message.

Since it was a Saturday, Olivia would be home any moment now. Sarah had to hurry to finish dinner. Pete was quick to blame Sarah if it wasn't ready when he wanted to eat. He liked the family to sit together, the storybook family.

Sarah had learned efficiency was far better than the punishment for being slow. A pan-fried steak and microwave baked potato would do in a hurry. Sarah sliced the lettuce, marveling briefly at the clean, sharp blades whisking through the lettuce head. Only for the briefest of moments, she allowed a morbid fantasy of running the kitchen knife across Pete's bearded neck and watching oxblood liquid ooze out among the scraggly hairs.

Sarah immediately said a prayer to Jesus, asking his forgiveness. "Forgive me, Father, for I have sinned," she whispered faintly. Trusting Jesus, she felt relieved she had such a powerful supporter. Her devout belief made life bearable.

Olivia slammed the kitchen door, announcing her arrival. "Where've you been?" Sarah asked lovingly, but curiously. "I thought you'd be home a couple of hours ago."

Olivia grimaced but answered, "I stopped by the church. Reverend Thomas needed a volunteer for some things." Innocently wanting to help God's house. Sarah felt proud of her daughter.

"Do I need to offer to help too?" Sarah asked.

"No!" Olivia snapped. "I'm volunteering, and that's all the help he needs. You're always butting in."

"Well, let's eat then," Sarah said and left the subject alone. Olivia could be so difficult at times. Pete's temper was always boiling in her psyche, and Sarah certainly didn't need two difficult companions.

"Olivia, would you call your father?" Sarah was fighting back the tears, momentarily remembering the demeaning and hostile behavior Pete had administered only minutes before.

Entering the kitchen door, Pete blew a kiss to Olivia. He loved his daughter as only a man with his limitations could do. She was his blood, which was paramount to Pete.

Sarah sat down after Pete and Olivia had taken their seats. She was a good cook, and the steak was juicy and filling. The all-American family ate mostly in silence, emotional distance overwhelming the need to connect.

Olivia suddenly announced she had to go and left the table. Pete frowned, but Sarah never disciplined Olivia in Pete's presence. The girl seemed hurried and ran upstairs to her room. She returned donning a jacket, as the fall weather brought chilly nights.

"Where are you off to?" Pete questioned Olivia.

"Just with friends, Daddy," she answered as the door slammed and she was gone.

Sarah's instincts had been on high alert with Olivia over the last few months. She suspected an unknown boyfriend, maybe alcohol, and even drugs.

But what could she do? God said in the bible, "Spare the rod and spoil the child" didn't he? Sarah felt that Olivia was getting away with things she shouldn't because Pete provided cover for his only daughter.

Sarah observed Pete carefully as he slid the chair back to get up from the table. She desperately hoped for no more altercations. All she looked forward to for the remainder of this Saturday evening was being left alone, cleaning the kitchen quickly, and praying under the covers that Pete was too tired to say a word.

Sundays were Sarah's favorite day. She left early for Sunday school and always stayed for Reverend Thomas' powerful message from God. This weekly four-hour respite provided Sarah with the strength and sanity for another six and one-half days.

There were many weeks Pete didn't lay a hand on Sarah but instead chose to batter her emotionally. Belittling her looks, her aptitude for most anything, and speaking in harsh tones were his specialties. Pete only complimented his wife in the presence of others, and it served him well. He particularly liked to mention how he'd married a woman of God and that she'd never do anything to disappoint God.

"Sarah doesn't believe in divorce," he'd proudly state when neighbors announced another couple was breaking up. Sarah would nod dutifully in agreement.

Through beatings and insults, Sarah had begun to question her family bible. Weren't there instances when a broken family was better than an abusive one?

She trusted Reverend Thomas completely and stopped by his office to discuss this issue on a Wednesday afternoon under the guise of taking food to church members in need. His door was ajar and she saw the ever patient and wise Reverend Thomas bent over his bible in deep thought and obvious communion with God. Sarah was hesitant to interrupt. Lightly moving the heavy wooden door to his chambers, the reverend called out, "Sarah, is that you?"

Startled at his use of her name, Sarah instantly recoiled, afraid Pete would somehow find out she was discussing their marriage with a stranger. This might be grounds for another trip to the hospital where Sarah would have to feign a nasty fall again.

"Reverend Thomas, I'm so sorry to bother you," she began.

"Never a bother, Sarah," he said. The minister smiled and she relaxed. "You're one of my favorite regulars. I wish everyone at church was as devout and God-fearing as you."

Sarah slipped into the dark red upholstered chair in front of the massive wooden desk housing many books. Reverend Thomas sat in the creaky oak chair and rocked a bit, never taking his eyes from Sarah's face.

"Problems at home?" he quietly questioned.

Sarah could only manage a slight nod.

"Let's talk about it," he soothed. Sarah's eyes welled with tears, and her hands trembled.

"It's okay, Sarah," Reverend Thomas said. "Together we can overcome Satan's test. I'll help you be strong." By then Sarah was sobbing.

"Sarah, do you believe God forgives us regardless of our sins?" he asked.

"Yes sir," Sarah affirmed.

"Do you believe that murderers, adulterers, thieves, and so on can be forgiven if they ask God?"

Without hesitation, Sarah said a determined, "yes."

"Then if you trust God so thoroughly, why did you come to see me?" he wanted to know. "What keeps you from praying to God to ask for your sins to be forgiven? Have you done something you think our loving God won't forgive?"

"No, sir," Sarah said. "But I do think about maybe getting a divorce sometimes. I know God doesn't like divorce."

"No, he doesn't," added the reverend sharply. "In your wedding vows you made a covenant with God and your husband to love and obey your husband for better or for worse, for sickness and health..." His voice trailed off. "Do you now think this covenant is gone? That God forgot about it?"

"No, sir," Sarah said, wanting to set the record straight. "I believe in my vows." She looked down, not wanting to face a disciplinarian minister. "I just wanted to get your advice."

Reverend Thomas' demeanor changed instantly. Suddenly his voice was soft and loving again, and he stood up and knelt beside Sarah's chair. Taking her folded hands in his, he said, "Let's pray together. God tells us when there is more than one gathered in his presence, he will be with us." Together, their bodies near and heads almost touching, Sarah and Reverend Thomas prayed for Sarah to be a loving and obedient wife, asking God to forgive any meanness or resentment in her heart.

Sarah sat feeling relieved by the end of the prayer. Reverend Thomas suddenly pulled her close to his kneeling body. Nuzzling her ear and trying to kiss her skin lightly, he assured her that she needed a man's attention and strength. If her husband wasn't providing this, he would perform the task. It would ultimately make her marriage more solid and not hurt anyone.

Sarah felt baffled and guilty. Had she done something to entice Reverend Thomas?

"Lord, please forgive me," she begged in silence. Suddenly frozen with the possibility of Pete's retribution, she pulled away, saying nothing.

Gathering her purse and the tiny white leather bible her grandmother had given her when Sarah took Jesus in her heart, she hurriedly apologized to the preacher and left his office. She hoped he would not follow her or try to talk to her about what had happened, not ever. She desperately didn't want to lose her church family.

***

Sarah grew up in a small West Texas town called Nocona. Her parents were quintessential post-war working poor. Dad was a railroad worker and Mom sold Avon beauty products to stay-at-home mothers. Sarah was one of three children, a middle child who caused little disruption and grew up primed to please others. Her brother was an early Vietnam fighter, and her younger sister got pregnant in high school and left their town for the next little settlement down the road nearer to her young husband's family. Sarah was left at home with parents who were wounded by their own disappointments, including the trilogy of children they had produced. Sarah appeared to be headed for the same road to nothing when she graduated high school and stunned her parents by enrolling in a community college in hopes of a bright future.

A solid B student, Sarah remained in her parents' home to keep college costs down. They agreed to pay her way until she married, and Sarah did most of the housework in return. Never fathoming that a small-town Texas girl could have a future without a husband, her parents explained that the minute she married, she was her husband's responsibility. This was the way of the Lord. The woman leaves her parents and cleaves to her husband.

Sarah was raised in the Church of Christ, one of the most conservative religious groups in her county. No drinking, no dancing, no sexy clothes, and most other things "no." Along with her mother and sister, Sarah rarely missed either sermon delivered on Sunday mornings and Sunday nights. Wednesday night was for organized bible study, and she spent other times during the week at ad hoc meetings and volunteering.

Dutiful and devout, Sarah made one terrible, unforgivable mistake as a young adult. It would forever impact her well-being. At a weekend church retreat, one of the young men brought along his cousin, Pete Sears. Pete had just returned from Vietnam and was ready to cash in his Veterans Administration loan and find a suitable wife. Pete never liked courting women and was already unhappy with his station in life.

After a couple of unremarkable dates, Pete brought up marriage, quizzing Sarah about her plans for her future. A second-year psychology student, Sarah wondered how she would ever use her education. Her eyes were opened to the problems of mental health and unsavory behavior, but Freud's theories still sounded far-fetched to her within the limited surroundings of her community college.

Pete took Sarah to meet his mother and, pending her approval, planned to ask Sarah to marry. Pete's father chain smoked and had died young of lung cancer. Mother Sears was a leather-skinned, depressed matriarch who berated her two boys at every opportunity. It seemed she blamed her children for her undeserved poverty and ill health. She did read her bible, however, and was impressed that Sarah was a godly young woman.

At the first dinner Sarah shared with Mother Sears, Mother lambasted hippies, feminists, and abortion. She warned Sarah she would not stand for either of her boys marrying one of those crazy women. Pleased to allow Mother to have her way, Sarah assured her that although she'd gone to college a couple of years, she would be very happy making a wonderful home for Pete. The deal was sealed.

Sarah and Pete married at Sarah's parents' home one month later. Sarah's sister was her matron of honor. Pete's brother was his best man. Both Sarah's parents and Mother Sears sat at the head table at the reception, barely speaking yet hospitable for show in front of the neighbors who came by for barbecue.

Sarah had memorized the wedding vows. She promised God she'd be a great wife and meant every word of it. Pete seemed annoyed that the vows took so long during the ceremony. Sarah didn't understand why he obviously didn't like her pastor.

Pete was complicated in a simplistic country way. Sarah had studied bi-polar disorder but refused to allow herself to think about her new husband having such a serious malady.

She thought the war had taken a toll and with enough of her love and attention, he'd be okay. Pete was the younger of two boys and was drafted, while his daddy had feigned flat feet and got out of going to World War II. That lie lived with the Sears family, exacerbating Papa's guilt because two of his best friends and one of his cousins had died in France. Papa Sears took to drinking and cards. He established a mechanic shop in the backyard, and local men took their cars to him for a cheap fix.

By having his own scrappy little business, he could have a drink at his pleasure and rarely missed a card game when invited. His nasty temper got him ejected from higher class poker games at the VFW hall, so he mostly participated with the poor blacks and low-class drunks. An occasional black eye or cut across his greasy cheek showed his penchant for cheating the other players.

Sarah never met Papa Sears but instinctively knew she would not have liked this man. She heard horror stories of his abusive ways, beating his boys as children just to make his demons feel better. He was kind to no one and had no identified friends. His existence was animalistic, lashing out at his perceived enemies, existing on simple meals Mother pushed in front of him in the ramshackle kitchen, and sleeping alone on a cot stuck in the living room corner.

Four years before he died, Daddy Sears coughed up nasty brown phlegm. He didn't trust doctors and wouldn't pay for medical care of any kind. If any of the family got sick, Pete told Sarah they were expected to "suck it up."

When the cancer finally overwhelmed him at 48, he

looked decades older. A waste of a life, Daddy had done little for very few. His death was barely mourned by anyone. His sons lacked respect for their father, and Mother Sears paid him the only compliment she could muster. "He never beat me," she'd say when people asked about her dead husband. "He didn't believe in hitting a woman." With this, she seemed to show a smidgen of respect for the drunk.

At community college, Sarah had attended a beginner's course in child psychology. During the hastily arranged wedding plans, the nagging thought of an abused child likely becoming an abuser as an adult would creep through Sarah's psyche. Although this fact worried her regarding Pete, she willingly chose the path that she and Pete took and genuinely believed they would have a fairytale life. She'd keep the home spotless and make delicious meals. They'd hold each other into the wee hours and eventually when God chose, they'd have sweet, innocent babies. There was no hesitation in her mind that Pete was a family man.

Sarah's mother was obviously disappointed in her choice of husbands. She didn't say much and tried to go along with Sarah's excitement for her upcoming wedding. Together they planned the food, cake, and punch. There would never be any liquor in a Church of Christ parishioner's house, especially at weddings. Sarah would wear her best lace dress and carry fresh flowers. The wedding would be simple but lovely, much like its female participant.

During the ceremony, the pastor asked both Sarah and Pete to repeat after him as he spelled out the religious vows—Sarah hopeful, Pete resentful, the pastor suspicious of Pete's motive and Sarah's innocence.

The wedding was short, the bride kissed, the fresh bouquet thrown to a small gaggle of single church girls. Sarah was expected to take off her garter and give it to Pete. Embarrassed, she shyly raised her skirt and slowly slipped the band from her leg. Pete was instantly irritated. Under his breath but certainly loud enough for Sarah to hear him, he snapped, "Why the hell are you being so slow? Get the goddamned thing off." Sarah was startled and hurried to tear the elastic off her leg and thrust it into Pete's hand. He threw it to his buddies who were whooping and hollering by now.

The record player belted out a popular Frank Sinatra tune, and the guests urged Pete and Sarah to dance the first dance. Pete held Sarah tightly, making sure she was close enough to hear him whisper, "Let's get out of this place and go fuck."

Sarah was disturbed by his choice of words.

"Honey, there are guests here who came to our wedding," she reminded him.

"Fuck them. Your old man and old lady can feed them. That's the only reason they came—for a free meal."

Sarah was helpless. "Let me tell my parents we are leaving," she begged.

"Hurry up. Remember, you're mine tonight and from now on," he said, and a shiver ran down Sarah's back.

She made her way to her mother. "Pete wants to leave," she explained and tried to smile.

"What?" her mother asked and looked stunned. "All these neighbors and friends came to see you and congratulate you."

"I've got to go, Mama. I love you," Sarah said. She went toward Pete, and he grabbed her hand and led her outside to his used Chevrolet he'd bought when he returned from the war. Off to the honeymoon and a new life for Sarah and Pete.

***

Pete had insisted that they drive to Amarillo, Texas, for a few days. They'd call it their official honeymoon, but he just wanted to scout out some places to hunt deer and antelope in the fall. Pete was a huge fan of hunting any animal. He loved guns and was a good marksman. He made it clear before the wedding that he'd be gone hunting every fall, either alone or with some other guys. Either way, he planned on killing something, hopefully a big buck.

The Sears wedding day took place during the perfect late October weather on a warm, sunny Indian summer day. Driving to Amarillo, the weather started to change. West Texas wind gusts began blowing drifts of snow across the lonely highway. Darkness soon fell, and the only sound in Pete's Chevrolet was the radio. The dashboard lights cast a shadow on the glass, and Sarah could see herself in the window. Tiny tears had formed and were meandering down her cheeks. She rubbed the moisture and wondered what in the world was wrong with her. She should be laughing and happy.

After a couple of hours traveling through the snow flurries

and darkness, Pete wheeled into a motel in Childress, Texas. Reading the unfamiliar city limits sign, Sarah inquired, "I thought we were going to Amarillo for the night?"

"Well, aren't you the curious one?" Pete chided her. "What's wrong with this place?"

Sarah replied meekly, "Nothing."

The room was sparse and cheap. But Sarah was determined that her first married night would be romantic. She brought a lavender negligee set, gown, and robe and sprayed Chanel No. 5 on her wrists and neck. A neighbor of Sarah's mother had given Sarah a lingerie shower. Ladies throughout the small town brought negligees in all colors, along with pajamas, perfume, and make-up mirrors and brushes. Sarah loved it all. It had been difficult to decide which outfit to wear for her honeymoon night. She wanted to wow Pete and make him proud he'd married such a sexy woman.

Sarah was the last to bed that night. Pete was awake but under the covers when she exited the bathroom. Sarah, being a virgin, was new to this scene. Should she turn out the lights or leave enough light on to see Pete and he her? She slid in the bed and touched Pete on the face. He immediately rolled on top of her.

"Are you a virgin?" he demanded. Before she could answer, he half-shouted, "You better be!"

Then without tenderness or hesitation, he entered her vagina and thrust repeatedly until he stopped. Sarah was hurting, bleeding slightly. She wasn't sure she liked this new thing called sex. But she knew it was a part of being a good wife; God mandated it. So when Pete wanted sex, she would comply, faking happiness.

Pete seemed satisfied that it was Sarah's first time.

"Good," he sighed afterward. "I had whores in Saigon, and I sure didn't want to marry a woman some man has already soiled. Rape or not, I didn't want a whore for my wife." Sarah was oddly happy she had pleased Pete.

Sarah laid awake for hours, raw between her legs. Pete snored and took up much of the bed. He offered no gentleness or kindness, and Sarah quickly learned these would never be part of their relationship.

When dawn peeked through the cheap curtains, Sarah went to the bathroom and checked the overnight weather outside the small window. A thin coat of ice was spread over everything in sight. Sarah wanted coffee and something to eat. Instead, she climbed back into bed. Pete was awake and wanted to relieve himself inside Sarah.

"Dear God," she thought, "is this what the wife has to endure, sex anytime the man decides?" Sarah silently prayed. Again, salty tears spilled onto her cheeks as Pete grunted, heaving inside Sarah. Her rawness was sharp and painful. Pete was quick but hard and powerful. Neither said a word, before, during, or after the act. Pete got up and started the shower. Sarah took out a new outfit to wear before realizing it was too light to wear in this cold environment. She had no coat, boots, or gloves.

Silent and brooding, Pete went outside the motel room and started the car engine. It needed to warm up. Skipping a shower to be ready to go on Pete's timetable, Sarah made sure she got ready quickly. Today was the beginning of years of being prepared at a moment's notice. Pete would rule at all times; Sarah would comply.

A few miles from Amarillo, Pete announced he was hungry and that they'd eat at the next truck stop. Like long, straight and flat ribbons, the roads were dotted with brown, muddy snow. The truck stop Pete chose had provided overnight shelter for 18-wheelers and a few other snowbound travelers waiting out the storm. Pete wheeled the Chevy to a stop outside the newspaper racks by the front door. Sarah wondered what had happened back in her hometown overnight.

Opting for a booth, the skinny, unkempt waitress poured hot coffee for the honeymooners. She looked at the two, guessing they had eloped.

"What can I get you two?" the waitress smiled through a few missing and yellowed teeth. Pete seemed irritated with her. Sarah had learned the signs of methamphetamine use after observing some of her classmates at college, and this woman was most certainly a user. How sad, Sarah thought to herself.

"I'm starved," Sarah announced to both Pete and the waitress. "I'd like the pancake stack with whipped cream and strawberries."

Pete glared at his wife and then added he'd have two eggs over easy, bacon with biscuits, and white gravy. The waitress left for the kitchen.

Several men were talking and laughing loudly in a booth several feet away. Discussing the best times to get their rigs back out on Highway 10, they seemed unhurried. A tall driver who looked like a cowboy crawled out of the booth, headed toward the men's room. He smiled at Sarah and slightly winked. Embarrassed, Sarah suspected he instinctively knew she was no longer a virgin. She nodded at him, barely smiling and diverting her eyes.

The waitress brought more hot coffee, filling both their mugs. Pete's demeanor changed, and he looked agitated and nervous. Under his breath, he seethed at Sarah.

"You like that son of a bitch trucker?" he questioned her, mad as hell.

"No," Sarah whimpered, scared of Pete's temper.

"Bullshit," Pete hissed. "You know you were flirting with him."

"What are you talking about?" Sarah asked, barely whispering.

The waitress set the eggs and pancakes in front of the couple. She asked what else she could get them. Pete answered firmly, annoyed that she was interrupting. "We don't need anything else, thank you," he said.

After the waitress went back to the kitchen, Pete resumed his demands. "I asked if you like that son of a bitch."

"No," Sarah answered again.

"Liar!" Pete half-screamed at Sarah. "Let's let him see you like this and see how he likes you." Pete picked up the plate of pancakes and smashed the whipped cream in Sarah's face. Startled, Sarah shrieked.

"Come on, bitch," Pete said and pulled Sarah from the booth. He threw down some dollars and pushed her into the

Chevy. Reviving the engine and peeling out of the driveway onto the interstate, Sarah began to cry. Pete reached over and grabbed her hair, pulling her toward him.

"Unzip my pants, bitch. Suck me off," he yelled as he forced Sarah's head over his hard penis.

Another new act for Sarah, oral sex repulsed her. Sarah had dreamed that sex would involve sharing passionate kisses, long embraces, and whispering loving thoughts to the other person. Sex with her husband resembled none of her expectations and would not change in the years to come. Most times after Pete demanded sex and Sarah complied, she prayed long prayers to God to soften Pete's behavior. Someday when God was ready, she would tell herself, God would hear her and save her from her husband's crude and harsh behavior.

The city of Amarillo finally appeared in the windshield before them. A dusty, scrappy oil field town, Sarah was ready to go home to her mother. Of course, this wish was between her and God. Pete rented another cheap hotel room for a few hours and seemed in better spirits.

"Tonight at dusk, we're gonna drive to Dalhart," he said. "There's lots of antelope up that way, and maybe I can shoot one from the highway. Got to get there before total darkness."

"Isn't that against the law? Don't you need some kind of license?" Sarah inquired.

"Well, Miss Goody Two Shoes, what do you know about hunting?" he asked.

Intimidated, Sarah grew very quiet.

"You just shut the fuck up, and we'll be okay." Pete was pissed that Sarah had pointed out an error on Pete's part. Pete Sears didn't allow any criticism from his wife.

The day was long with Pete watching the little black and white television and Sarah writing thank you notes to people back home for their wedding gifts. Thankfully, no more sex. Sarah went out about noon and brought back two What-A-Burgers with fries and cokes. About 4:30 that afternoon, they got in the Chevy and headed for Dalhart.

***

Dalhart, Texas, is a long forgotten stop on the way to Colorado. Most people pull in only for gas and pre-heated tacos or chicken wings available at the local convenience store. Agitated that he didn't see any wildlife on the lonely stretch of state highway, Pete was even angrier that Sarah was worthless as a hunting companion.

On the way back from the dirty West Texas outpost, dusk was beginning to limit the view of the hills dotted with small, struggling cactus and other dryland plants. Pete demanded that Sarah keep a vigilant eye for antelope, but she often mistook a plant for an animal. This irritated Pete. "You're not good for nothing," he criticized. "Guess I'll have to drive and spot the antelope myself."

Over a small hill in the distance a small herd of antelopes froze, seeing the car lights. Pete whispered, "Don't move, you'll scare them." He quietly got out of the car, opened the trunk, and pulled out an enormous rifle. It had a big scope on top and seemed to Sarah about three feet long. She was paralyzed by fear, as were the magnificent animals.

A shot rang out, and one of the beasts fell over to his side and screamed in pain. The others scampered away almost in slow motion, unsure as to whether to aid their wounded relative or try to save their own hides. They left the scene, scattering to regroup later when their safety was less in peril.

The wounded animal was moving, dragging itself along the ground. Another car was approaching, its lights getting closer. Pete closed the trunk, laid the 30-30 rifle underneath the car on the ground, and slid in beside Sarah. "If that car stops to see what's the matter, tell them we were watching the moon. No problem. Show them your new wedding ring."

The car slowed, peering at Sarah and Pete. Country people stand ready to help travelers. It's not uncommon to find vehicle occupants frozen to death on the long stretches if there's car trouble. Pete signaled an "okay" sign, and the driver slightly smiled and drove past them into the darkness.

Pete hurried to grab the rifle, climb over the fence, and run up the hill to shoot the struggling animal. The second shot silenced it.

"C'mon!" Pete yelled to Sarah.

"What are we doing?" Sarah asked, slightly in shock after having witnessed a murder.

"We're gonna put him in the trunk," he said.

"What? Why?" Sarah gasped.

"Shut up and help," Pete demanded. Pete and Sarah together dragged the animal to the barbed wire fence.

Getting its carcass over the fence was a big problem. Sarah wasn't strong enough to lift it, and Pete couldn't do it alone.

Another car approached. "Dammit," Pete hissed, disgusted that a second vehicle was approaching. "Act like you're peeing."

Sarah looked perplexed.

"You heard me! Squat down and act like you're peeing!" Sarah did so and it worked. The car slowed and then gunned the engine, scurrying over the hill.

"Now let's get this damn thing in the trunk before we get caught," Pete commanded. He smashed the barbed wires to the ground, and he and Sarah heaved together pushing the antelope over it. Already bleeding from the rifle wounds, the animal was now scratched and bloody over its whole body. Sarah and Pete were also covered in blood.

This was Sarah's first time to watch a death. Although it made her feel squeamish, it was strangely exciting. Her heart beat rapidly. Once in the car headed back to Amarillo, Sarah glanced at Pete wondering what kind of sounds he might make if he was shot, death overtaking him.

Throughout her life, Sarah occasionally fantasized. The fantasy's subject matter varied depending on Sarah's experiences. Fantasizing about her husband dying was a new, odd experience. Sarah felt shame and guilt.

"Forgive me, Jesus. I am a sinner," she mumbled to herself and God.

"What did you say?" Pete demanded, instantly provoked.

"Nothing," Sarah answered. "Just coughing from the cold night air."

Pete grumbled under his breath. He knew an Amarillo taxidermist who asked no questions. Pete pulled in front of his shop and popped open the trunk. A foul smell permeated the air. The shop owner, a grizzly and fat West Texas man, was chewing a cigar when he spit—almost hitting Sarah's bloody flats.

"Well, I'd better get on this tomorrow," the man said. "We'll stick it in the freezer for tonight."

"How much?" Pete asked the animal stuffer.

"Oh, I dunno. About $200 and a few antelope steaks," the man offered.

"Deal," Pete said and nodded in agreement.

They both pulled the stiff, bloody carcass from the temporary car casket. Sarah stood quietly, aghast at her blood-stained clothing. She never planned on a hunting trip during her honeymoon.

Pete and the nasty meat cutter spoke a few more minutes before Pete told Sarah to get in the car. They drove back to the motel and peeled off their clothes that now had a disgusting stench. Pete got in the shower, making Sarah wait her turn. "Call Godfather's and get us a large pizza," he said from inside the shower. "Make sure they deliver it. And we'll need a six-pack of Budweiser." He ripped the plastic curtain back from his body and added, "Hey, put on some of that perfume," smiling faintly at Sarah.

As she mulled the phone book looking for the pizza delivery place, Sarah was so pleased that Pete had shown her some tenderness. Perhaps his tough demeanor was just temporary and part of his recovery from Vietnam. Sarah was certain things would get better.

Pete's hair was wet, and his body had the smell of Dial soap when he laid down on top of the bedspread. Sarah always pulled the covers back before lying down in her bed at home. She was meticulous inside her house, and these habits carried over wherever she was. But Pete was the boss, and if he wanted to lay on the bedspread, Sarah would stay quiet. She gathered her things and entered the bathroom.

Pete pulled twenty dollars out of his wallet, knowing the pizza man would be there shortly. "Hey, hurry up. You've still got to get the beer," he called out to Sarah as she was in the shower.

Sarah hurried, not taking time to let the hot water cleanse her body of the murder she'd just witnessed. Sarah pushed back any guilt and instead quickly washed her hair and tied it up in a rubber band. She dried each limb and pulled on one of Pete's shirts and her own pants.

"I'll be right back," she assured Pete. He nodded drowsily, and she headed out to find a Quick Stop or local liquor store. Sarah was twenty-one and had her driver's license. She didn't anticipate any problems getting a six-pack of Pete's favorite beer.

The pizza man was getting back in his car when Sarah wheeled into the motel parking lot a few minutes later. They exchanged pleasantries, and Sarah lightly rapped on the motel door, again very briefly disappointed in the outcome of her one and only honeymoon. Pete cracked the door, but upon seeing Sarah there, he seemed relieved. "Boy, am I hungry. Get in here," he said.

They opened the pizza box and tore into the sausage and cheese pie. Two bottles of brew completed the meal. Sarah sat on the edge of the bed, and Pete used the nightstand for a table. Although he was busy chomping his dinner, Sarah felt he was pleased that he had taken down an antelope. This success had put him in a good mood. Sarah realized then how important hunting animals was to Pete.

Pete looked at Sarah when they finished eating and said, "I thought you were going to put on that perfume."

Sarah smiled, gathering her negligee and dashing to the tiny bathroom. She would wear the red one tonight because she remembered reading once that men like women in red. She sprayed Chanel No. 5 on her wrist and neck and looked in the mirror. Sarah was satisfied with her looks.

Re-entering the bedroom, Pete had the light on. He stared at Sarah, who was becoming unsure of his mood. He grabbed her and pulled her onto the bed. Like the night before, Pete was forceful, not taking the time or making the effort to ask Sarah for input. He finished quickly and seemed ready to disconnect, both physically and emotionally. Suddenly Pete looked closer at Sarah's negligee. "Red is a whore's color," he stated. "In Saigon, the whores wore red panties. I had lots of whores. They cost about ten dollars every time. That sounds expensive, but whores might be cheaper than keeping you around. After all, I have to make you a living."

Sarah held her breath, and her stomach felt queasy.

"Well, I guess having you is better than a bunch of whores," Pete mused. "After all, I don't like sticking it in where another man's been. You better never have another man. I'll kill you both."

Somehow Sarah knew Pete was saying the gospel truth. The next day Pete was ready to go back to the little town of Nocona they would call home.

***

Pete had secured a VA college tuition loan and would enter the nearby two-year college in Gainesville in January. He thought a degree in the growing field of computer science would fulfill his need to make a living. The little wooden house Pete and Sarah rented needed a lot of work to make it presentable. The newlyweds stayed at Sarah's folks' home, while they scoured the garage sales and used furniture stores for a few pieces they needed to keep house. Pete was very helpful and mostly let Sarah make the decisions regarding what furniture to have in their new place. Sarah's mother made sure Sarah had a hope chest filled with dinnerware, towels, and bedding ready for use.

Pete received $400 per month from his VA check. His Chevy was paid for. Rent was $115 per month. The remaining money could stretch monthly without Sarah having to get a job. Pete was adamant that his wife not work outside the home.

A bit of luck landed in the Sears household the first few months they lived in their new home. Their neighbor was disabled and seemed very frail. She hobbled across the yard one day and knocked on Sarah's door.

"Hi, honey," she murmured. "I'm Mrs. Knox. I live next door."

"Hi," Sarah said and welcomed her inside. Mrs. Knox came in and sat briefly with Sarah in the spotless living room. The older woman seemed to take pride in the fact that Sarah knew how to make a home. She told Sarah of her advancing Parkinson's disease and how it had become impossible for her to do her laundry and change the sheets on her bed. Mrs. Knox explained that she got a small pension from her dead husband's social security. The two of them had also managed some savings, so she had enough money to pay someone to help her in the house. Would Sarah be interested? She would pay ten dollars per week, which would mean a little spending money for Sarah.

Sarah said she would have to talk to her husband. One problem was that she suspected she might be in the first few weeks of pregnancy. She had missed her period and felt nauseous last night when serving Pete's dinner. She didn't mention this fact, however, when she talked about the proposal to Pete that evening. He looked at Sarah warily. "Well, okay if you want to help her. But two things; don't you ever tell anyone I asked you to get a job, and the money is for the family, not just you."

Sarah agreed.

The arrangement worked very well and would stay intact for years between the two neighbors. Sarah was a godsend for Mrs. Knox. She never asked for more money, but occasionally Mrs. Knox would slip an extra ten-dollar bill into Sarah's hand, telling her she didn't have to tell Pete.

When Sarah discovered she was indeed pregnant, she worried about Pete's rough sex. One night, she mustered the bravado to mention that sex was painful, adding that she seemed to have a lot of urinary tract infections. Sarah had been to her doctor only once since confirming the pregnancy, and she told Pete that she burned upon urination and was worried.

Pete seemed concerned. He looked Sarah in the eye, never touching her, and said, "You'd better have that checked out. I got a venereal disease in Vietnam. I got treated right before I came home. You could have it."

Sarah felt faint. She made her way to the tiny bathroom and vomited. Her hatred for this man suddenly loomed clear. Her thoughts clouded her disgust.

Hidden in her mind was a fantasy where she could see a much stronger version of herself catching Pete unaware as he slept on the couch. She wanted to put her hands around his throat and cut off his air. She wanted to see him struggle, flailing his arms and kicking his legs until his last breath.

The doctor eased Sarah's mind later that week, letting her know there was no sign of venereal disease. He seemed ill at ease discussing this with the woman he had delivered when she was a baby. The kind doctor wiped away her tears, smiling and patting her tummy.

Baby Olivia was born September 15, 1973. Sarah saw the birth as a gift from God. She was a natural mother, and much to Sarah's surprise, Pete was a good father. He loved the baby and was less abusive to Sarah during the pregnancy. Quietly disappointed that there was not a Sears baby boy in the household, Pete never mentioned his preference to their precious daughter.

Regardless of Pete's random moments of kindness, Sarah had learned that she lived with an unpredictable, hot-tempered, demanding narcissist. But she believed wholeheartedly in her vows and the part about "whatever God put together no man should put asunder." She would be Pete's wife until death do them part.

However, Sarah did have a secret. While pregnant with Olivia, Sarah conspired with her physician to get birth control pills. She knew Pete would not have his wife killing his baby in her belly every month. Sarah prayed time and time again about using contraception. After months of stress and guilt, she decided God would forgive her for protecting herself against pregnancy. Sarah was particularly concerned about Pete's family's mental illness and passing on defective genes.

Before Olivia's birth, Sarah drove 18 miles to the next town and filled her prescription at the local pharmacy. She gave them the wrong phone number just in case they ever called her house. Her birth control pills were her savior. She looked forward to making the 18-mile trek every month and kept the pills between her bed frame and the mattress. Pete never made the bed, so this sanctuary proved a safe harbor.

Her husband hated his college courses but despised the thought of blue collar jobs even more. Forced to take the basics, including language arts, history, and science, it all proved a waste of time for him. His classes took up his mornings, and computer lab was in the afternoons.

This gave Sarah most of the day to care for Olivia, prepare nutritious dinners on a shoestring, and watch game shows as she waited for Pete to come home. She straightened and cleaned their tiny house in only moments every day.

Many nights Pete would demand Sarah to read his textbooks and do his papers. He would hand in the assignments the next day and try to stay out of the line of questioning in class. Sarah, having been a good student, was very helpful and Pete got high grades on her essays. Finals were particularly stressful as Pete was unprepared. Sarah usually got punished during this time, Pete berating her for not preparing him sufficiently.

Daydreams of a more interesting life would creep in Sarah's psyche, but knowing how to pursue any other course was impossible. Some afternoons, Sarah's mother would stop by for a visit. Neither of her parents was close to Pete, and Sarah's father especially kept his distance. Olivia wasn't close to either grandparent and would cry if they tried to hug her too close.

Pete and Sarah spent holidays with Mother Sears, who became more cynical and hateful by the day. Nothing was right or just in her narrow world.

Two years and several beatings later, Pete graduated with a computer science degree from the community college. Sarah invited all the family to his graduation, but only Sarah and Olivia attended. A little reception was planned at their home. Pete's brother and Mother Sears drove over for the gathering. Sarah's parents sat beside Mother for the first time since the traumatic wedding years earlier. Sarah's sister brought only her teenage daughter because rumors swirled that her husband didn't want anything to do with the uppity side of the family. In Sarah's world, that meant anyone with any college training. A college degree was almost unbearable for the small-minded hometown neighbors.

Even Reverend Thomas came by for a glass of mint ice cream punch and white cake. Sarah sat in uncomfortable awe of the pastor and could hardly take her gaze away from his deep-set eyes that never looked up. Sarah felt uneasy around him but wouldn't allow herself to ponder her feelings. The reverend patted Pete's back and hugged Sarah a little too tightly in an overly familiar manner. Only Sarah noticed. In small country towns, the man of the cloth was sacred.

***

Handy with tools and guns, Pete fixed up an old camper and planned a driving vacation to Colorado. It would be the first Sears vacation since killing the helpless antelope in Amarillo years before. After they returned home, Sarah would be thankful that no similar incidences had occurred.

Olivia was precocious and demanding. At four, she already seemed to have the upper hand against Sarah and knew that Pete would invariably support her. Sarah had much the same demeanor with her child that she chose with Pete: go along to get along.

After Sarah served his breakfast, she cleared the table quickly and it transformed into Pete's office where he made calls for the telemarketing job he landed after graduation.

The small house offered no respite for Sarah. She had to stay totally quiet because Pete was on the phone all day. The situation was claustrophobic. If Pete got a difficult client, he often diffused his temper by banging Sarah's head a few times.

After a while in these unbearable quarters, Pete said they could move to a bigger place if they could find something affordable. Sarah was ecstatic.

She perused the newspapers and kept an eye out for sale signs whenever she drove to the grocery store. There was a tiny, new subdivision outside of town. The houses looked similar in style but might be perfect for a small family.

Pete was somber about having only one daughter. Sarah had hesitatingly mentioned one day that her doctor had said Pete's venereal disease might have spoiled their chances. Pete wasn't totally convinced, but he didn't want to face anything that might lessen his manhood. So the Sears stayed a family of three.

Pete and Sarah drove out to see the little 1500-square-foot boxes. The inside was quite pretty with cheery kitchen wallpaper and a big fireplace in the family room. The master was on the west side and the other two bedrooms on the east upstairs. Pete could use one of the rooms for an office. The yard was red clay dirt, begging for seeds and water.

It was decided that Pete would take care of buying the house. Sarah was to pack everything and oversee the move. They could borrow a pick-up and take most of their dilapidated furniture over to the new house themselves. When moving day came, Sarah was so excited and believed

God was responsible for this new start. Pete, on the other hand, was stressed.

While trying to organize the essentials in the refrigerator, Olivia demanded milk at that moment. Sarah, bone-tired, found the child a clean glass and poured what was remaining from the carton. But Olivia wanted chocolate milk and Sarah couldn't find the Nestles. In defiance, Olivia spilled the white milk on the tiled kitchen floor before breaking the Libbey glass. Pete overheard the commotion.

"What's going in here?" he demanded.

"Olivia spilled her milk," Sarah replied.

"I did not," Olivia lied.

"Olivia, God will punish you for lying," Sarah said forcefully.

"And I'm the one who will punish you," Pete yelled at Sarah. Grabbing her hair, he pulled her shoulders to the floor, grinding her face in the milk and shards of glass. "We will see who gets punished!"

"Please stop," Sarah begged. This seemed to irritate him more. He grabbed her face and punched her right eye. "Never tell my child God will do anything to her. You keep your damned mouth shut!"

Sarah's expectations of a softer life in the new house diminished with this encounter, followed by more years and more beatings. "Dear God, why me?" she often questioned. With no warning, thoughts of seeing Pete's face being torn off the bone with sharp pieces of glass, him crying out for mercy, delighted Sarah. She shut it out instantly and pleaded, "What's wrong with me, God? Please purify me!"

The Sears household portrayed a simple, but sweet life to outsiders. Sarah carefully masked any tension that resided inside for the benefit of others, except Mrs. Knox. During the times Sarah couldn't camouflage her wounds, she drove over and hurriedly gathered Mrs. Knox's laundry to avoid an encounter with the old woman. But this plan usually failed, and Mrs. Knox saw Sarah's arm or face where the marks were evident. Mrs. Knox would shake her head and say how lucky she'd been as a wife to avoid being abused.

Within a few days after these encounters, Sarah could usually expect to find a few extra dollars in cash hidden in the laundry. The note would invariably read, "Dear Sarah, save this for you. You may need it someday. With love."

At the bottom of the note was a scribbled capital letter L, which was Mrs. Knox's signature for her first name, Lorene. Sarah would smile through tears and squirrel away the cash between the bedframe and the mattress, never considering what she might use it for.

***

Pete collected guns, far too many to fit the Sears' limited budget. He kept the weapons in the garage, most under lock and key. The car stayed outside, as it was less important than the arsenal Pete acquired throughout their years of marriage.

Rather than resenting the guns, the weapons fascinated Sarah. Working at home, Pete had many reasons to visit the office supply store. In his absence, Sarah would sneak into the garage and run her hands over the sleek wooden shafts of the shotguns and the rifles, never leaving a fingerprint. The handguns were even more interesting. The thought that a woman of Sarah's stature could carry a gun and so easily take someone's life would slip into Sarah's psyche. She wanted one of the pistols, not because she needed it but because she liked it.

She wondered what she could do to get Pete to offer her a handgun. Since he was at home most hours, she had no excuse to be afraid of burglars. Pete was an expert marksman, and a burglar would likely be easily foiled. The trees around their little subdivision were so young, even squirrels didn't climb the skimpy bark. So there was no need to shoot the squirrels in the trees. Maybe she should offer to go hunting with Pete, not knowing how this idea would settle with him. This way she could learn to handle guns of any size.

November first was coming, the opening day to hunt deer in Texas legally. Pete never missed opening day. He planned to go with two buddies he grew up with. They would spend a couple of nights in an old rotted out camper on ranch land about 120 miles west of their hometown. A butane stove kept them warm and allowed them to cook simple meals.

The hunting trip was Pete's pure joy. Packing for this adventure was one of the few times Pete smiled. Sarah made herself useful and packed a fully-cooked turkey and ham. These meats would keep a few days without refrigeration.

"Take care of Olivia and don't spend any money," Pete told Sarah as he climbed in the twelve-year-old pick-up he bought a few years before.

He rumbled off with two big rifles placed in an overhead gun rack near his head. The rifles showed through the back glass and enhanced Pete's tough guy image.

Sarah had saved about three hundred dollars from Mrs. Knox. This fund was dear to Sarah and totaled her entire savings. Pete often reminded Sarah she had no income, which equaled having no worth. Because he was quick to point out what a drag she was on his earnings, she tried to be very careful at the grocery store and never ordered much in the way of personal items for herself.

Sarah had these three days in November to ponder what to do with all her money. Why these greenbacks suddenly imparted to her a certain power and pleasure was a curious phenomenon to her. On the second day of her husband's absence, she hatched a plan. Olivia, now a pre-adolescent, went to stay with a neighbor's daughter several blocks away beyond eyesight of the Sears house. Sarah decided to go shopping.

She had little interest in buying anything for her appearance. Luxuries like new dresses, perfume, or shoes were rarely considered. Sarah was going gun shopping. Wal-Mart had a big, impersonal gun department.

She felt relatively safe buying from that retailer as Pete would never befriend Wal-Mart employees. She rolled the money into a tight ball, slipping it in the side pocket of her purse. Sarah breathed shallow breaths as she parked, went in, and walked toward the sports department. She could see scores of guns hanging on the walls, but she took special joy in seeing the handguns laying side by side in the glass cabinets.

A tall, lanky twenty-something man with two sizeable winged eagle tattoos, one on each arm, approached Sarah, who was staring at the gun cases.

"Do you want to see something, ma'am?" he questioned.

"Um, I'm not sure," she said. "I don't know anything about guns, especially handguns." Sarah continued her fascinated relationship with the guns beneath the glass counters. She was perplexed about which one she wanted to touch but was not hesitant about wanting to own a firearm. The thought of having her own gun seemed to quell the fiery stomach knot that had lived inside her belly since her wedding. But Sarah would not allow herself to think of using the gun, not even for her own safety.

"Well, ma'am, let's try this .38 special and maybe this 9mm," the skinny sales associate suggested as he took them out of the case. "These are great for a woman."

Looking at the man, Sarah reached for one of the weapons. Putting the cold steel in her hand, Sarah smiled. She imagined talking to Pete and proclaiming how now she'd be worth something.

"Do you have any more that a woman might like?" Sarah asked excitedly. The employee pulled out a .45 caliber handgun. "This one's awful big and powerful," the man warned Sarah.

With three weapons laying in front of her, Sarah debated her choices silently.

"Pick 'em up and see which one you like and how they feel," he told her.

Sarah fingered each one, cradling them and aiming them toward the wall. She liked them all but felt particularly comfortable with the .38.

"Do you have any bullets?" she asked.

"Of course," said the man. "A gun is no good without the bullets."

"Good," she said. "I'll take a box of bullets."

Sarah was unhappily surprised to learn that she had to register the gun. This was state law, the man explained. Should she lie or just hope this purchase never came to light? Sarah decided she'd be honest and take a horrible beating if Pete ever found out.

When the transaction was completed, Sarah practically skipped as she left the store, silently hoping none of Pete's acquaintances had seen her at the gun counter. Again, she had to take her chances.

In the car, Sarah ran her hand over the gun, hardly believing she owned it. She was in a hurry to get home with her prize, and she drove very tentatively, desperately hoping to avoid a car accident. A policeman would be a disaster for Sarah.

The gun would reside between the mattress and the bed frame beneath Sarah's head during the night, along with her birth control pills. She had a warm feeling knowing the weapon was there, loaded and ready to help in a second's notice.

Pete suddenly came into Sarah's thoughts that evening. She briefly imagined his forehead with a precise hole above his right eye, blood spilling into his eye socket. Shaking her head as if to scare away the demons, today was the first time she didn't ask God to forgive her. The .38 special would be her savior. The line was now crossed. Sarah could take care of herself.

***

Olivia returned the next morning, excited from being at her girlfriend's house, but she was as hateful as ever with her mother.

"Can I help you unpack?" Sarah asked lovingly.

"No, just leave me alone," Olivia snarled. Sarah's concern kept growing as Olivia showed more signs of the internal anger Sarah believed emanated from the Sears family gene pool. That night she prayed, "God, please purge my child from Satan's grip. Give her kindness and godliness."

The old pick-up's muffler announced Pete's arrival on the third day of the hunting trip. He propped up a deer rack in the bed of his truck, and the bloody carcass lay motionless while blackish liquid drained through the tailgate crack onto the ground. "Got one this morning," Pete said matter-of-factly. "Wasn't sure if I'd have any luck out there. Not many deer around." Pete seemed pleased he'd had success with such poor odds. Sarah wasn't surprised. Pete had been designated an expert marksman in Vietnam.

Thoughts of the Amarillo honeymoon and a dead antelope raced through Sarah's mind when Pete yelled out, "Help me get him out of the truck." Sarah helped Pete tug the animal out of the truck and into the garage. Laying it on plastic, Pete told Sarah to get the sharpest butcher knives out of the drawer in the kitchen.

Sarah promptly delivered two knives. "Let's carve up the meaty part of this," Pete explained. He didn't ask; he expected Sarah to participate. Sarah touched the cool steel of the knife's blade and then stabbed it in the deer's hide just above the leg bone. The ripping noise was distinctive, and the bloody flesh was faintly warm to Sarah's touch. She was not repulsed and wondered what it would be like to quarter fresh meat off a creature that had been alive at dawn that same day. Her mind thought of Pete and what it would look like for him to have a butcher knife sticking from his side, his warm blood puddling next to his feet.

"Hurry up," Pete demanded. "The meat will rot."

Sarah worked efficiently, slicing off big pieces that would become deer roasts and sausage. This job was one of the few times Pete and Sarah worked as a successful unit. The deer was scalped and its meat stripped within an hour. Pete left to take the remnants to the city dump and wash out the pick-up bed.

Sarah ran hot water over the knife blades. Just touching the heated steel caused heart palpitations. She went back into the garage to clean up the mess. Olivia walked into what looked like a crime scene and screeched, "What is all this meat?"

Sarah told her about the deer.

"Ewwww! I'm not touching this stuff," Olivia declared. Sarah knew that if Olivia didn't want to eat the deer, she wouldn't.

The little revolver under her bed crept back into Sarah's mind as she finished cleaning up. A sharp knife or a small gun, either one made Sarah feel strangely empowered. That night she slipped quietly to her bed, placing a sharp butcher knife next to the gun. Sarah had an arsenal.

***

Months and years went by and little changed for the Sears. Pete occasionally had fiery and abusive fits of anger and Sarah was the recipient. When Olivia became a teenager, Sarah could see that Pete's angry temperament festered in her body and surfaced toward Sarah whenever Olivia experienced any stress. Sarah was saddened that her baby and her husband shared the same bi-polar mental illness. It seemed unfair that poisonous semen tainted the Sears children and passed from one generation to the next.

Pete's employer, meanwhile, was now a regional service company experiencing overwhelming competition and considering a friendly buy out. This change of circumstances caused Pete distress and exacerbated the danger of spousal abuse for Sarah. He grew more withdrawn and suspicious. Sarah felt medication might help him but knew better than to make any suggestions.

Sarah's angst worked overtime in her daydreams and head games. With Pete withdrawing more into his office upstairs, Sarah was left with books and television. She read mostly either self-help or psychological thrillers. Television offered her a steady diet of murder mysteries. She particularly focused on shows that highlighted the sorrowful plights of women being abused. The anger inside her grew when women with no means of escape were interviewed on talk shows. Naturally drawn to psychology, Sarah felt a strong need to help those women, often divorcing her mind from her own state of misery and abuse. But Sarah's devotion to God remained unwavering. A woman who takes the wedding vows is married for life.

However, in drowsy half-awake moments during long nights, Sarah's thoughts grew hazy, yet purposeful. Women could be saviors for other women. After all, God sanctified motherhood, and Jesus revered his Mother Mary. Sarah's mind began edging to mania after each encounter with an abused woman she read about or saw on TV. She desperately wanted retribution for the woman and could vividly imagine the woman thanking her. Sarah knew she'd feel proud if she could help another woman in a similar situation. But at this point in Sarah's life, it was all a dream. Sarah was a homemaker and an abused woman. That spelled her whole existence.

2

Pete grew increasingly hostile and focused on money after his boss cut his hours at work, leaving him more time to sulk and blame Sarah for most everything. The Saturday morning when Pete chatted with his neighbor and Sarah at the fence line would change the Sears household in profound ways.

Sarah could not erase that Johnny had mentioned an opening at the county sheriff's department. She was intrigued. Seeing abuse firsthand would offer her opportunities to help so many women. How could she convince Pete to allow her to pursue this opportunity? He was easily agitated and intimidated if Sarah asked for any type of freedom.

Sarah became convinced that she must have this job, although she had no idea what the duties would be. She needed to act fast, as jobs dried up quickly in small towns. That evening she made an especially nice but small pot roast. She ate none of it, leaving all the meat for Pete and Olivia.

Olivia was at church for a youth event, leaving Sarah alone at the dinner table with Pete. Sarah hesitatingly brought up the conversation with the neighbor.

"I was thinking about the job that Johnny mentioned at the sheriff's department," she said. "I know money is tight. If I went to work, maybe it would really help out. I'd never let the housework or anything for you or Olivia go undone."

Total silence ensued before Pete finally answered hatefully, "You were thinking? Do you know how much trouble it is for everybody when you start thinking? I'll do the thinking around here. You just do what a wife's supposed to. Maybe more time in bed might work." Sarah's heart sank.

After Olivia made it home, Sarah warmed up a plate of food for her and then got ready for bed. Pete rarely went to bed early. He often sat in front of his television for hours late at night. Sarah stayed up late sometimes too when their daughter was older. She made sure Olivia did well at school and even assumed the role of a student once again to make sure Olivia received good grades. Sarah spent many nights working on Olivia's homework and special projects if the need arose.

Depressed and disappointed, tears dripped down Sarah's cheeks, and her hands shook as she washed her face and then got into bed. Anytime Sarah approached Pete with an idea, she felt his slap, either physically or from his angry rebuke, declaring her disgusting and incompetent.

Laying her hot cheek on the cool sheets, Sarah once more let her troubled mind take charge of her thoughts. The little voice inside her head swirled with questions that reminded her of life's inequities. *Why did God make men the stronger sex? Was the wife always expected to submit to her husband?*

As she slowly drifted to sleep, images of an antelope crying out and bleeding in Pete's trunk entered her mind. Years later the memories of pulling the bloody animal through the rancher's fence still induced excitement in Sarah's mind. She also felt a sense of fairness from knowing that others suffered pain in this world, even innocent creatures. Pain was a common denominator for Sarah and for so many others she related to.

Hours later, Pete crawled in bed, waking Sarah. She didn't move, barely breathing at his presence. For the briefest of moments, Sarah recalled *The Godfather* movie she and Pete saw years earlier. The gruesome scene of a bloody horse head underneath satin sheets had stayed with her for decades. What would Pete's head look like on their sweet-smelling white sheets if it were sawed from his body? Perhaps his scratchy, unkempt beard would be bloodstained, or his yellowed teeth would he clenched, a permanent look of terror in his eyes. It would take a large, sharp blade to get through his bony neck. To decapitate a man would be physically exhausting for the smaller, weaker sex. Sarah surmised that God must have decided women could be physically weaker, but mentally stronger, for a reason.

Within minutes, Pete was snoring and making grotesque sounds, sometimes gasping for breath. Sarah was sure he had sleep apnea and often wished his heart would stop so that his craggy breathing would stop mid-breath. Whenever she had these thoughts, Sarah would quickly beg God's forgiveness. She was a wife, and therefore was ordained to care for her one and only husband.

Slowly drifting to sleep, Sarah dared to hope Pete would soften his stance on her getting a job. Going to work could be her escape and therefore her salvation.

Nightmares often invaded Sarah's psyche, startling her awake at odd hours. Tonight was no different. The clock's bright light said twelve minutes past three. Sarah sat up in bed, trying to regain her wits. Tonight's dream was particularly upsetting. A man with a hood over his face was chasing a woman into darkened woods, pushing her into a brushy pit and throwing dirt over her. Gasping for breath, Sarah saw Pete standing on the edge of that pit, laughing and throwing clods of wet ground onto Sarah's back. Sarah clawed at the muddy bank of the slippery mounds but was quickly covered in sludge, Pete's laughter growing fainter.

At that moment, her eyes opened just in time to see Pete roll over in bed and turn toward Sarah, mouth agape. Sarah's urge was to grab a feather pillow and with all her strength cover his ugly mouth until he no longer moved.

"Stop it," she thought. "This is just a dream. Forgive me, God." She eventually slept again.

Sarah had Pete's coffee brewing and two eggs over easy when she heard rapping on the front door. "Who was knocking so early?" she thought. Johnny Campbell, dressed in his sheriff department khakis, grinned at Sarah as she opened the screen door.

"Hey," he said. "We've not found a good person to work in the sheriff's office. I thought I'd ask one more time."

Sarah didn't answer and did not invite him in, but

instead called up the stairs to Pete. "Pete, Johnny Campbell's down here, and your breakfast is ready."

Pete came down the stairs and went out on the porch, frowning at Sarah before slapping Johnny on the back. "What's up, John? You here to arrest me?" Pete joked.

"Nah," Johnny said. "I'm here to see if you'll let your wife at least fill in a few days while we look for a permanent clerk at the department."

Sarah didn't look at either man.

Johnny persisted. "We really need someone, and you could probably use a break from each other." Pete looked suspicious, as if Johnny knew the Sears' marital situation. "What do you say, man?" Johnny looked at Pete.

"Okay, but just a few days," Pete relented. "She's a mother and needs to be here taking care of our daughter."

"Shoot," Johnny said. "Olivia is almost grown. She should be taking care of you two."

"Would you like some breakfast?" Sarah asked, hoping to divert the tension.

"No thanks," Johnny replied. "I gotta get to the office. Sarah, can you be there at eight tomorrow morning?"

"Okay," Sarah agreed as Johnny slapped Pete on the back and stepped off the front porch, headed for the patrol car.

Pete's eyes pierced Sarah's back as they made their way back into the kitchen. The hair on her neck stood on end, expecting his fist at any moment. Sarah's body instinctively reacted to Pete's threats, much like a cowering animal. Bracing for a blow, Sarah did not lift the hot skillet off the burner, afraid she'd drop it if her body defended itself from

Pete. Instead, she reached for the bread slices in the toaster oven.

It looked like no beating would take place this morning, just Pete's sarcasm.

"If that son of a bitch would mind his own business, we'd all be better off," Pete was obviously mad at their neighbor. "Goddamn it. Why can't he get some other bitch to answer the goddamned phones at his goddamned office?" Pete stared at Sarah. "You better not let this house go while you're playing good cop, bad cop. You'll see what your husband thinks of you being Campbell's assistant, and it'll be a lesson you won't forget."

"I won't," Sarah whispered.

***

Sarah prepared a lunch of smothered steak, whipped potatoes, and freshly baked biscuits before she left for the sheriff's department. Up at 5:00 am to get everything done, Sarah had been too excited to eat a bite before pulling out of the driveway. An apple tucked in her handbag, Sarah would prove to everyone at her new employment how helpful and hardworking she could be.

She walked in the glass front doors and met two women who introduced themselves.

"Hi! I'm Ruby. This is Peg," one of them said and shook her hand. "Johnny said to be expecting you. We will show you what to do. If you have any questions, don't fail to ask," Ruby said and smiled. Peg nodded her head pleasantly at

Sarah.

These two women were the clerks. The men were the enforcers. Sarah didn't waste time worrying about equal employment or equal pay. Pete had trained her to be submissive. Sitting at a desk was more than she'd hoped for since marrying Pete.

She learned she would be the new voice of the Montague County sheriff's department as the main receptionist. This would be a dream come true.

Sarah was pleasant and efficient. Taking copious notes and cheerfully summoning the correct extension, the hours on her first day flew by. Ruby and Peg invited her to lunch, but Sarah didn't have money for food. She politely turned down their offer, thanking them profusely. When she got hungry, she bit into her apple, thinking how much she loved being with these women and helping victims on the phone.

"This is God's doing," she dared to admit. "Thank you, God!"

The next few nights were fraught with tension, and Sarah tried to steer clear of Pete after work. She made sure to have supper on the table at six. These days it was typically just the two of them, with Olivia gone more often than not at church or some youth activity. Never once did Pete ask about the new job.

On the second Friday of Sarah's employment, Ruby, who was the official office manager, handed Sarah an envelope. Sarah was reticent to open it, afraid it was a message that she was no longer needed. Instead, it was a check payable to Sarah Sears. Sarah thanked Ruby and beamed at both the women, safely putting her first paycheck in her purse. Sarah Sears was a real employee, a receptionist, a coworker.

"Thank you, Jesus!" she whispered as she made her way into the parking lot to go home.

Sarah proudly handed Pete the envelope when she walked into the living room.

"What's this?" he demanded, ripping open the top. "Oh," he acknowledged. "It's a paycheck. Well, ain't that special." He could not be happy for her, but Sarah could see signs that even Pete knew this little bonus would be helpful to the Sears household. Pete put the check in his pocket and later sat down to the meatloaf dinner Sarah had put in the crock pot that morning before work. They ate in silence. Olivia was volunteering at the church again that evening.

Pete was less combative after Sarah's first paycheck. He often made fun of her meager job, but the perceived threat to his manhood did not lead to a beating. Sarah believed God was working in Pete's soul, and a slightly softer Pete was emerging.

"God works in mysterious ways," Sarah thought as Pete's abuse diminished over the following months.

***

Both Sarah and Ruby were worried on Monday morning at 8:15 when Peg hadn't clocked in. Arriving at 8:25, Peg closed the office door, a rare occurrence.

"I need to talk to you both. I'm retiring next month after 32 years," Peg announced. Her eyes watery and her face flushed, Peg had obviously been crying.

"Why so sudden?" Ruby wanted to know.

"I need to rest," Peg continued. "I have pancreatic cancer, and the doctor gave me six months to a year. This place doesn't need a sick woman, and besides, you two can handle it."

Sarah was stunned, and Ruby began crying.

The silence was deafening. No other words were shared between the women the rest of the day, only police business and persistent phone calls. Sarah was even more efficient than ever, wondering how this turn of events would affect her job.

The county sheriff's department was a small coterie of dedicated but unhurried locals who enjoyed working at a steady government job. Small towns and rural counties have mostly petty crimes, often related to alcohol and drugs. Meth labs, drunken homegrowns, and violent divorces often filled the court dockets.

Sarah loved the esprit de corps the group exhibited. A prisoner could complain about the food, or being behind bars, but complaining about any of the department staff would only exacerbate his problems. His mealtimes might be forgotten, and his bread and dessert would mysteriously be left off his tray.

The county offered good benefits in an area of the country where jobs were nearly impossible to obtain. Sarah knew she was very lucky to have known Johnny.

Pete had little knack for education but an acute sense of the potential to lose control of his family. As his telemarketing hours continued dwindling, Pete grew increasingly agitated, spending more time watching television into the wee hours of the night. Paranoia was slowly overtaking his mind.

Sarah tried to avert any direct conversation with him and never mentioned her job. After Peg's resignation, Johnny Campbell urged Sarah to apply. If she got the job, she'd be the full-time supervisor of the clerks. Ruby, Sarah's coworker, was sixty and had no interest in furthering her career. She wholeheartedly supported Sarah wanting to apply for the job.

The night Sarah decided to discuss her opportunity with Pete, Olivia was once again absent at the dinner table because she was volunteering at Reverend Thomas' church. Pete and Sarah ate silently. Sarah mentioned Peg's pancreatic cancer and her inability to continue her duties. The department had posted her job, Sarah said, and several people thought Sarah should apply for it.

He violently pushed his half-eaten chicken toward Sarah, backing his chair from under the table. "I guess you think you could be the head clerk," he hissed. "Not surprising for a college girl," he mimicked Sarah. Her stomach was a knot and shoulders tense.

"Don't look at him," she reminded herself. "Please, God, help him settle down," she prayed.

Pete left the kitchen, leaving Sarah alone. She knew his behavior patterns. Leaving the room did not mean he was now peaceful. Sarah braced for his re-entry and the pounding blows or a slam to the floor. To her surprise, he stayed away.

She began to clean the table, still conscious of his presence in the adjoining room. He was pacing like a caged animal, lighting a cigarette and blowing smoke. He suddenly re-entered the kitchen, watching Sarah work on a sink load of dirty dishes.

"You clever, little bitch. Do you have the hots for one of those uniformed sons of bitches?"

"Not at all," Sarah said, furrowing her brow.

"You better never let me catch you. I'll kill you both! A deputy doesn't scare me," Pete bragged. "You seen those rifles in my pick-up? They work on humans too!"

Sarah was barely breathing.

"Okay, cunt," Pete said and stared at Sarah. "Take your little job, but don't think you can get away with not taking care of your family. I expect dinner and breakfast. And you better not be late coming home."

"I won't," Sarah uttered.

"We can use the money right now, but don't complain if you have to quit," he raged. "I figure you'll fuck up either here or at that shitty little sheriff's office. And don't try to sneak any money to the side. I'll know your tricks," Pete snarled and went upstairs to catch an episode of *The Rifleman*.

Sarah could hardly wait to go to bed. Tomorrow she could apply for the head clerk's position at the Montague County sheriff's department. God had smiled on Sarah tonight, and she thanked him as she dozed off.

***

With bacon frying and oatmeal cooking on the burner, Sarah was frantic to leave the house before Pete changed his mind. He had an early call list, and Sarah could hear him walking the call through the company sales protocol. After covering Pete's plate of eggs and bacon and placing a lid on the cereal, Sarah changed into her favorite of the five dresses she owned that were suitable for the office. The green color made her happy, and she felt it brought her the "luck of the Irish," although she wasn't sure she had any of the Emerald Islanders' bloodline.

Sarah brushed her hair and hoped soon she could get a haircut, but now was not the time for daydreaming. She had application papers to fill out. As she hurried down the stairs, Pete stood braced at the front door.

"Off to your stupid job?" he smirked.

Sarah nodded.

"Just so you won't forget who's boss," he stepped closer to Sarah and punched her right eye. Her neck felt the blow and careened back, giving her an immediate headache.

"Any problems remembering now?" he laughed at her.

"No, sir," she capitulated.

"Now get the fuck out of my sight, but you'd better be home on time, boss lady," Pete said, mocking Sarah.

Sarah's right eye had been colored many times in her married years. She knew how to cover the bruise and swelling with make-up she carried in her purse, but she still cried a few tears after every blow from her husband. How many women were in her situation? Sarah wondered, but she had no way of knowing.

Entering the small headquarters, Sarah stepped into Johnny's office. He looked up, suspicious of her swollen face. "What happened to you?" he asked, alarmed.

"Oh, just bad allergies," Sarah said and smiled, momentarily looking away from his questioning eyes.

"I'd sure like to apply for Peg's job," Sarah asked, slightly holding her breath.

"That's great!" he said. Johnny's chair made a screeching noise as he pushed it out from under his desk and opened a file drawer. "I'll get you the paperwork, and we'll see where it goes." He smiled at Sarah.

"Thank you, God," Sarah prayed under her breath. "I know you are good."

She went back to her desk and began working. The investigators' office was a wall away from Sarah's desk, and she often heard the two middle-aged white men assigned to various crimes laughing about some of the cases. A "crazy bitch" calling in about her old man hitting her was not uncommon. Wife beatings earned last place among the detectives' workload.

The investigators, Darrel and Homer were buddies and often worked a case together. Their day was a good one if a case closed, even though most often the final assessment was actually premature. Their day was a bad one if they got a call from state headquarters or had to assist a neighboring county.

Homer's teeth were heavily stained from chewing cigars, rarely lighting the ends. His belly overtook his khakis, making them ride perilously low on his torso. He heaved as he walked any distance more than five feet.

Darrel, Homer's' brother-in-law, was the stereotypical inept and lazy investigator. Taking advantage of his relationship with Homer, Darrel often claimed worsening allergies to stay home for the morning. If he was at the office, he often spent time flipping through hunting magazines.

Whenever Homer yelled, "Let's go get 'em!" Darrel recognized it was code for leaving the office to grab an oversized breakfast at the local Rosa's diner.

Sarah was the first person callers spoke with before she connected them to the detectives, and she always made detailed notes. She was empathetic with the victims, especially the whimpering, panicked women who reached out to the police for protection against a drunk, ranting husband, or lover. Sarah would promise these callers that an officer would be there shortly. Sometimes that happened, but most often Homer and Darrel ignored the domestic violence requests. They figured time would take care of the "mean bastard" and he'd sleep it off. Abused women were mostly a waste of time for law enforcement. The detectives also hated any Jews, despised the black part of town, and mostly ignored anyone they considered "white trash."

They snickered when an Indian-owned convenience store was robbed one time. Unless there was physical harm done to the proprietor or customers, calls from minority communities went unaddressed. Blacks were often pinned with any petty thefts such as stolen hubcaps or missing bicycles. Residents of Montague County mostly fended for themselves or asked for a neighbor's assistance. Homer's family was longtime friends with the elected county sheriff, Will Townsend, and felt certain any transgressions would be overlooked.

Rural sheriffs are typically the most powerful individuals in the county. They can incarcerate virtually at will and often dole out favors with the same fervor. Sheriff Will was a popular lawman because the crime rate for Montague County was practically absent, except for an occasional pot-head committing petty theft or a drunk roughhousing a buddy or his wife. Two detectives for such a sparse population wasn't unusual. If Sheriff Will felt two men were all that was needed to investigate crimes in his county, no one would question him.

Homer was a regular at the local diner, Darrel often in tow. Rosa's diner and gas station was the hub of local gossip, and citizens enjoyed rehashing crimes over hotcakes and biscuits and gravy. Nothing upset Homer more than being interrupted at a meal by a call from headquarters spelling out the latest misdeed. If a black was involved, Homer would make sure he had his Billy club handy and take Darrel to assist in the likely case that Homer would end up beating the suspect.

Homer's pals back at Rosa's would compliment Homer on his work when he returned to finish eating, commenting on how efficient Homer and Darrel were at keeping the peace. To Homer, investigating a crime was simply pinning someone with the misdeed and then beating out an admission of someone—guilt or innocence was unimportant.

Sarah learned the office routine quickly. Around 10:00 every morning, the two detectives would enter the back door, grab a cup of stale coffee, and question Sarah on any calls that might demand their attention. Most often, Sarah had already handled the situation. Afterward, the men spent the morning chatting—Homer smoking a cigar, often a good one he was given or had confiscated, and Darrel working on a pack of Camel straights.

Although disgusted with the men's attitude and demeanor, Sarah was fascinated with the crimes they so lightly dismissed. A crackhead cashing his grandmother's social security check; a worthless, unemployed child abuser reported by his neighbors; or a bar brawl from the night before ending in someone hospitalized and a demolished business.

Sarah often fantasized that she could stop these incidents if she was allowed a gun. A gun was a great equalizer in difficult situations.

Sarah particularly hated the abusers. "I'd show them," she'd think. "Damn bullies." She prayed for Jesus to take the hatred from her heart, but her resentment of thugs in power would not leave her.

Weekends were a flurry of housework and cooking for Sarah. She'd promised Pete she'd take care of the house just as she did before she entered the workforce. Pete had been even more critical of her homemaking and cooking skills since she was employed. Often spitting out her meatloaf or angrily pushing away her chicken-fried pan steak, he'd complain that a man should never have to eat such trash. However, Pete also seemed to like the extra money in the Sears budget.

One Saturday night Pete and Sarah were eating dinner when the wall phone's ring jarred their silence.

"Answer the damned thing," Pete demanded. Sarah ran to catch the next ring.

"Yes," Sarah was listening intently to the other end. "Okay, I'll make sure," she assured the caller. "I'll be down tomorrow afternoon," Sarah said and hung up the phone.

Sitting back down with Pete, Sarah announced that Homer had keeled over at Rosa's diner earlier that day. "He died at Memorial Hospital about an hour ago," she told Pete. "A heart attack they said."

"Why are they calling to tell you?" Pete inquired, anger in his voice.

"Homer's nephew, Darrel, is the assistant investigator. He wants me to handle the funeral, call all Homer's relatives, and make sure the county employees hear the news," Sarah explained. She was calm and factual. "I guess Homer's wife is in no shape to handle anything."

"Why that fat old broad probably couldn't get out of her chair to call anybody," Pete snapped. "I hated that man anyway, always driving his county patrol car, chewing on a cigar. Fat bastard deserved to die." Pete sopped a bite of steak in the cream gravy and stuffed it in his mouth.

"I told Darrel I'd come down to the office tomorrow afternoon and get everything organized," said Sarah.

"Of course, you did," Pete said with a mouthful of food. "Miss Efficiency. Miss Pleaser. Miss Do Good." Pete taunted his wife relentlessly. "Why don't you try to please your old man?"

Peter continued chewing and rattling his fork on the plate just to upset Sarah. She realized how much she hated this man but worried God was reading her mind. "I'm sorry, God," she thought. "I'll try to remember the good things about him."

The night brought crazy dreams again. Sarah pulling a gun and shooting Homer in his fat stomach; blood spurting out of his bulbous abdomen; and Homer's eyes bulging when he realized his time had come. Sarah imagined both the blacks and the white trash townspeople congratulating her at a 4th of July parade. Sarah Sears, their hero.

Sarah felt smug and happy that Home, the town bully, was dead. And she had done the deed. Just like Wonder Woman. Jolted awake by the noise of her husband's snoring, she realized it was only a dream, one of many she'd had since joining the sheriff's department. She dismissed the nightly fantasy and readied herself for the day's work informing everyone she could that Homer Wilson was dead.

The funeral was smaller than expected. In attendance were the county sheriff, a few neighboring county lawmen, Homer's immediate family, and a cadre of white supremacists angling for a fight with any blacks who might show up nearby to celebrate Homer's death. Darrel fidgeted in his pew, and he glanced around many times during the service. He knew his job could be on the line because Homer had shielded his inept performance for many years.

The funeral service was over quickly, and a few cars waited in line for the casket and the pallbearers to leave the chapel for the cemetery. Sarah looked professional wearing the black suit she'd bought on sale a few weeks earlier. "Why do I need a black suit?" she'd asked herself at the time. She now knew it was God's plan, as was everything in life.

The next day was Wednesday, and the morning was spent back at work as usual. Sarah handled the phone lines and typed reports.

Darrel came in early around 8:30 reeking of stale beer and sporting a scruffy beard. He probably had not shaved since Saturday, Sarah assumed.

"Will Townsend is here to see you," Sarah said to him. Will officed at the courthouse, not with his county staff, but he was stationed at Homer's desk this morning. Darrel was shocked to see his boss sitting in Homer's old chair.

"Darrel, this department is going to need you to step up and take Homer's place," Will announced, staring at the assistant investigator. "I'm afraid to post this job, as it might get attention from the state office. They've been wanting me to cut staff. If I cut out a job, I'll never get it back." Will knew how to play the government's game.

"Do you know anyone you trust to take your job so you can move into the lead investigator role?" Will was pursuing his plan not to make any waves in his personnel. Darrel looked at Sarah, who was standing next to his desk.

"Yes," Darrel said, seemingly more assured. "Meet Sarah Sears, this woman right here."

Sarah slightly gasped, muffling her surprise.

Will did not react. "A woman?" he said and raised an eyebrow.

Darrel continued, "Sarah handles most of the phone calls around here anyway and really understands the law." Sarah was stunned that Darrel was promoting her in front of the sheriff.

"Might look good to have a woman, now that I think about it," Will said, as much to himself as to Darrel and Sarah. "I'd be seen as progressive. Austin likes that." Austin was the state capital and the seat of government for Texas.

"I can't believe what I'm hearing," Sarah thought, reeling in shock. "Me. An investigator!" She tried to maintain her cool and simply nodded her head toward both men in agreement.

"What do you think, Sarah?" Will asked her.

She regained her composure and said, " I'll do my best, sir."

"Okay, then," the sheriff said and stood up from Homer's chair. "Let's give it a try. Don't let us down," he warned. "There's always gotta be a first."

He shook her hand and announced that he'd be back later to swear her in. Darrel and Ruby would serve as witnesses.

Sarah floated through the rest of her day, not believing she'd just been handed a job as an assistant investigator. She'd be given a state-owned official vehicle, a badge to wear on a uniformed shirt, and a state-issued handgun. These symbols of power aroused Sarah, and she continually glanced out the window eyeing the unmarked Ford that might become hers during the work week.

Darrel, meanwhile, sat in Homer's office all morning, half-pouting and half-smug. He was the new chief investigator, and Sarah Sears, his assistant investigator, could now do all his work. Nothing would have to change. Truth be told, he had grown tired of Homer being his boss, and now he was the boss. He reached in Homer's desk drawer and pinned on his bigger badge. Chest out and hand on his revolver, Darrel smiled at Sarah and went outside to get in his new state-owned Ford. Darrel was off to Rosa's diner.

That afternoon, Will returned and announced that his supervisor in Austin had hesitatingly agreed to try this experiment using a woman in a traditionally male role. He had warned Will that this better work and there better be no whining, crying, or complaining from her. Sarah smiled as Will relayed this information, but not too wide.

Oath taken, gun issued, and car keys delivered, Sarah was to stay at her current desk until another office clerk could be hired. Will would not allow a public job posting for Sarah's old position, again wanting to fly under the radar screen. Sarah was to find her replacement without fanfare.

No crimes were reported that day, and Sarah typed reports as usual, laying her Colt .45 beside her in case she was summoned. Sarah felt a strange power, much like her dream had foretold. It was as if God had transformed her into a real Wonder Woman. Sarah Sears had a mission now; crime would not be allowed to go free. Like the Old Testament offered, it would be an eye for an eye and a tooth for a tooth in this county. Montague County would not be the devil's workshop any longer. Sarah Sears was to be feared by criminals and cheered by God's people.

"Thank you, Jesus," she said softly, smiling as she packed up to go home and tell Pete the incredible news.

Sarah prevented any sour thoughts of Pete's reaction from invading her psyche. Somehow she'd convince him that if she was to work, she should try to make as much money as possible. This would be a second raise within a year of her employment. Of course, she'd never bring her achievements up to Pete; he'd likely slap her around for bragging. She'd downplay her promotion and gently mention getting her own car to drive. Sarah knew this entire scenario was fraught with danger. Pete's reactions were often inconsistent and hard to predetermine. But she had to let him know. Surprises were not allowed in the Sears household.

Dinner was the best time for discussions, and most often it was the only time to approach Pete when he wasn't already agitated by something else. Sarah was ready for flying dishes, a man's fist, or verbal abuse.

However, her newfound power began to well up in her body and mind.

"Will Townsend came over to the office today and asked Darrel to do Homer's old job," Sarah said flatly as they finished eating.

"Oh, another blind pig sucking up our taxes," Pete snarled. Sarah was silent.

"Darrel asked me to help him in the investigator's department," she stated flatly again. She held her eyes down away from Pete's.

"La tee da," Pete mocked. "So you're going to catch Alcatraz criminals in Montague County? How stupid. You and stupid Darrel, what a waste of taxpayer money."

Sarah sat motionless waiting for an eruption.

"Does this mean more money?" he inquired, almost civil.

Sarah answered, "For sure. It's a little more." She sat quiet again, nervous.

"Whatever," Pete said and acted disgusted. "One thing, bitch. No shrugging off your duties as a wife and a woman. This house better be clean, and you better not get uppity with me. I'll beat the hell out of you."

Silence befell the rest of the meal. Pete stared at Sarah when he finished eating, and he left the table without a word and without a tantrum. Sarah was relieved.

On Thursday morning, Sarah Sears reported for duty officially as Assistant Investigator for Montague County, Texas. She was ready for anything. God had a plan, and Sarah was his willing messenger.

***

The long, hot Texas summers seemed to mimic Satan's fiery hell and brought out people's demons. Summer typically saw crime rates increase, and even Montague County's rural population turned mean when the days and nights scorched the earth and stifled their breaths.

The phone rang more often in the sheriff's department,

keeping Sarah and Ruby busy manning the calls.

Johnny stopped by Sarah's office to congratulate her. He had just been promoted himself and would soon be the assistant sheriff in Gainesville, Texas. "Hey, Sarah," he said and smiled, spotting Sarah at the reception desk. "First, congratulations, and second, when are you getting out from behind that desk?"

"I will," Sarah answered and smiled back, careful to never appear flirty. "Just as soon as I find someone to replace me."

"Oh yeah," Johnny said. "I meant to mention that. My cousin's son is 21 and needs a job. Zach is a good kid, but he's not college material. All he really likes to do is look at his damned television and watch crime movies."

Sarah raised her eyebrow, wondering where this conversation was going. Zach sounded like a loser, among the many losers she already knew. Johnny continued, "He's really smart, but just kind of weird. He likes men."

"You got something against homos?" he asked in a lowered voice.

"Not really," Sarah said, hesitant.

Johnny continued, "You know, the sheriff doesn't want to post this job. Austin just waits for us to have an opening so they can freeze hiring. It's best to get the position filled right away."

Sarah nodded.

He continued, "Will you interview Zach? It would really help him and his parents for him to get a job."

"Sure," Sarah agreed, unsure where this conversation was going. "Monday okay?"

Johnny seemed glad she'd agreed to meet Zach. "Consider it a favor," Johnny said quietly and moved toward the front door.

"Johnny," Sarah said. " I really want to thank you for helping me get this job."

"No problem," he said. "What are friends for?"

Monday morning marked Sarah's first full week in her new role. The weekend had been tense as Pete took turns pouting and snapping at Sarah. She had fortunately evaded his hand and felt grateful to endure only his verbal outrage instead.

Sarah pulled up the driveway of the office and parked her new state car in the back parking lot. Johnny pulled in beside her, a young man sitting in the front seat beside him.

"Sarah Sears, meet Zach Turner." Johnny was happy to introduce the two. Sarah was slightly embarrassed and felt suddenly unworthy of her powerful position. She hoped this young man didn't think she was uppity.

"Hi Zach," Sarah said and smiled. Zach smiled back. "What a pleasant young man," Sarah thought. Although Zach was too skinny, he was good-looking with some feminine aspects.

The interview went well between Sarah and Zach. They bonded over a cup of coffee in the office kitchen while Sarah explained her old job to him. Sarah was anxious to get started reading all the criminal files and wanted to learn everything possible about the professional thugs who repeatedly broke the laws. Determined to be the best investigator ever in Montague County, Sarah agreed to recommend Zach for the front office job.

"A goddamned fag working in the sheriff's department?" Will would later exclaim, aghast at the idea initially when Sarah told him about the new hire. Then Will sat quietly and after a few minutes said, "What the hell? A homo should sit well with Austin. If you want to try him out, okay. But make sure he doesn't want to fuck the prisoners."

"Yes, sir," Sarah said. Sarah hid her surprise that Will would use such foul language. She'd heard much worse from her husband, but somehow felt the county sheriff would be more professional.

Zach seemed happy he was going to work and thanked Sarah for her support. "You won't be sorry. I'll be totally supportive of you. We can be friends," he promised her.

Sarah didn't know what to say about this comment.

3

The following week Sarah taught Zach how to answer the phone in a kind yet efficient way. She silently wondered if hearing a man's voice answer the phone would frighten women who might already be spooked by dialing the sheriff's department, but she kept quiet and let Zach answer each call, instructing him on the next step. Nothing too serious happened all week, just a runaway dog and a couple of fender benders on the county highway.

Sarah often fingered her newly issued Colt .45 in the holster throughout the day to give herself a sense of power and calm. She could hardly wait to investigate a real crime, hoping Darrel would let her take the lead.

The weeknights seemed to fly by, and Sarah had lots of chores to keep the house in perfect order and have meals prepared. Pete was surly and distant. He rarely came to bed when she did and often sat in front of his television watching *Gunsmoke* re-runs until after 2:00 in the morning. Sarah never addressed his odd night owl behavior, happy that he was preoccupied.

Early mornings were slow at the county office, and Zach liked to chat with Sarah to pass the time. Ruby played solitaire with a deck of cards. Although an unlikely duo, Zach and Sarah soon found they shared a common history, especially regarding how others had treated them all their lives. Zach explained his affection for other men to Sarah and described the heartache of growing up as a homosexual in a small, backward Texas community. The townspeople had taunted him, he said, and Sarah noticed how Zach's eyes turned cold whenever he recounted his past. Abuse was familiar to both Sarah and Zach.

They'd talk a while and sometimes fall silent into their private hells not disclosing further thoughts to the other. Zach did admit there were times he wanted to kill the straight, white homophobes who called him names and occasionally roughed him up. Sarah surprised herself when she told Zach her dreams about blood and decapitation. They would both smile devious smiles, vowing never to share such morbid secrets with anyone else.

One afternoon Zach answered the ringing phone in his now polished and professional voice, but raised an eyebrow and looked at Sarah as he took the message. "Yes ma'am," his voice lifted. "Our investigators will be right over. Have you contacted the police department?"

Sarah's heart starting pounding. Slamming down the phone and smiling at Sarah, Zach reported there had been a robbery at 1133 Bodark Street. Reading his notes, Zach explained that the intruders had tied Judy Franklin to her bedposts and taken her purse and her wedding ring before running out her side door. She watched them take off in a black pick-up before wrangling herself free. "Mrs. Franklin wants the sheriff to get the sons of bitches," Zach exclaimed, laughing.

Sarah told Zach to try to contact Darrel and tell him she would be the first one going to Mrs. Franklin's house. Sarah would take her statement and get on the case immediately.

The car threw gravel rock as Sarah sped out of the parking lot. She was excited and nervous at the same time. What if Judy Franklin wanted a man to investigate this crime instead? Sarah sped on toward 1133 Bodark.

"Goddamned sons of bitches," Mrs. Franklin said as she opened the door to let Sarah inside. She was not as frightened as she was just plain mad. "They're probably on drugs and needed money," she proclaimed, welcoming Sarah to take a seat in her living room.

Sarah nodded and opened her notebook to a clean page to take notes.

"I hope you find them and lock 'em up," Mrs. Franklin continued, enraged. "I don't give a damn about my wedding ring, and they didn't get much money. I'm just pissed off because they think they can get away with treating an old lady like that!"

Sarah took Mrs. Franklin's statement, inquiring how many men there were and getting a description of each one. She assured Mrs. Franklin that the sheriff's department would find these thugs. Instead of being grateful, the old lady sighed impatiently, lighting up a cigarette before tuning in to a morning television show and ignoring Sarah. When it was clear that Mrs. Franklin was tired of talking, Sarah excused herself and got back in her vehicle, aware that neighbors were watching.

A small town rarely let any kind of mischief go unnoticed. Prying eyes were always looking out for strangers and no-gooders. Sarah felt intimidated and uncomfortable walking in Rosa's looking for Darrel to update him. She saw him sitting in a booth behind a stack of pancakes. When he saw her coming toward him, Darrel yelled out, "You already got 'em, Deputy Sears?"

Sarah smiled and said, "No, sir. But I'm on it." Darrel returned to his pancakes.

She walked to each booth and asked the customers if anyone knew any younger men who drove a black pick-up. "The make and model are unknown as of yet," she explained. They shook their heads, seemingly disappointed to be in the dark about such a momentous event happening in their town. A burglary in Montague County was big news.

Relentlessly questioning more townspeople finally yielded Sarah her lead. The Turners lived on the edge of town. Their nephew showed up a few weeks ago and had been staying with them until he found work. He drove a black pick-up and had apparently upset everyone on the road into town as he sped down the lane every day. His careless driving scared the old people who liked to stand at their mailboxes and chat with neighbors.

"Yep, this one's a wild child," said one of the Turners' neighbors. Just the kind to rob an old lady, Sarah thought.

Sarah staked out the Turners' street and waited patiently

one afternoon. Two days had passed since the crime occurred, and Sarah was anxious to pull her gun if she needed to. The roar of an engine whirred past her parked car. Sure enough, it was a speeding black pick-up. Sarah took off behind it. Dust bellowed up and made it impossible to see inside the vehicle. Then a beer can flew out the passenger side, telling Sarah there were more occupants than the driver inside. Following the truck to the Turner home, Sarah saw two young guys hop out and pulled in the drive behind them.

Hurriedly, she got out of her car and yelled toward the men, "I'm Deputy Sarah Sears with the county sheriff's department, and I'd like to have a word with you."

The two scraggly boys grinned at each other and jumped back in their truck. They almost clipped Sarah's car as they sped out of the drive. Sarah was stunned. Feeling incompetent, she got back in her vehicle and raced after them.

"Dammit," Sarah said aloud. "Why didn't I get their license plate number? Come on, Sears, use your head."

She drove every nearby street looking for the two hoodlums, but saw no black truck. Stopping for gas, Sarah spied a twenty-something male working in the gas station garage.

"Hi, do you happen to know anyone around town with a black

pick-up?" she asked.

The kid nodded. "Yeah, I put a muffler on one the other day."

Sarah was encouraged. "Do you know the owner's

name?" The young man eyed her, barely answering, "I think it's Jake Turner, but not sure."

"You wouldn't happen to know where he hangs out, would you?" Sarah spoke gently to the mechanic, as she didn't want him to clam up.

"Well, I know he and his buddy Clem Dodson like to drink beer and fish a little in Red River under the Oklahoma bridge. Maybe they're over there?"

"Thank you," Sarah said and gave him a couple of dollars. She'd never been under the bridge, but she had heard the stories of druggies and drunks hanging out there.

Turning off her car engine and parking hundreds of feet before reaching the bridge, Sarah pushed back the prickly brush on the side of the road, trying to see under the bridge without being seen. However, even before she spied the two men, she could hear them laughing and cursing. Sarah pulled her gun. Her hands shook and her heart pounded as she approached two males sitting on a couple of tree stumps.

She pointed the gun at them and yelled, "I said I want to talk to you both!"

Startled, they both stood up and stared at Sarah. "What for, ma'am?" the driver asked her in a polite voice. Sarah assumed this was the Turner boy, but she did not recognize his companion.

"You know," Sarah growled. "I think you robbed Mrs. Franklin on Bodark Street."

"Are you crazy?" the Turner kid smiled at Sarah. "That old bitch wouldn't have anything we'd want."

"Still, I need to ask you some questions," Sarah answered,

her hands visibly trembling.

The other man reached his hand in his pocket, making Sarah nervous. She turned to look at him and Jake Turner suddenly grabbed her arm and peeled the gun from Sarah's hand.

"Well, well, lookey what we got here, Clem. A pretty law woman. What'd you say? Let's show her what sneaking up on two fishermen can get her. Tie her up."

Clem got some ropes from the old black truck while Jake held her own gun on Sarah. "You make a move, little law whore, and this gun might go off. Wouldn't that be a shame?" he said.

Clem tied her arms to a dead tree trunk that was on the ground and then with a second rope tied her legs to the trunk, spreading them apart. Sarah was gasping for breath, yet she was afraid to fight back and agitate the men.

Suddenly Jake unbuttoned and jerked her khaki patrol pants off her legs and pulled her panties down. He started laughing, eyeing Sarah's naked body before he rammed his hand up her vagina.

"Never follow two fishermen, bitch. You might get caught," he said, grinning. Climbing on top of Sarah, he relieved himself hurriedly inside her and then invited his accomplice to take a turn.

"Go on, Clem. It might be a while before we get some more pussy," Jake said. "Hers ain't bad for an old sheriff bitch."

Clem was rough but didn't say a word. He finished quickly and rolled off Sarah. Hot tears welled up, but she refused to cry. She was afraid these two might decide to kill her and throw her body in the Red River. She lay silent.

"Come on, Clem," Jake said walking away from her. "Let's get the hell out of here. Let's go to Oklahoma. She ain't going anywhere soon. We'll go across the bridge and be in OK City before anyone finds her. I'm tired of this two-bit town."

The black pick-up careened out of the mud and made its way back up on the country road.

When she was sure they were gone, she began struggling to untie the ropes. No one knew where she was. Vultures flew overhead in a circle, and the muddy red water lapped at the river banks inviting Sarah to join its watery grave. Sarah was determined to live but told herself that others would die. She'd had enough of being the victim. From now on, Sarah Sears would control the scene. Finally getting some slack in the rope, she slipped a hand through the knotted loop to work her way free.

"I'll kill those assholes," she thought, "and I'll do it my way. They will suffer. An eye for an eye and a tooth for a tooth."

On the way back to the sheriff's office, Sarah stopped at the convenience store to wash herself in the public bathroom. No one must know about the rape. She alone would get her revenge.

Sarah saw Zach when she returned to the office.

"How's it going?" he asked, anxious to get details.

Sarah didn't comply, keeping her secret for now. "Haven't found them yet," she lied, "but got some good leads."

"Anything I can do to help?"

"Nope, just make sure Darrel doesn't get a wild hair to help on this case. I really want to catch these jerks myself. Tomorrow I won't be in. I'm going to track them down."

"Okay," Zach said, "but be careful. Sarah, you're just a woman."

"Thanks, Zach, and you're just a man," Sarah answered, trying not to laugh.

Zach smiled with brotherly concern for Sarah.

***

Leaving her house before daylight the next day, she could hear Pete snoring on his little sofa in his office. Sarah had become so preoccupied with catching criminals that she didn't have the energy to focus on protecting herself from Pete's ire. He seemed less ominous as her world expanded.

Heading north across the Red River Bridge to Oklahoma, Sarah had a plan in mind. She remembered her rape in detail. The ordeal was quick but rough, neither man having respect for Sarah or himself. Much like rabid dogs in heat, they'd acted like animals, overpowering the weak. And what did you do with rabid dogs? Put them to death.

Sarah was prepared this time with Pete's ropes and some sharp kitchen knives carefully stowed in the patrol car. Sarah would become a cunning prowess hunting her prey and use her Colt .45 and any other means to help her overcome these offenders. Death was appropriate for dogs like Jake Turner and his sidekick.

Southern Oklahoma's hardscrabble farms were hostile to the easy life. Some properties had sandy soil, ideal for growing watermelons. But others were red clay, and anything proved difficult to grow. Farmers drove their hay bailers on the highway, waving as Sarah veered around these slow-moving workhorses. Most Okies were kind, docile people, but not the two escapees traveling these roads. Sarah was determined these two would pay.

Waurika, Oklahoma, was a small farming town with a greasy café on the main drag. Wrapping around the restaurant on both sides was a mostly vacant motel, each room's door opening to the pavement where guests parked their cars for the night. A muddy, battered black pick-up was parked in one of the spaces.

Sarah parked her patrol car in the shadow and grabbed the handle of the big kitchen knife on the front seat. She wrapped several lengths of rope over her shoulder. Quietly she crept beside the pick-up truck and stabbed each tire with the knife's sharp point as air spewed out.

Sarah hoped to corner the men in their room. She rapped on the door in front of the hobbled truck.

"Maid service," she chirped.

"Get out of here! We're sleeping," a male voice said. Sarah recognized Jake's voice.

"Sorry, sir, but I have something for you."

She heard someone coming to the door.

When Jake cracked it open, Sarah pushed her way in and rammed the .45 into his stomach.

"Sit down on the bed!" Sarah ordered. "I know how to

use this gun." Jake stepped backward and fell onto the twin bed, stunned. Clem was snoring on the other twin bed, likely fighting off a whiskey hangover.

"I will kill you," Sarah assured Jake. He believed her. "Lie down on the bed and keep your mouth shut."

He did as she demanded. She tied his arms to the bedposts, just as he'd done to Mrs. Franklin, and unzipped Jake's jeans before pulling his briefs around his ankles. Clem was next. She secured his arms to his bed, waking him only after she had him tied up. She pulled down his pants likewise.

"Shut up," she hissed at Clem, "or you'll die." Sarah rammed a washcloth from the bathroom in Clem's mouth, rendering him speechless.

Sarah's mind had taken control of the situation. She was no longer the obedient, frightened victim but rather the master over these criminals' fate. The one who would rid the world of them and other sorry souls. Her purpose was clear: kill Jake Turner, and save the women he'd likely abuse in the future. Sarah had no choice. She stuffed another washcloth into Jake's mouth and shoved it down his throat as he struggled against her. Placing her gun on his scrotum, she slowly pulled the trigger and shot Jake point blank. Blood spurted from his sack, oozing onto the bed and onto the floor. Jake Turner's life was draining out on the dirty carpet of a cheap motel.

Clem's eyes showed his panic. He whimpered, begging like the cowardly animal he was.

"You made your choice, Clem," Sarah explained with no emotion in her voice. She was determined that no woman would ever suffer anything this man might attempt in the future. Her vagina twinged, remembering Clem clawing at her breast, as she aimed and shot Clem's penis clean off his body. Blood shot straight up and soaked his torso.

"Good bye, Clem," Sarah said and smiled. The sight of so much blood thrilled her. She sat down in a chair, watching both men succumb to Sarah Sears. She had cleansed God's world of two devils.

The gun she cherished was now a problem. The bullets could be traced to her weapon and implicate Sarah in the boys' deaths. Quickly she concocted a story that would surely suffice in the lazy Montague County sheriff's department.

After ransacking the room and making it look like the scene of a robbery and murder, Sarah drove immediately back to her office. She stopped briefly on the lonely bridge over the Red River and wiped her gun clean of fingerprints before she threw it in the muddy water. Sarah was confident she'd be issued another Colt .45 because she'd report that the two thugs had stolen her gun two days before. She felt sure Zach would gladly serve as a witness to anything she said. Zach was becoming vital to Sarah's plan of becoming a better crime fighter. God and Zach were her partners.

Since the double murder would be reported in Oklahoma, Darrel would write it off and be happy he didn't have to do anything more. It would soon be back to business as usual, exactly how Darrel liked the sheriff's department to run. No doubt he'd criticize Sarah for losing her gun, but he would issue her another one so that she could keep doing her job. Doing her job assured him the opportunity of more lazy days eating and drinking.

Sarah had a slight feeling of nausea as she parked outside the office, but mostly, she felt smug. An eye for an eye and a scrotum for a vagina, in this case, hers.

"Thank you, God, for giving me the strength to do your will," Sarah prayed. After she left the office and headed home, she remembered she would need to have Pete's supper ready on time.

***

Olivia and Pete were standing on the driveway when Sarah drove up. Wary of interacting with Pete, she got out of the car, looked at Olivia, and asked, "What's going on?"

Olivia looked anxious to tell a story. "Mom, you know my friend Cynthia Stevens?"

"Yes, why?" Sarah inquired.

"She died today."

Sarah was shocked. Cynthia was a positive role model for Olivia. She was a good student and was always helping at their church.

"What happened?" Sarah asked.

"Her mother said it was a drug overdose."

"Olivia, did you know Cynthia was taking drugs?"

"No," Olivia said a little too quickly and looked away, appearing pale and shaken.

Sarah didn't believe her, but she knew better than to question Olivia more in front of Pete. No reason to agitate Pete, she reminded herself, and let her suspicions drop.

"Has Mrs. Stevens contacted the police?" Sarah asked.

Pete mocked, "Oh yeah, that's right, Miss Important. Miss Annie Oakley needs to make sure the law is involved. That's all you think about, meddling in other people's business."

Sarah smelled trouble from Pete, so she walked inside the house, letting the conversation die. She decided the best course of action was to make sure Pete's dinner was on the table. Then she'd call Mrs. Stevens and ask how she could help, including making sure the proper authorities were notified.

After supper Sarah picked up the phone and called Cynthia's mother.

"Delores," Sarah began when Delores Stevens answered the phone, "this is Sarah Sears, Olivia's mother."

Mrs. Stevens mumbled something unintelligible, obviously grieved.

"I'm so sorry to hear about Cynthia," Sarah continued. "Is there anything I can do?"

A long pause ensued before Mrs. Stevens answered Sarah. "Yes, you can do something. Don't you work for the police?"

"The sheriff's department," Sarah replied.

"Can you find out who was giving her drugs? They killed my baby girl." The distraught mother began to cry.

A lump instantly formed in Sarah's throat, making it difficult to answer Cynthia's mother. "I will sure try," she assured Delores. Sarah took a few more minutes with the mother to get her statement on record. Delores explained that she did not want an autopsy performed.

"Reverend Thomas is doing the funeral on Saturday," Delores added before hanging up the phone.

Pete grunted and pushed his chair across the kitchen floor. "Come clean up this mess, Inspector Clouseau. You know our deal."

Sarah began putting dishes in the sink. She loved her job and needed to keep Pete as calm as she could to keep it.

"I got stuff to do upstairs," Pete said and left the kitchen.

"Good night," Sarah offered. Pete didn't answer.

Suddenly Sarah felt odd, almost as if a trance was overtaking her. She remembered every detail of killing those two thugs—tying them to the bedpost, aiming the gun, and pulling the trigger. As she recalled how the blood spurted from their bodies, she felt strangely satisfied. Sarah Sears loved justice and was happy she alone could administer it.

As she got ready for bed, her mind moved to Cynthia. So young, pretty, and vivacious—how could the devil get to this innocent girl, hooking her on drugs and rendering her helpless? Sarah imagined some bastard offering pills to Cynthia and the poor girl wanting to please him and not hurt his feelings. This person deserved to die. Sarah would hunt him down and kill him just as he killed Cynthia Stevens. An eye for an eye.

Sarah slept fitfully, waking around 2:00 in the morning with the sensation of hot blood running through her hair. She imagined Jake and Clem's faces as no longer part of their bodies. Sarah could only see blood running off their shattered pelvises. She realized she had been dreaming. It wasn't a nightmare, just a dream, because she and God had a pact. She would be his instrument to fight the devil and help win God's war against evil.

Now acutely aware of her next mission, Sarah planned how she would find the drug dealer and kill him. This work had to be done to save more girls like Cynthia and maybe even Olivia one day.

She would begin her search in a few hours. Sleep eluded her the rest of the night, and dawn brought renewed faith that Sarah was the one for the job. God had planned Sarah's life, and she was fulfilling it.

***

After putting Pete's breakfast in the skillet to cook, Sarah dressed hurriedly and returned to the kitchen. Sarah spooned out scrambled eggs and placed three pieces of bacon on his plate. Suddenly she realized his toast was not ready.

"I'm sorry," she addressed him. "I'll get your toast in a second."

"A second, a minute later...it's always an excuse with you, bitch," Pete said. He was seething at this offense.

Sarah leaned over the counter to take bread out of the toaster oven when Pete suddenly grabbed her from behind and pushed her forward. He pulled down her work pants and her panties, unzipping his jeans. Without a word, he started thrusting her from the back, ramming her head into the wooden cabinet door. Sarah was quiet, taking his abuse. Pete was gratified to realize that he still controlled his wife.

Afterward, he sat back down in front of his plate as if nothing had happened. Sarah put his toast on the napkin beside him and hurried upstairs.

"Dear God, please use your power to make Pete a kinder husband," she prayed. She washed up, smoothed her wrinkled clothes, and rushed out the door. Sarah had a job to do: find a murderer who dealt drugs. He would die before he killed other innocent little girls.

Sarah headed back to the office and walked in to find Ruby talking on the phone.

"Okay, Darrel," Ruby said, seeming nervous. "I'll have your office all cleaned up by then."

"What's happening?" Sarah asked.

"The sheriff's coming here tomorrow and meeting Darrel, who is all pissed off because he has to be here at 8:00," Ruby explained.

"I'll make sure we are all here, also," Sarah said. Sarah was always a bit anxious when the sheriff was around. She wanted to impress Sheriff Will so much.

With another quiet, uneventful night behind her, Sarah hurried to the office the next day. The county sheriff was always on time, and Sarah wanted to be early.

Sheriff Will pulled in beside Sarah's unmarked patrol car, hurriedly exiting his black sedan.

"Morning, Sarah," he said. Will pulled down his sunglasses. "How do you like your job?"

Why was he asking that? Sarah did not know. "I really like it, sir," she said.

"Good. It's important to like your work," the sheriff

said and went inside. He made his way to Darrel's office and sat down in a chair in front of his desk. Darrel was conspicuously absent. Ruby and Zach were both stationed at their desks when Sarah walked in. Everyone was focused on Sheriff Will.

Darrel bounded in the front door a few minutes after eight o'clock, breathless from hurrying. He grabbed a mug and some coffee from the office machine, then offered the sheriff a cup.

"Ruby makes great coffee, Will," Darrel said.

"No thanks," Will said and scowled. "This won't take but a minute." He closed Darrel's door.

Less than ten minutes later, both men walked out of the office. Darrel went outside without looking at anyone or saying a word. The lanky sheriff looked relieved and draped himself over Ruby's desk in sight of his three remaining county employees. "Darrel is leaving the department," he explained. "I don't have any budget money to replace him. But hell, our crimes are mostly petty anyway." He paused. "Sarah, I'm making you the county investigator. No raise and no help. Can you do it?"

It was Sarah's turn to be breathless. Stammering, Sarah answered, "I'll sure try, sir. I'd love to try."

Will's face contorted into a frown. "The county investigator isn't about love. It's about finding criminals, Sarah," he said.

Sarah stopped smiling. "I understand that, sir," she said quietly.

Will was still scowling. "You move into Darrel's office,"

he said. Addressing Zach, he said, "Pretty Boy, you can move into Sarah's old spot. Ruby, Pretty Boy can help you and Sarah. We gotta stretch this office. I don't have any more money to hire anyone. Does everyone understand?"

Sarah, Zach, and Ruby all shook their heads, agreeing in unison.

"Well, let's all get busy," Will instructed. "And call me if you need anything. Ruby, pack up Darrel's stuff. Sarah, go through the files. Hell, there's probably open cases none of us knows about."

Sheriff Will Townsend was in total control, and his smile returned as he left the room. Everyone had their orders.

The atmosphere was hushed as the three went about their duties—Ruby packing up Darrel's office, Sarah going through his files, and Zach doing all the other morning tasks. No one asked a question or said anything to each other, seemingly frightened at the thought that Sheriff Will might hear them from wherever he was working.

But Sarah's mind was racing quietly. The official Montague County Sheriff Department Investigator... Sarah could hardly believe she had the job. Her heart was pounding, and she promised herself to catch every criminal. No one would escape Sarah Sears. Women would thank her, children would grow up safely, and men would fear her. Sarah, for the first time in her life, was in charge. "Thank you, God!" she prayed.

***

Sarah was excited but afraid to mention another promotion to Pete. Within a short time at the sheriff's department, Sarah had been promoted three times, and she was convinced her God worked in mysterious ways. Somehow she'd endure Pete's wrath when he found out the news and possibly even escape his brutality. She hoped Olivia would one day be proud of her mother.

The remainder of the day was quiet with the three employees settling into their new roles. Ruby dialed every neighbor she knew to tell them of the department upheaval. No more Darrel. Sarah Sears was now in charge. And a homosexual was the acting assistant investigator.

"A senior citizen working with a fag and a woman," she exclaimed into the phone. Ruby was a little worried what folks would think of this set up, but she amused herself with people's opinions.

Nocona was quiet lately, and Bowie, the little town to the south, only produced a couple of drunks last evening. Sarah often read old unsolved cases in her office on a slow crime day like this one. A label marked "serial" caught Sarah's eye on one of the files she was reading. Flipping open what appeared to be a freshly marked record, she was quickly interested in the many pages contained within. Henry Lee Lucas was the name at the top of most of the papers. Sarah read quickly but thoroughly. Lucas was a suspect in the killings of several women, but he had not been charged at the time Darrel noted the file.

The folder was missing any photos or identification of the suspect. The brief instructions issued by the state were to be "on alert" for his man. He was a scheming drifter and perilously dangerous. Sarah began reading more case notes about Lucas. She didn't know it then, but he was someone who would come to be known as Texas' most wanted criminal. Suspected of rape, murder, cannibalism, and theft, Henry Lee Lucas was the worst of the worst.

She was not surprised that Darrel had ignored this case. This was not a man to tangle with. The latest notice in the file read that Lucas was suspected of being in the Montague County vicinity, probably hid out in an abandoned building or along Red River where Sarah had been raped by thugs who were now rotting somewhere in a cemetery covered by muddy Texas red clay. They would never rape another woman or child. Sarah had done God's work.

Laying the Lucas file to the side, she read the other shorter files Darrel had ignored. Petty thieves, drug offenses, and even a suspected child abuser and child molester. "Tomorrow I'll focus on this last one," she thought. There could be no more crimes against women and children in Montague County.

Locking her office door and preparing to leave for the day, Zach asked why she had locked her office. Did Sarah already have secrets unavailable to him or Ruby?

"Just precautions," Sarah answered dryly. "Zach, tomorrow I want to pick your brain."

Zach smiled, glad to be in her good graces again. "Guess

I better not smoke pot tonight or get drunk," he joked. "You're gonna be a tough boss."

***

Pulling in the driveway of her home, Sarah was edgy. She needed to tell Pete about the office changes before the local newspaper ran a story. Changes in law enforcement always made headlines, as these things affected every resident for better or worse.

Pete hated surprises, so she decided to deliver the news right away. Maybe he would be hungry and want to eat more than he'd want to rough up his wife. Assuming he was upstairs, Sarah quietly climbed the staircase and stood in his office doorway.

"It's about time you're home. I'm ready to eat," he complained, quickly shoving a magazine he'd been looking at under some papers on his desk. Sarah thought for a moment that she'd seen two naked women on a page in the magazine. She quickly looked away.

Pete seemed flustered and yelled, "Get the hell downstairs and get me something to eat, bitch. What are you doing up here anyway?"

Pete Sears was mad, and Sarah was the target. Her familiar "fight or flight" instinct kicked in, and she hurried to the kitchen. The pork chops left over from the night before might do, but not by themselves. She thought she should make him a fresh baked potato and warm up the apple pie from Sunday. Sarah's meals could never look haphazardly prepared. She'd be punished.

While the potato was baking, Sarah attempted to rouse Olivia from her afternoon nap and turned the doorknob to her bedroom. Trying to open the door, Sarah heard Olivia shout, "It's locked. What do you want?"

"Come to supper," her mother said cheerfully.

"I'm not hungry," Olivia said sharply.

This brief conversation ended the nightly exchange between mother and daughter. Sarah knew better than to beg, so she left Olivia alone.

When supper was ready, Pete came downstairs. The kitchen chair screeched as he slid it back from the table. Sarah quickly spooned his servings and asked what toppings he wanted for his potato.

"Leftovers," Pete grumbled and stared at the pork chops. "That damned job of yours is ruining our lives."

Maybe tonight was a bad time to announce Sarah's promotion. If her husband didn't dole out physical punishment, he'd likely make fun of her news and then demand to know how much more money she'd make. Pete's repertoire of three types of abuse—physical, mental or emotional—was exhausting.

Sarah bit her lip, remembering her relationship with Jesus Christ. Why didn't God step in? It was not for her to know.

"You'd better tell him," a little voice in her mind said.

"Darrel got fired today, and Sherriff Will Townsend asked me to fill in for him."

"What?" Pete asked, staring at his wife.

"I'm going to fill in for Darrel's job."

"What does that mean?" Pete stared harder, his steely gaze narrowing.

"I'll be the chief investigator for a while?" Sarah answered his question with a question.

Pete's anger was rising, but he attempted to hide his surprise. His stupid wife was the county sheriff's chief investigator?

"Are they fucking crazy down there?" he exploded. "A woman investigator? Townsend must have gone fucking crazy."

Sarah kept her eyes off Pete.

Picking up the steak knife beside his plate, Pete sloppily sawed at his pork chop and then stuck the knife holding the bite in his mouth. Sarah had an overwhelming desire to grab the knife and plunge it down his throat. She wanted Pete Sears' blood to gush through his neck, and she relished the idea of hearing his animalistic gurgle while he choked on the pig.

"Dear God, I must stop thinking this way!" Sarah caught herself. Walking to the sink, she anticipated feeling a blow from Pete's hand against her body. He liked to call it a "bitch slap." But he sat in silence, tearing bite-sized pieces of the chop and eating them off the end of the knife.

No more words passed between the spouses for the rest of the evening. Sarah lived two lives: a battered woman in her own household, and an efficient protector of other women in their homes.

Sleep was difficult, and Sarah's dreams became

disturbing. She woke abruptly thinking she was sleeping beside Henry Lee Lucas. In her dream, Pete's face had become the face of a rapist, murderer, thief, cannibal. Sarah vowed she would find this animal Lucas and kill him. He must die just like the others. If her neighboring counties had lazy law enforcement and allowed killers to run loose, Montague County would draw the line. Sarah would hunt him down, slit his throat, and castrate him. Lucas would no longer hurt anybody. Instead, he'd be the one hurting.

Sarah's second day as chief investigator was her first day to begin the hunt for the notorious criminal. She was not afraid. God was her sidekick.

***

"Morning boss," Zach said cheerfully when Sarah entered the office the next morning. Ruby was on the phone chatting as usual and smoking her Virginia Slims.

Sarah's extension rang non-stop the rest of the day as neighboring police congratulated her on her promotion. She politely accepted their messages and vowed to help them in any way she could. Sarah would be a team player. Her goal was simple: never let a criminal escape. Killing the bastards was the surest way to protect her neighbors.

A late afternoon call from the Cooke County police asked for the Montague County department to be on the watch for a white pick-up traveling through the area. Two men from Dallas were wanted for drugs and a rural bank robbery. They were last seen driving in the northern Texas counties.

Sarah was anxious to track these two, but the clock striking five prevented any further activity that day. She was on high alert, anticipating her husband's unpredictable behavior. Pete Sears could get nasty this evening, so she prayed for her safety while driving home and saved making plans to catch criminals for bedtime.

Dinner slipped by without incidence. Pete ate in silent rage, and Olivia sailed through the kitchen, grabbing a chicken leg on her way to church. Sarah was proud of her daughter and wished they had a strong mother-daughter bond like the one they'd shared years before. Olivia's teenage years changed her. She had no tolerance for her mother's maternal instincts anymore. Sarah prayed for the sweet Olivia to return once she grew out of adolescence.

The next morning, Sarah slid a pot roast in the crock pot and called up the stairs to wish Pete goodbye. She thought she heard Pete barely grunt in return. Her work was consuming and delighting her. Self-worth and purpose were now her companions.

***

Zach was already hard at work when Sarah arrived at the office and busied himself foraging through more yellowed files that had been left untouched for years by the formerly dismissed and dead investigative team. Zach was an unlikely compatriot for Sarah with his tattoos, scraggly hair, and ragged jeans. But a minute spent with him uncovered a brilliant and inquisitive mind behind his fine features, along with a soft heart.

He could not hide his sexual orientation, yet his sad eyes told of some kind of horror he had endured. Sarah guessed extreme schoolyard bullying and possibly more. She sometimes wanted to wrap her arms around this little boy-man and show him compassion. This was not possible, of course. She was the county crime investigator; there was no time or space for Zach's mental health counseling when she was on the job.

Zach liked working with two women every day and vacillated between being their protector and the one needing protection. His nerves were raw and edgy but never allowed him to be unkind. Zach was a complex human with hurt and betrayal etched in his psyche. Lacking the courage to dream of future plans or goals, he was too vulnerable to hope for anything. The best he could do was to rely on his loyalty to Sarah and Ruby. He wore it proudly like a favorite badge.

Every rural community has a public servant like Ruby, efficient and dependable with highly-honed gossip skills. Ruby knew most of the county history. She could name numerous thugs and drug users and identify all the poor bastard children born out of wedlock. She relished in sharing all the details of cases with her women's Sunday school class and never missed a funeral, wedding, or her weekly beauty shop appointment. Should a gray hair escape her Lucy Ricardo red coif, she would sweetly remind her hairdresser, "Your job is to keep me a redhead. Is that asking too much?"

Ruby could not tolerate having a broken fingernail or running out of cigarettes at work. She'd leave the office unannounced just for a smoke run or to fix a chip in her manicure. Ruby had one purpose: to collect the meager retirement 30 years would supply her for staying with the county. Every year marked another milestone. Ruby was happy.

The smell of Ruby's coffee brewing every morning was comforting to Sarah. She instinctively recognized this trio of misfits would be most effective at extinguishing Montague County's hoodlums.

Other big shot law enforcement offices throughout Texas would soon know Sarah Sears and her staff. With no further leads on Henry Lee Lucas, she decided she would kick start her reputation by finding the escaped bank robbers if they dared to leave a trace in her county. Her heart raced at the thought of pulling out her gun to arrest the criminals. If necessary, she'd use it without hesitation.

"Come into my office, Zach," Sarah said as she passed by him. She offered Zach the visitor's chair in front of her desk and got down to business right away.

"I have a case I want you to concentrate on," she began. "Please read this file and then let's talk." Sarah pushed the Lucas file toward Zach. With a raised eyebrow, he said, "You got it, boss. I'm all over it!" He left, tucking the file under his arm.

An hour later, Zach respectfully knocked on her office door.

"Wow," he seemed breathless. "This guy's a doozy. You

sure you want to try to catch him?" Zach appeared stricken by Lucas' profile.

Sarah shook her head, affirmatively. "Never been surer," she replied. "You and I will take him down."

Unlikely simpatico partners, Zach and Sarah exchanged a look that communicated complete cooperation and agreement. A crime novice and a killer—not good odds, but they had enthusiasm for the task ahead.

4

HENRY'S STORY – ONE WEEK EARLIER

Henry Lee Lucas had been on the lam from Florida's inept law enforcement and was traveling through the South headed to Texas. His traitorous friend, Ottis Toole, had just been captured and had ratted on him to the Florida officials. Toole was ignorant and mean, a babbling fool. Lucas was a crafty smooth talker, filled with hate. If Lucas had been brought up with any stability and kindness, he might have functioned as a normal family man, probably working for his pay instead of killing for joy and sustenance.

No fiber in either Lucas or Toole contained empathy for man or beast. Toole had kicked dogs to death with steel-toed boots and regularly tortured stray cats with lighters or threw them into fire pits. Lucas delighted in Toole's sickness and had even sought a demented sexual relationship with the man.

Lucas was not only a homosexual but a heterosexual rapist. Young, old, bony, or obese, his disturbed mind satisfied his sexual appetite while forcing women and men to carry out his deviant and demanding acts. He often finished his sexual fantasies by killing the prey by various methods. A friendly gas station attendant, a smiling housewife opening her front door, or a shop clerk bidding him hello could set off his animalistic killing instinct. Stealing rations and automobiles for pleasure was merely a necessary afterthought.

Toole and Lucas were the perfect murderous playmates, often accompanied by Toole's niece Becky. Repeatedly raped by both men, she became a willing accomplice, fulfilling her teenage angst with their evil deeds. Lucas was the mastermind, and the others were his assistants.

However, Toole was at times belligerent and uncooperative, and that worried Lucas. Both men despised anyone with authority. "Ottis, you're a crazy bastard," Lucas would say and shake his head whenever Toole was particularly wild, sometimes smearing a tortured soul's blood on his arms and body, smiling through his black and rotted teeth.

"Don't be stupid or you'll get those fucking police bastards coming after us," Lucas had warned him. As Lucas drove west, he thought back on the night it had all gone so horribly wrong when Toole got caught.

***

The Florida Panhandle had been hot and humid, the kind of weather that agitated the killers. Toole particularly wanted trouble. Lucas had seen a young mother loading groceries in her sedan and harbored a desire to keep her a few days chained to his bedpost. He described her beauty and innocence to Toole, who grew more enraged with Lucas' glowing description of his prey. Toole liked having Lucas as his lover, and he was highly disturbed that this bitch could take his place in bed with Lucas.

Henry had followed the young woman home and noted her house and street number. "I'll get her tomorrow," he told Toole.

Staked out in an abandoned shack, the men slept that night on a filthy mattress, a small fan whirring in the corner. The niece was on the floor. Toole couldn't sleep, knowing his lover would soon have a sex slave he had no desire to share. He cared little for rape but enjoyed watching the pain he could inflict on another human. This bitch would give him no pleasure, only stirring more jealousy regarding his lover. Toole hatched a plan: find the bitch's house and kill her before Lucas could take her from her family. If anyone got in his way, Toole would kill her husband or kids. But the bitch was his real target.

Typically, Lucas drove the getaway car, but around 4:00 in the morning, Toole revved up the old Chevy's engine and drove toward the nearby small town. Ottis Toole was on a murder mission. No cunt would replace him with Henry, if even for a few days.

The night air was slightly cooler as Toole drove down the little burg's short streets. He rubbed his eyes, trying to see the street signs without using his high beams. The small, well-kept houses cradled the town's families, unaware of the presence of a bloodthirsty killer.

Lucas had described the home to Toole, and there it was: the tiny white clapboard house with two small clay flowerpots on each side of the front door. Toole, never a planner but rather an explosive personality, thought to himself, "I'll knock and whoever answers the door, I'll kill first. But I'll make sure I get the woman."

Parking on the street directly in front of the house, Toole walked around the car, opened the passenger door quietly, and grabbed his shotgun. This would prove to be a poor choice of weapons for his crime. Sneaking across the tiny yard toward the unpainted porch, Toole tightened his grip on his gun. A cop car suddenly turned the corner, flashing its headlights on Toole. The young cop had been assigned to the night shift for that neighborhood and had spotted a shadowy man toting a long gun.

Toole ran for his car. The officer hopped out and shouted for his suspect to stop. Instead, he turned and aimed his gun toward the officer, cocking the trigger.

The cop would have been a dead man, had the young woman's husband not heard the ruckus outside in his yard. Recently returned from military service, the husband was an expert marksman. From the front porch, he shot Toole in the leg, rendering Ottis helpless and leaving him yelping like some of the dogs he'd delighted in torturing.

Both the officer and the shooter ran toward Toole, wrestling him to the ground and handcuffing him. By sheer luck, a rookie cop on a new beat had captured a serial killer.

The marksman husband grabbed Toole's shotgun and helped the policeman slam Toole's torso against the hood of the patrol car while the cop called for back-up. Ottis Toole, a demented killer, was on his way to jail while his lover and partner, Henry Lee Lucas, slept until daylight.

When the sun streamed through the broken windowpanes, it woke Henry. He looked around and saw that his partner was gone. He yelled for Toole but got no response. Becky was still fast asleep on the floor.

"Where the hell is he?" Henry wondered. He had a strange feeling that Toole had gone on a solo murderous spree. Henry often worried about being outed due to his lover's stupidity.

Henry yelled louder for Toole. Nothing. Becky awoke.

"He must have took the car, the stupid bastard!" Henry concluded, baffled. "Where the hell would the fucker go this early?" Mornings were typically reserved for a little grub and planning whatever mischief the two thugs could devise.

Vowing to curse Toole when he returned, Henry heated water for instant coffee and cold cereal. He switched on the small radio he kept and tuned into the local news. A reporter was telling a story about a man named Ottis Toole who had been arrested for attempted burglary earlier that morning and was being held in jail. Most small-town radio men loved to announce criminal apprehensions, and locals loved for their tax dollars to pay for heroic acts of law enforcement.

Henry knew his friendship with Toole was likely at an end. He'd better pack his few things and get out of town today. Henry would make sure Toole's niece would go with him, as he didn't need anyone left to talk to the police. Toole better keep his mouth shut, or Henry would kill him too.

Henry was rarely without stolen transportation or enough money for necessary travel. He was an expert at picking a car door lock, and today was no exception. Walking a half mile up the road, he saw an empty blue Chevy sedan on the front lawn of a small, yet well-kept clapboard house. Unlocked. This was a cakewalk for a seasoned thief.

Henry was slightly saddened to continue without Toole. Although the fool was dim-witted and overly careless, Henry would miss having a partner. Clever and cunning, Henry decided he'd head west to Texas and determine his next move.

***

Henry and the girl rarely said a word during the long, hot drive across Florida's Everglades toward the Texas border. Becky was on edge, leaving behind the only relative she had ever known, although he never showed her any empathy. To her, Henry was scary yet beguiling. When she occasionally shot a glance toward the driver, she experienced a sudden sexual stirring. Her short skirt offered her the opportunity to rub her crotch to entice Henry. He took his eyes off the road to eye her and her legs. "I'll take care of you later, little girl," he snarled, yet he was happy this young girl was willing to please him.

Henry would be labeled a bi-sexual in future newspaper

articles written about him and his crime spree. Man or woman, he only knew that he liked to satisfy himself occasionally. This girl might work out fine for a while. But Lucas fully realized he was easily bored and would need others to keep him stimulated. If he had to kill them, so be it.

Driving throughout the night, Henry stopped only to "take a piss" and get gas and food. He wasn't concerned when the girl went to the bathroom and bought soft drinks and chips. She'd been schooled by Toole and knew to keep her mouth shut.

Hitting the Alabama line, Henry was careful to stay within the speed limit, not alerting some local cop that he was breaking the law. Lucas was careful and admired his own ability to fit into society.

Mile after mile, Henry silently planned his next moves. He was adept at providing himself the necessities such as food and transportation. If the girl became too much trouble or talked too much, likely getting both of them in trouble, he'd be forced to dispose of her. Lucas never felt remorse for his life of crime but considered himself superior to others. He didn't have the burden of an eight-to-five job like most men. Henry was only burdened by the moment, finding vulnerable prey and then doing any clean up that protected his deeds. He hated to mop up blood, so most often the tortured lay dying in their own pool of blood while Henry moved on.

The girl slept most of the way through Alabama. Henry was aroused by the innocence of his accomplice, her miniskirt hiked up around her thighs. Henry caught glimpses of her emerging breasts showing through her open blouse. He needed to fuck this girl and many others.

When he could take it no longer, he pulled off the highway onto a crooked country road.

"Where are we?" Becky asked, wide awake now.

"In the middle of bumfuck," Henry said and smiled. "I'm going to fuck you."

The girl smiled and pulled up her skirt. Henry pulled her toward him in the front seat, thinking it would not take long.

Usually careful of his surroundings, Henry didn't expect the old pick-up advancing toward his parked car. The girl was giggling and laughing as he heaved against her.

"Shut up," Henry demanded.

She let out a yelp.

Henry was agitated now.

An old Alabama farmer was looking through the driver's window, not sure if these people were consenting adults or maybe cheating on their spouses. Perhaps the man was even raping the girl. He decided to rap lightly on the pane. Henry was highly irritated at the old man, the stupid girl, and himself. But he was a capable sociopath, so he controlled his rage.

Remembering his handgun was under the driver's seat, Henry sat up and let down the window.

"What's going on here?" the old man asked. He looked curious.

Henry smiled and said, "Just a little pussy this morning."

The old man frowned and starting walking away. The guy might talk to his coffee shop buddies later that morning, and Henry could not chance that. He warned the girl not to make a sound.

Sliding out of the driver's seat, Henry called out, "Hey, mister!"

The man turned toward Henry and gasped before Henry pulled the trigger on his handgun, hitting the farmer in his chest and firing a second shot to the man's stomach. Another killing was no problem, just a distraction.

Henry started the car, which lunged forward and made its way toward the interstate. Henry thought, "I don't owe redneck Alabama anything. I'm gonna keep going to Texas."

***

Driving all night to distance himself from the farmer's body, Henry was hungry and tired. The road sign ahead read, "Welcome to Texas." Henry and the girl had finally made it to Texarkana on the border between Arkansas and Texas. The girl slept most of the drive once again, which annoyed him more.

"Bitch," he thought. "I'm not sure she's worth a little pussy. I'd rather have a real woman." Henry made plans to ditch her when it was safe. Instinctively, Henry knew he'd have to kill her. He didn't like witnesses; they were too dangerous.

Henry wheeled in a small diner, shook the girl awake, and opened the driver's door. "I'm gonna pee and eat something. You'd better do the same," he told her.

Clothes wrinkled and beard unshaven, Henry sat in a booth. The girl slid in the other side. She suspected Henry was in a foul mood because she was accustomed to reading Ottis Toole's moods. Henry exhibited little difference from her uncle. Anger mixed with anxiety were both men's constant companions. She knew when to keep quiet and go along.

Eggs and pancakes on the way, Henry sat next to the window. He never sat with his back to strangers. Bells on the dirty glass door jingled as two patrolmen walked in. Their guns in holsters and badges proudly pinned to their chests, these men were younger and much stronger than Henry. He sensed trouble.

Henry waved to the skinny waitress by the coffee station, and she smiled back at him. "Whatcha need?" she said as she walked over and looked at Henry.

"I gotta get my daughter back to her mother and need to get goin'. Can you put my grub in a box or two and make the coffee to go?" She agreed to do so, and Henry added politely, "Thanks for hurrying it up."

The cops were talking to a local townsman when Henry paid the ticket with cash. Leaving a big tip, he and the girl walked to the getaway car and drove west. The Texarkana police had let a serial killer slide through the border town unnoticed. Henry slightly smiled, thinking how dumb most cops are. Evil can sit right beside lawmen, and they are more worried about what they will have for their next meal.

"Stupid bastards," he said under his breath. "I'm gonna

kill me a Texas cop just for fun." Henry drove west with the morning sun coming through the back window of the car.

Nocona, Texas, was located about three-and-one-half hours from Texarkana. About 2,000 residents made up the little town on the Red River, whose banks form a natural border between Texas and Oklahoma.

Henry had successfully driven unnoticed through several other Texas border towns overnight. It was morning now, and he was too tired to go on. He pulled in the Nocona Dairy Hut drive-thru to order a sausage biscuit sandwich for breakfast and to ask directions to a motel nearby. This spot would suffice for a night so Henry could sleep.

***

Sarah was in the same drive-thru line at the Nocona Dairy Hut in her unmarked state vehicle, waiting on her Diet Coke with vanilla. Sarah could nurse her soft drink all morning. After the blue Chevy sedan in front of her pulled away, Sarah was next in line and greeted the kid working the window. He handed her a large drink, and she headed to the office.

Main Street, Nocona, Texas, was virtually non-existent—just a few remaining stores from a bygone era carrying sparse merchandise. One building boasted a bed and breakfast. It was basically a hotel connected to a café next door, the product of a poorly concocted renovation. One clerk worked the front booths, while also providing the hotel reception duties.

Although disheveled in his appearance, Henry could still deliver crude charm when a lonely woman was nearby. When he walked into the hotel to see about getting a room, Henry sensed the buxom blonde clerk was a willing sexual partner, yet was mostly ignored by the townsmen. She would welcome a stranger, but his sleep was too vital right now. Henry paid in cash and said that he and his daughter would be leaving within a few hours. The woman seemed disappointed by this news and offered coffee to the killer. Henry declined.

The tiny room had a twin bed and one small chest of drawers. Henry ordered the girl to sleep on the floor, and he sprawled across the mattress. He pushed open the window, allowing the Texas heat to fill the room. The open window gave Henry both a bit of air and the ability to hear the street sounds.

Henry tried to sleep but grew angry that the tiny room was so hot. A breath of air blew the dingy curtain but provided little relief. "Dammit," he said. "I need a beer and some grub. Shit, I'd better get some money somewhere." Two five dollar bills would buy a hamburger and beer. The girl, he reasoned, could get by on a candy bar from the little convenience store Henry saw at the edge of town.

He left Becky napping and went down the creaky stairs. Approaching the same clerk he met earlier, Henry turned on the charm again. She was wearing shorts and a loose blouse that tried to hide the rolls of fat she acquired from eating too much fried chicken and too many fried pies. Henry leaned across the little counter separating them, staring at her generous breasts. A sick mind but a healthy libido, Henry briefly considered fucking her but decided that could wait. He was too hungry to get it up.

"How 'bout one of them burgers and a beer next door, young lady?" Henry smiled toward her. She smiled back.

"Yes, sir, how was your nap?" she asked. "Where's your daughter?"

"Still asleep, gorgeous," Henry said. This one would be too easy. "Maybe I'll stay a day or so and fuck her brains out," he thought as he stared at the woman.

"Got any idea where I might pick up a few bucks, maybe an odd job or two?" Henry touched the young girl's shoulder. "Say, what's your name anyway?"

"Lysette," she said. "But everyone around here calls me Lee."

Henry grunted thinking about how he was gonna have his namesake suck his dick later. He laughed out loud at the thought.

"Well, little Lee, I'm Hank. I hope we can get to know each other better," he told her.

She winked and said, "I bet we can" before leading Henry next door to fix him some lunch at the café.

The greasy hamburger and beer helped put Henry in a better mood. Shoving the two fives toward Lee, he was ready to drive west. But Lee wanted this new man to stay longer. She remembered that a customer had tacked a note on the hotel bulletin board asking about a handyman. She hoped he might fit the bill and stay in Nocona. Lee wanted a boyfriend, and this guy was good enough for her.

"I think there's an old lady named Rose Mooney who was needing a handyman. Are you handy?" Lee was flirting now.

"What do you think, little girl?" Henry was flirting back. "How do I find the old lady?"

Lee excused herself to go next door and find the note. Henry followed her into the empty hotel lobby. Pulling the young lady into the men's room, he grabbed her ample tits and started kissing them, chewing on her nipples. Lee was compliant when Henry unzipped his pants and pushed his cock in her mouth. She had tasted a man's cum before and happily drank the killer's juices. He decided he liked this country girl and wanted more of her favors.

"I'm gonna find the old lady, and I'm gonna fuck you again," he said to her. Henry zipped up his pants and left Lee in the men's room.

"See ya around, bitch," he thought.

Opening the door to his room, Henry's traveling companion was waiting for him on the bed completely nude.

"Where you been?" she asked flirtatiously.

"None of your business, you little slut," Henry said. "Get dressed! We gotta find some money."

***

A few miles west in the blinding Texas sun, Henry looked for the address Lee had given him. He eyed an unpainted shack with a small flower bed overrun with weeds and climbing red roses.

He saw a rocker on the porch with two wooden chairs and a small table nearby. Henry pulled in the graveled drive, rocks crunching under his worn tires and observed that the house sat close to Highway 82, providing a getaway efficient and likely if necessary. The porch, which was barely clinging to the little frame house, led to a front door with a torn screen and a loose frame. Rabid-looking dogs kept out anyone who chose to enter.

"Mrs. Mooney?" Henry called.

He heard a woman's grunt.

"I'm here. What do you want?" the old woman's voice crackled. Cigarette smoke billowed through the sunlit front room, illuminating a hunched elderly woman's frame in a starched apron. Her mouth was caved in yet somehow managed to hold a Camel straight between her gums. Henry's demented mind questioned how much money the old lady might have stashed somewhere in the hovel.

"Ma'am, I believe Miss Lee down at the hotel called you to say I would be coming by to see about doing some handiwork around here," Henry explained.

"You're Hank, are you?" the woman asked, eyeing him.

"I can see you're looking for someone to help," Henry said convincingly.

Mrs. Mooney could hardly see the killer through the west sun pouring in through her windows. He seemed nice enough. If she planned to continue living in her home for the next few years, she would need to keep it up. Her kids had vanished, scattering to distant jobs and lives, but Rose

Mooney had stayed put. Montague County was her home.

"Where'd you come from?" she asked.

"Texarkana, ma'am," Henry said, happy he remembered the name of the East Texas border town and briefly thinking of the two dumb cops he'd fooled.

"What're you doin' in Nocona, Texas?" she said, peering at him.

Henry was getting angry, wondering why the old witch was questioning him. He took a breath and answered, "I broke up with my wife and decided to leave town. I brought my daughter with me, and we decided to go west. We like this little town and the hills. It's nice."

"Huh," the woman grunted. "I don't know how nice it is, but it is my home. My husband is dead, and I'm by myself. You wantin' a job, are ya?"

"Yes, ma'am," Henry said. He detested questions.

"Well, I guess I could let you stay here a while and get some things done. Are you good using tools and a paint brush?"

"Why sure!" Henry said, hiding the fact that he was even more agitated. He considered snapping her neck but decided spending a few days in one spot would be okay. Henry was just plain tired of running.

"Well, you can sleep on the screened-in porch, and put the girl in the little bedroom," Mrs. Mooney explained. "No drugs and no drinking, 'cept maybe on Saturday night. A beer won't hurt. My old man drank himself to death, and I don't want to see that again."

Henry nodded gratefully.

"If you need to wash up, go ahead," the woman said and opened the screen door to welcome him in. "I'm making some fried eggs and sausage for dinner. Are you hungry?"

He nodded and smiled at the old lady, knowing he'd win her over in no time. Henry Lee Lucas turned on his charm again.

***

"Ma'am, did your husband leave any extra clothes after he passed?" Henry asked the woman after dinner. He pointed to his dirty trousers and shirt. "I sure need to wash these up," he added.

The woman was beginning to like this traveler. He was polite to her, which was more than most of the townspeople ever were. In town, she was known as "white trash" and her old man no better. This man reminded her a little of her husband.

The Mooneys had come to North Texas as a young couple 60 years ago looking for work. They settled outside the little burg of Nocona and started farming as sharecroppers in the cotton fields. They later scraped together a little money and bought twenty acres and the old house where she still lived. The junkyard started naturally as they both were pack rats, and selling old car parts became their business.

The Mooney kids grew up and left town, ashamed of their parents. Their father drank cheap whiskey and slept most days and nights. He wasn't mean, just weak and addicted. Rose ran the used parts business, raised a few chickens, and tended to a cow and calf in the little pasture. Once a week, she'd drive three miles into Nocona and buy a few groceries. Life became a lot easier when Rose collected her social security checks.

She became more haggard and unkempt through the years and was mostly misunderstood by locals. Kids thought she was a witch, and men only went to the Mooney place to find car parts or deposit an old vehicle onto her land, and she paid them a little money for it. She was a businesswoman by necessity and seemed destined to die on her small plot outside Nocona.

She agreed to find Henry some clothes. What was left of her dead husband's clothing was piled in a small chest in the closet. Bending over, Mrs. Mooney let out a little groan, steadying herself on the side of the chest. She grabbed a handful of items and walked back into the kitchen where Henry was sitting.

"Here," she said and pitched all of it on the floor. "Take anything you want. I don't know why I even kept them."

Mrs. Mooney grabbed at her back and struggled to stand upright. "Throw your dirty stuff on the back porch, and your girl can wash them. I got a washer and a clothesline." Henry agreed to come back in the morning with his daughter to start working.

***

When Henry went back to the hotel that evening to pack up and grab Becky, he warned her not to say a word to Mrs.

Mooney. "Act like you're my daughter," he instructed her.

"But what about us fucking each other?" Becky said and touched her pussy underneath her skirt.

"Shut up, little cunt, or I'll kill you. Act like you're my kid, you hear me," Henry growled.

Becky looked down, afraid of this maniac. She knew what he was capable of doing to her or to anyone he chose.

In the morning, they packed quickly and drove in silence to the Mooney place.

"Becky, this is Mrs. Mooney," Henry said when Mrs. Mooney opened the front door to welcome them inside. "We're gonna help this nice lady around the house," he told Becky.

"How long will we have to be here?" Becky asked, looking around at the mess. Henry frowned at her and then smiled at Mrs. Mooney.

"As long as she needs us," he scolded Becky.

"Well, hell," Mrs. Mooney interrupted. "Can we quit jabbering and get you some food and clean clothes?"

Henry smiled again at Mrs. Mooney.

"Yes, ma'am," he said and closed the door behind them.

Henry dropped off their belongings and headed to the bathroom to wash up.

Clean shaven and with combed hair, Henry was a fairly good-looking man. He had a young man's body and youthful smile, although he needed dental work badly. Poor hygiene and crooked teeth were common and accepted among country people. Money for a dentist was sparse, and most people only visited the dentist for painful teeth extractions.

As he sat down to eat with Becky and Mrs. Mooney, Henry decided he was going to like North Texas.

***

The next day he left the Mooney place and drove to town to get some supplies to work on Mrs. Mooney's porch. He met a man named Donnie at the hardware store. The only danger was that Henry was new in town. Small towns loved to spot a newbie, their curiosity taking control of all the small talk. Who's the new guy? What's he doing here? Where'd he come from? The questions were never-ending until answered. Henry knew this was a potential problem. He explained to Donnie that he was Mooney's nephew doing some work around her place.

He kept a low profile in town, but he felt strangers' eyes were on him all the time. He carefully approached Mrs. Mooney that evening to attempt to rectify the situation. "Ma'am, I don't like a bunch of chatter," he began. "I don't want Becky to have to tell about her momma, who is a drug addict and slut. Would it be alright if I said you're my aunt and you wanted us to live with you a little while?"

Mrs. Mooney was a little taken aback but liked this man and girl. "It's okay with me, but I don't expect anyone to ask. The folks around here would rather gossip behind your back."

Mrs. Mooney spat her snuff in a jar and continued, "I'd tell them to shut up. But suit yourself." The old woman had turned crusty to most people in the county and wanted nothing to do with anybody except the occasional junkyard customer.

Satisfied with this arrangement, Henry knew the lie he'd tell if anyone asked how he ended up in Nocona. And Becky would say anything once he instructed her. Deep down, the girl was frightened of Henry. They both knew it.

5

The next day the sheriff's office was quiet when Sarah arrived. Zach was looking at a magazine, and Ruby was making oatmeal in the kitchen. Sarah could hear the microwave running. Ruby ate often and took her breaks in the office kitchen. She liked to talk to her daughter on the phone and set aside mornings for this ritual.

Sarah brought up Cynthia Stevens' death when Ruby came back. She explained that she'd go to the funeral tomorrow. Zach and Ruby were interested in why a young girl like Cynthia would die suddenly. Sarah said her mother thought it was a drug overdose. If she did not want an autopsy, no one would be certain. Sarah pulled out her notes on Mrs. Stevens' statement and asked Zach to record it for the sheriff's records.

"Zach, do you know any drug dealers in our county?" Sarah asked.

"Not personally. But I got some friends who do a lot of pot. They may know someone." Zach seemed edgy about answering Sarah's question. "Why are you asking me?"

"I just thought you might know since you're young," she explained and added, "Zach, do you believe someone should sell drugs to young girls, making them targets for overdose?"

Zach shook his head. "No, but there are people who do sell all kinds of drug," he explained. "I don't have anything to do with them."

"Good, Zach. That's what makes you a good employee of the county sheriff's department," Sarah told him and smiled. "What do you say we catch the dealer?"

"Yes, ma'am!" Zach said, grinning.

Ruby was back in the kitchen talking to her daughter again, complaining about her son-in-law.

"Ruby, can you handle the phone?" Sarah called out. "I need Zach to go with me. I've never been through the druggy part of town alone."

Ruby was slightly disturbed by the interruption but agreed, shaking her head up and down without breaking stride on her phone conversation. Sarah put a jacket on over her uniformed shirt since she was going to need to be incognito for a while. Zach and Sarah headed out the door to the patrol car, and he seemed pleased to slide into the passenger side. The vehicle did give its occupants a sense of power, Sarah recalled.

"Go out south of town, that's where most of the thugs stay," he instructed. "There's a trailer park out there, and there's probably lots of drugs in those trailers."

Sarah knew that park and always warned Olivia to stay away from that part of town.

Criminals can spot a cop car immediately, Sarah thought

as she pulled her unmarked car into the middle of the collection of mobile homes. Ruddy-faced little kids were playing with dirty dolls and sticks in one of the yards. They were too young for school and too young to be left alone, but their mothers were nowhere in sight. A skinny, grease-covered man was hunched over an old car working on the engine. Sarah and Zach parked close by.

Not knowing exactly how to question this man, Sarah rolled down the window and tried a direct approach. "Sir, do you know anyone I could talk to about getting a fix?" she asked.

The man smiled through black and broken teeth. "No, ma'am," he said. "The only thing I fix is old cars like this one."

Sarah thanked him and rolled up her window.

"Sarah, let's go back to the office. I need to come out here alone," Zach said. "We stand out like a sore thumb. I can get you the name of the dealer, but I can't have you with me."

"You're right," Sarah said, disappointed. She was afraid it would take a long time to identify the dealer. Other girls might die before she could eliminate him from this earth.

***

Reverend Thomas was especially kind and approachable during Cynthia's funeral service. He seemed genuinely sad and empathized with the family. With Sarah's permission, Olivia had skipped school to be there, and about fifty people were in attendance. Sarah watched from several rows back as

Reverend Thomas hugged Olivia afterwards and whispered something in her ear. What had he told her? Sarah then saw Mr. and Mrs. Stevens and Cynthia's two younger brothers wearing their best Sunday clothes. Mrs. Stevens had wailed during the reverend's service and muffled a scream when the casket lid was closed.

Later after the casket was lowered into the grave at the cemetery, Sarah reached for Olivia's hand, but she brushed it aside. When they had paid their final respects, Sarah offered Olivia a ride back to school.

"No, I want to go pray with Reverend Thomas," Olivia said in a harsh tone. Sarah was surprised the pastor would schedule a prayer session so soon after the funeral.

"Okay, honey, I'll see you tonight."

Olivia walked toward the preacher, each step taking her farther away from her mother.

On the way back to her car, Sarah happened to catch a glimpse of a thirty-something man who looked out of place. His vehicle was parked away from the others, and he was leaning against it, looking directly at Reverend Thomas. He saw Sarah staring at him and immediately got in his dark blue Chevy sedan.

Sarah suddenly realized this man might be important in her hunt for the dealer. She hurried to his car to get his license number but was unable to make out the plate before he drove away. However, Montague County was so small that a certain vehicle could be found fairly quickly.

***

Henry decided he'd keep his old blue car around the back of the shack. No reason to alert anyone about his presence until he was settled in. Mrs. Mooney okayed the parking spot.

He was working outside the next day when a news delivery boy threw a rolled-up copy of the Nocona News in Mrs. Mooney's yard. Henry quickly retrieved it. Resting a few minutes on the front porch, he flipped through the pages. He noticed a story about a lady investigator who worked for the sheriff's department. There was a picture of Sarah Sears standing beside an unmarked car wearing a holster. Henry looked closely at the photo, quickly determining this woman needed a good fucking and he'd do it. He particularly liked the intrigue of overpowering a female policeman.

He'd follow this woman, stake out her office, and catch her off guard one day. Henry was getting antsy for blood, and what a good story killing this woman would provide. Catch her, gag her, rape her, and kill her. Henry Lee Lucas looked forward to his prospects. He shoved the paper into a large, black plastic yard bag he'd been collecting trash in all morning.

It was a hot and humid day in Montague County. Henry much preferred robbing and killing to physical work, but spending a few days with Old Lady Mooney would allow him cover until the cops got distracted by another crime.

Becky, however, was too chatty with the old woman. Henry would need to slap her a few times and get her attention. Becky was young, but not dumb. She'd shut up if he threatened her.

***

The next day the plastic blinds covering the office windows were closed when Sarah arrived early. She pulled the string to open them and immediately recognized a blue car parked nearby. It was the same car she'd seen parked nearby during the funeral. Sarah felt a strange stirring, her body sensing danger.

Should she walk to the car and question the driver? She was a law woman now, and Sarah would not allow fear to be her companion. She stood up and walked toward the front door with the intent of at least getting the license of the car. Gun in her holster, she fingered the trigger.

The front door banged shut louder than she would have liked, and suddenly the blue car started, immediately lurching forward from its parking place before Sarah could get close enough to identify the plate. That same uneasy feeling flooded over her, and she now believed this vehicle housed a demon, someone Sarah might encounter in the future. This blue car symbolized danger.

Sarah decided to visit local places to yield information on the Cooke County bank robbery suspects and maybe the owner of the blue car. The local Dairy Hut was a hot spot for retired men to drink coffee and talk. Through the greasy windows facing the parking lot, Sarah could see all eyes turn toward her as she entered the café. Then the men looked away, whispering and sneering. Two or three nodded their heads toward her in quiet greeting. She easily overheard one loudmouth declaring how the sheriff's department was no place for a woman. "Sheriff Will has lost his mind. I plan to vote against that asshole next year," another man said, practically shouting.

Sarah looked past him and smiled at the crowd. "Has anyone seen a suspicious-looking white pick-up around town?" The café went silent, everyone straining to hear the first woman in such a dominant position address them.

Someone in the back said, "What is Montague County coming to? Next, it'll be a black man getting some fancy job."

A few played along with Sarah's questions and piped up, "nope" and "not me," shaking their heads. Others just stared, and a few looked away, refusing to show respect for the bitch playing cop. Sarah persisted.

"There's also a blue car running around town," she said. "Does anyone know the driver?"

Donnie Dick, a greasy mechanic who lived west of town, spoke up. "Yes, ma'am. I met him," he said. Everyone else fell silent.

"Who did you meet, sir?" Sarah asked, flipping to a new page in the small notebook she carried with her.

Donnie smiled, taking delight in being called "sir" for the first time in his 31 years. "I met the guy who drives a blue Chevy. He's the nephew of Old Lady Mooney out west of town. He's been cleaning up her junkyard."

"Thank you so much, sir," Sarah said and left to get in her car. She sped out of the Dairy Hut lot, heading west toward Mrs. Mooney's house. She'd get to the bottom of the blue car owner's intentions.

Everyone knew about the Mooney place full of rotting junk left by the old lady's dead husband. Hungry pit bulls and far too many emancipated cats roamed the dilapidated house. Old Lady Mooney rarely left the place and only to drive a few miles to the Piggly Wiggly grocery store. Social security checks kept her in food, and a broken-down couch provided a soft place to watch her game shows for hours during the day.

On occasion, a man might stop by and ask to search the junkyard for an out of date car part. If they were successful, the old lady would chuckle. She'd grin, showing her gums missing every tooth, and ask way too much money from the customer. Mrs. Mooney was not a fool, just a pitiful person. Time and circumstances had not smiled on this decrepit widow.

The sparkling clean sheriff's department car easily stood out in the Mooney yard. Dust boiled up as Sarah pulled in. Not a blade of grass or a green plant softened the filth surrounding the homestead. The pit bulls and some other strays ran toward Sarah when she opened her door, hoping for a few crumbs or at least an entertaining diversion from their measly existence. Sarah thumbed her revolver. She might have to use it if the beasts decided she was a target.

Scolding the dogs with mostly nervous bravado, Sarah

was relieved when they allowed her to walk onto the creaky, unpainted porch without bothering her. Two cats tried to rub against her boots, but Sarah kicked them away lightly.

Sarah knocked loudly on the screen door and could hear *The Price is Right* blaring on the television.

"Who is it?" Mrs. Mooney yelled out.

"Sarah Sears with the sheriff's department." She could hear the old woman heaving as she got out of the sofa to come to the door.

Old Lady Mooney opened the door and stared at Sarah. "A woman working for the sheriff..." she let her words trail off. "Where's that lazy old bastard who used to have your job? I hadn't seen him in years?"

"He died, ma'am," Sarah explained patiently. "And Darrel, his brother-in-law, is no longer with the department."

"Is that right?" Mrs. Mooney said and shook her heard. "Everybody gotta die sometime. Ain't you lucky! Or did you kill 'em off?" She laughed at her own humor, her lungs crackling with what Sarah assumed was emphysema. "Well, good for you, now what do you want with an old lady like me?" She stared at Sarah, suddenly seeming suspicious.

Sarah realized she was on shaky ground. "Have you seen a blue Chevrolet around?" Sarah inquired.

"What kind of Chevrolet, lady? A pick-up? A car? A truck or maybe a bicycle?" Mrs. Mooney was toying with Sarah.

"A car," Sarah stammered.

"No, I ain't seen nothin'. Why?"

Sarah was at a loss. This line of questioning was going

nowhere. "Well, thank you, ma'am," Sarah said and handed Mrs. Mooney her business card. "Call me if you ever need me."

The old lady grunted as she reached for the card. She was glad Becky was asleep and her new handyman had taken his blue Chevy to town for some supplies. It was nobody's business who worked for her.

The cur dogs again tried to lick Sarah, and a few growled as she hurriedly got back in the car and began backing toward the gravel road. Old Lady Mooney stood on the porch staring at the cop car. Exhilarated and disappointed, Sarah vowed to return to Mooney's soon, determined to uncover the mystery of why Mrs. Mooney hadn't told her about her nephew staying with her. Why had she lied?

Just before Henry was going to pull back in the Mooney driveway, he noticed a car was already parked there. He looked closer at the sedan and saw its white brake lights were on, indicating the driver was backing out. Something about the nondescript vehicle told him it might be a cop car. He sped up suddenly and looked in his rearview mirror to see if he was being followed. Nothing. He waited for about an hour before he returned. What had this visitor wanted? It sure looked suspicious to Henry.

***

Back at the office, the lunch hour passed by slowly. Zach drank his third or fourth Dr. Pepper for the day, chomping on the contents of a Cheetos package and capping it off with an extra-large Butterfinger. Ruby often went home for lunch, usually overstaying a few minutes to finish a phone call she'd started with a neighbor. Sarah ate her sandwich and apple at her desk.

Sarah and Zach typically chatted about department business or small talk during lunch, but they would occasionally delve into more personal issues. Sarah learned that Zach's dad fixed boats at the lake a few miles out of town. He rarely said a word to his only son, detesting Zach's interest in the same sex. Zach explained that his dad felt that real men should lose their virginity to a woman by sixteen, never to another man. Zach was a huge disappointment. His mother was a cook at the high school and came home dead tired by 2:00 in the afternoon every weekday, and she took no interest in Zach's life.

Frequently abused, bullied, and teased growing up, Zach wore a big chip on his shoulder, clouding his judgment of most men. Being gay in Montague County was dangerous and psychologically crippling. However, the most devastating blow to Zach's mental state, Sarah discovered, was his sister's death three years before in a car accident. On a date in her boyfriend's dual cab farm truck, they both got distracted when things got out of hand. She was fending off the boy's rude advances and pushed him so hard that he swerved to the middle of the four-lane highway. An eighteen-wheeler could not miss clipping the cab, killing his sister and breaking Zach's heart.

Sarah hurt for Zach when she heard this story because his only sibling and understanding confidant was killed due to the bullying of a man. Zach would never recover, she mused, and the only way life would be fair again was if this boy died. In fact, Zach confided in her that he often dreamed of killing the monster.

Zach rarely had a lover, as the Montague County homosexual supply was scarce. He focused his attention on murder mysteries and crime shows and video games. An occasional trip to a Dallas gay bar depressed him deeply, as he felt "used by the fags" for their relief. Love was out of the question.

Sarah felt sorry for Zach but never showed him pity. He was her partner, and she needed him. Partners in this line of work used their minds to come up with ingenious ways to handicap their opponents and trap them.

One afternoon Zach answered the phone and Sarah could overhear a woman screaming, begging for help. "He's gonna kill me!" the woman shouted. "He's gone crazy!"

"Where are you, ma'am?" Zach questioned her calmly. "How can we find you?"

"Pine Street," she said, and the phone went dead. Pine was a hotbed for criminal activity.

"I'm off," Sarah said and grabbed her holster.

"Sarah, I'm coming for back-up," Zach said. "Ruby's here."

"This wife beater would rue the day Sarah Sears learned his name," Sarah thought to herself as she raced toward Pine, turning up the short street off the county road. An enraged man, short in stature with tattoos, brandished a long knife in the front yard of a shanty and was yelling.

Sarah pulled in the yard and stepped out of her car. "Sir," she said, "you're under arrest."

"Who the fuck are you, bitch?" he turned toward Sarah and screamed. "Get the fuck out of here, or I'll kill you."

Not moving, Sarah repeated, "Sir, you're under arrest."

The man lunged toward Sarah with the knife and fell to the ground, obviously drunk. Zach ran to Sarah, and they both handcuffed him while he shouted obscenities. A skinny, dark-haired woman opened the door and ran to Sarah. A cut over her eye and one on her arm bled into two towels she held against her wounds. Tears fell from her swollen eyes onto her torn blouse, evidence that she'd suffered a severe beating. Sarah had lived the same scenario many times.

"Where is he going? Where are you taking him?" The woman was near hysteria.

"Ma'am, are you okay?" Zach tenderly asked the woman.

"Yes, sir," she muttered. "I'm okay."

"We may need you at the police station," Sarah instructed the woman. "We work for the sheriff's department. We're not the police. But we have arrested him and will turn him over to the city cops."

Sarah was informative, but the abused woman just kept crying and saying, "He'll kill me for calling the sheriff."

Sarah looked the woman squarely in the eye and assured her, "He will never harm you again. Don't be afraid."

Sarah planned to drive the criminal to the police station. She had done her part. But Sarah knew wife beaters better than most, and if this animal obtained bail, his wife could die.

Sarah could hear the abuser cursing in the backseat and felt his spit hit her neck. Her mind suddenly took over her body. She could feel Pete's palm across her face. Pete's grip pressing her arms, then slamming her to the floor. Pete's fingers closing around her throat, his hands gripping her hair. Her body began shaking as she realized how much she intensely hated the man in her backseat. Everything he represented repulsed her. The crying woman, afraid and helpless, needed Sarah to act on her behalf.

Sarah was now sure of one thing only: everyone was better off if this man was dead. Sarah looked at Zach, wondering if he really meant it when he said he'd always have her back.

Sarah stopped the car and turned toward her partner. "Zach, that poor woman can never escape this monster. He'll get out and probably beat her to death. We have to stop this."

Zach looked befuddled. "What can we do? Let's get out and talk about this," he said in hushed tones.

Zach and Sarah stepped out and huddled beside the car away from the handcuffed man.

"You think we should kill him?" he asked.

Zach looked at Sarah, nervous but excited.

She slowly nodded, "yes."

"Every woman in the world would be safer. Somebody has to get rid of the world's scum. Maybe we can do a little good," she said.

Zach seemed unsure.

"God says an eye for an eye, Zach. It's in the bible. God wants us to help." Sarah was certain.

Zach then whispered to Sarah, "I have a different gun," pulling a weapon out of his holster.

"What do you mean?" she asked.

"This gun is not registered. We can kill this man with it, and no one will know."

Sarah slowly nodded. "Give me your gun. I must do it. I want to kill this monster, Zach. Do you have my back?"

"I'll never tell a soul, Sarah. The world is better off getting rid of him," Zach swore.

"Okay, then," Sarah said, looking at the drunk man in the backseat. "Let's get rid of this sinner. God is on our side." Zach handed her the gun, and she swung open the back door.

"Get out of the car," Sarah ordered the man. He swore and spat at her. "Where are we, cunt?" he demanded.

Sarah quietly ordered him again to get out. "We have car trouble," she lied. Their prisoner looked doubtful.

The suspect climbed out of the car, still handcuffed, while Zach held his unregistered gun on him.

"Start walking that way," Sarah pointed her finger.

Again, the man spat toward her and yelled, "I'll kill you, cunt. And you too, cocksucking fag."

"I don't think so," Zach said and smiled.

The prisoner began the death walk.

"Stop!" Sarah yelled. "Turn around."

As he turned toward Sarah, she shot a single bullet from Zach's gun, hitting the man's forearm. He began screaming, blood spurting from his appendage. Sarah shot the man again, this time hitting his forehead. Blood ran down into his eyes. He fell, and Sarah walked closer. The third shot to his heart stopped his movement. Everyone was silent.

"Zach, remove his handcuffs," she ordered. "It has to look as if he escaped and someone else killed him. Remember, we are the ones who have to investigate this murder."

Sarah and Zach quietly drove back to town, rehearsing their story. They both knew the dead man would be discovered and they'd be questioned. Their stories must jive.

Sarah filed the appropriate report on the incident and was pleased when Sheriff Will buried it under a mountain of paperwork. It turns out that the meaningless wife beater was someone nobody knew and nobody cared was dead.

***

Sarah's love for and fear of God were inextricably intertwined. She wanted to please her God more than anything, yet she feared he was often displeased with her. Her early religious teachings had pierced her growing ideas of a woman's independence. Sarah was proud of her newfound status, yet felt slightly ashamed when women would ask how Pete liked being a "kept" husband. Sarah feared only two men in her life: God, whom Sarah never doubted was male, and Pete. Fearing either one's wrath, God and Pete were Sarah Sears' sole judge and jury.

In her prayers every night, Sarah asked for God's forgiveness and begged for his help in righting the wrongs that mortal men executed against others. Sins like spousal and child abuse, sexual predation, theft, and murder—Sarah felt God needed her as his instrument for justice in all these cases.

Over time, she and Pete had become even more estranged. Pete rarely left his office upstairs and no longer approached Sarah sexually. She wondered if the magazine she'd caught him looking at had anything to do with the change in their relationship. This distance was appealing to Sarah, allowing her free rein to concentrate on her investigative duties for the county.

The two, it seemed to Sarah, remained married only for financial and convenient reasons. He had little interest in spending the Sears family money on clothing or home furnishings but instead had deepened his fascination with weapons and other hunting gear. When he wasn't working, Pete's days were consumed by magazines and books devoted to firearms.

Olivia was virtually a stranger to both her parents, as she spent most of her free time with friends or volunteering for Reverend Thomas at the church. Remembering her young friend's fate, Sarah highly suspected Olivia was on drugs, but she chose not to fight that battle.

Pete was Sarah's earthly judge, however flawed he was. She yearned for freedom but would not consider leaving the man she promised God she would obey. Pete's wrath, although it had waned in recent months, still intimidated Sarah. At the end of each workday, Sarah habitually entered the Sears house with dread. What was the current state of her husband's mind, and how would it affect her evening?

This Monday night was no exception to the routine. When she arrived home, it was quiet. Tense and anxious, Sarah climbed the staircase, entering the spare bedroom Pete claimed as his office. Pete was gone, and one of his hunting magazines was laying open on the desk. Sarah came closer and, gasping with surprise and dismay, saw the magazine was pornographic. The page was turned to an image of two pubescent girls naked and touching each other in a sexual pose. Sarah could hear steps on the stairs. There was no time to escape—Pete Sears was entering his lair.

"What the hell are you doing up here?" he hissed at Sarah. "No one but me is allowed in my office, bitch!"

Pete instantly realized Sarah had seen the porn. He reached for Sarah across the wooden desk, trying to grab her. Sarah was still in slight shock and total disgust at seeing two girls younger than Olivia arousing men like Pete Sears.

She instantly decided that she would not take a beating tonight from her husband. Sarah would stand up to his abuse this time.

"Stop!" she yelled back at Pete. "Not tonight!"

His wife's yelling was not something Pete was accustomed to. His anger boiled, but his better judgment prevailed. He stopped and stared at Sarah, his mouth gaped.

"Get the hell out of here," he demanded. Sarah walked around the desk and past Pete with a little air of superiority.

As she walked down the stairs, she admitted to herself and God, "I hate my husband, and for that I'm sorry. But Pete Sears will die if he continues to hit me. God, I hope you understand." Sarah was changing, and tonight was the beginning.

**

The next day Zach welcomed Sarah to the office by brandishing the latest crime sheet from the state that had come over the fax machine. They'd given up on the bank robbers from Cooke County. But several other heinous crimes had been committed the last few days, mostly in South Texas. One stood out. A farmer in Alabama had been shot, and the killer was on the loose. There were no witnesses, but Highway 82 was a possible escape path since the main highway went through town east to west. In the past, an occasional escaped convict or suspect had traveled through Nocona, but one had never been apprehended in the community. According to the crime brief, all the counties along Red River were to keep a lookout for strangers.

Zach smiled and said, "Any killer in Montague County better watch for Detective Sears."

Sarah returned the grin. "See you in a little bit," she told Zach and went into her office, a Diet Coke in her hand.

Looking out the window, Sarah immediately spied the same blue Chevy from the cemetery parked about 200 feet away. Her curiosity growing, she went outside and started walking toward the car when the driver started the engine and slowly pulled away. She suspected it was Mooney's nephew who might be a drug dealer, possibly the same one who sold Cynthia her dose of death. Sarah was reminded just then of the bible's promise that God blesses those who are kind to little children. This drug devil would pay.

6

Pulling in the parking lot the next day, Sarah noticed Ruby's car was gone, while Zach's motorcycle was in place. Sarah liked it best when Ruby was away so she and Zach could devise plans to rid more criminals in their little county. They were a formidable team, but that was a secret no one else would be able to guess.

By now, Sarah had grown familiar with her new position at work, and most of the tiny town's residents had learned to accept a woman as a lawman. She often smiled and waved to both women and men strolling on broken concrete sidewalks lining the few downtown city blocks.

She decided one day to go downtown and see if she could get some information from the townspeople about any suspicious activity. A tin overhang at the old feed store's front entrance provided shade for a few elderly men sharing decades-old stories about farming and the war. They tipped their ball caps and dirty western Stetsons as she entered the building.

Big Sam, the convivial store clerk, had spent decades

throwing feed sacks into pick-up beds. He was born in Nocona, and he would die there by all accounts.

"Hi, Sam," Sarah said and smiled. "Anything going on today?"

Sam paused before answering, "Nope, 'cept Mr. Adams bought 30 bags of cow feed. His tank is 'bout dry."

"Well, you know my phone number at the station if you see or hear anything," she replied. Sam had a good view of downtown and would spot a strange vehicle that did not belong there. Sarah knew almost every car in the county and who it belonged to. Any unidentified vehicle would arouse suspicion.

"Don't forget, I did give you a badge a few weeks ago," she reminded him. Sarah had determined early on in her new role to recruit vigilant citizens to help rid her county of any crime. Sam was one of the people she chose to give a badge to, with the instructions to keep an eye out. A badge meant a lot to most people, even if it was not official. It certainly empowered Big Sam.

"Okay, Miss Sarah," Sam said. He liked the policewoman. She bid him goodbye, and he went back to sweeping grain on the concrete floor. She talked with a few more townspeople and spent the afternoon catching up on paperwork.

Sarah once again dreaded closing up the office and driving the short distance to her house at the end of the day. She often asked God why her marriage to Pete was so traumatic, but most often ended her prayers thanking God for her life and that of her daughter. She desperately wanted Olivia to get a college degree, but that appeared unlikely.

Only church work seemed to satisfy Olivia. Sarah vowed to ask her more questions about the extended time she was spending at the church, even if angering her daughter was the outcome.

Pete was downstairs listening to the nightly news when she walked in her front door.

"Well," he said, "looks like North Texas may have a killer loose. Whaddya you know about it, Ms. Lawman?" He looked at Sarah incredulously.

"Not too much, just to be on the lookout for strangers or anything suspicious," she answered flatly.

"Who knows? Maybe you'll get to use that gun you like so much," he sneered.

For an instant, Sarah imagined his forehead with a bullet hole, blood oozing through his eyebrows. She immediately asked God for forgiveness. Pete was her husband, now and forever. She had promised God.

"The killer could be anywhere by now, but I guess we'd better lock the doors," Sarah said as she took a seat beside him on the couch.

"Yeah, but I'm so hungry, I might invite a killer to eat supper if that got you off your ass and made us something to eat." Pete's meanness never left him.

Sarah got up and went into the kitchen. She pulled some items out of the fridge and dropped two pork chops into a pan of grease, stuck a potato in the microwave, and opened a can of green beans. Add a loaf of bread and a piece of lemon icebox pie, and it would have to do for tonight. Then she planned to retreat to the bedroom.

Sex was seldom between the Sears, and Sarah liked it that way, although she sometimes had dreams that a man was rubbing her breasts and kissing her neck. She couldn't control her hormones from working, but she suppressed all sexual thoughts, as her husband repulsed her.

***

"Hey, Sarah," Zach greeted his boss as Sarah opened the office door the next day.

No Ruby yet, but sure as the morning sun, she would come in and ring up anyone she could gossip with.

"Old Seth Adams called a few minutes ago and said he saw an unusual car in town yesterday," Zach explained. "He thought you might want to follow up, as he'd heard on the news last night a killer was likely somewhere in North Texas."

Sarah smiled at Zach, appreciating his loyalty and confidence in her. She felt like a mother and a big sister to the young man who had been abused most of his life. Zach was a loyal comrade.

"Want me to go with you through town to see what we can see?" Zach offered, hopeful.

"Nope," Sarah said.

"You stay here, and if I need you, I'll holler. Old Seth usually sends us on a wild goose chase, but I guess you never know. I'll be back in a little while."

Zach went back to reading through the faxes that had come in overnight. Ruby arrived as Sarah was leaving, coughing into her hand as she nodded and smiling at her co-workers. Ruby was a chain smoker along with her husband before he died. Sarah was sure Ruby also had emphysema.

Sarah drove around a bit, but the usual suspects were the only ones on the Nocona streets. The First National Bank tellers had parked and reported for duty. School buses were headed to the north side to deliver kids. The local grocery store parking lot was virtually empty. There was nothing unusual in Nocona today.

Sarah found Seth Adams and a few old farmers inside the grocery store, sitting at a small table at the front of the store near an old coffee pot. Coffee was free until 10:00 each morning, and the locals took full advantage of anything free. The men turned when Sarah walked toward them. Some hesitantly smiled, and others frowned. A woman of the law in Nocona, Texas? Hard to believe and even more so to accept.

"Hi, fellows," Sarah said. She tried to sound friendly yet firm. "Have you seen anyone new in town?"

They glanced at each other and shook their heads, "no."

What was this woman up to now? They were all curious.

Just as Sarah had wanted him to do, Old Seth piped up. "I saw an older blue car parked in front of the hardware store yesterday, or maybe the day before. Never seen that car before in town."

"What did it look like?" Sarah questioned the old man, taking notes in her notebook.

The other men snickered when Seth answered curtly, "I told you. An old blue car."

Sarah nodded, thanked Seth, and walked away quickly. She hated hearing snide remarks about her being a female. "Sons of bitches," she thought. "Always the same. They think just because they have a dick, they're better than women."

Sarah was now on high alert. She was sure that if she saw the old blue car anywhere in Montage County again, she'd get a chance to question the occupant.

***

Old Lady Mooney was up early frying bacon. Henry shaved and put on a pair of too short khaki pants that had belonged to Mr. Mooney. He laughed to himself at his reflection in the full-length mirror. Henry Lee Lucas in a dead man's clothes. He'd liked to have met Mr. Mooney. No reason why; he just would have liked to.

"Mrs. Mooney, what can I do to help you today?" Henry was already hard at work charming her.

"Well, let's eat first, and then you can start by picking up the trash that has blown all over this yard. I'm too old and fat to bend over much."

Henry glanced at the old Westinghouse television on a stand in the small parlor. The clean-cut reporter was talking about a killer who might be traveling through North Texas, likely alone. Anxiety crept into Henry's mind. What if the old lady became wary of him?

Henry began a conversation with Mrs. Mooney, drowning out the newscaster. He also planned to gather up any newspapers in the yard, just in case they contained a story or notice. Henry was skilled at covering his tracks.

Becky was up too by now and threw her arms around the old woman, startling her.

"Thank you, Mrs. Mooney, for breakfast. I am starved," Becky said and sat down at the table. Mrs. Mooney was surprised and pleased the girl was so friendly and that she appreciated her. She had received so little gratitude in her lifetime.

Henry was proud of Becky. She could play up her acting when she wanted to. "Hi, Daddy," Becky said sweetly as Mrs. Mooney returned her attention to fixing breakfast.

"That's enough," Henry whispered. He didn't want Becky to trip up by blabbing too much.

He looked at his accomplice and said, "I need you to help me in the yard this morning."

"I'd like to help Mrs. Mooney inside," Becky said and smiled at him.

"No!" Henry snapped. Mrs. Mooney looked up from the pan of fried eggs. "Sorry," he offered. "I just need the girl to help me right now."

They sat down to breakfast and ate quietly. The old lady was well aware of the knot of worry in her stomach, taking in a strange man and a girl. But she liked having someone else in the house, so she disregarded her instincts. Henry went outside to work after he ate.

He didn't like to be sweaty and tired, so he took a break from repairing the front porch and opened the shabby front door of the home to grab a cool drink. He needed to head to town for some supplies.

Mrs. Mooney was slumped on the ragged couch napping.

"What's wrong?" she asked him, suddenly awake. "If you're already pooped out, you must be a city boy. In the country, we work sun up to sun down."

Henry wanted to stab the old bitch.

"I got to go to town," he answered softly. No reason to agitate or argue with the old broad. Henry knew to keep a low profile.

"Whatever," she said. "At least you got some of the trash. Oh, hell, tomorrow is another day. Is the girl going with you?"

"I'll go check on her," he said.

Henry eyed the teenager asleep in the small bedroom.

Closing the door behind him, Henry put his hands around the girl's neck, her eyes popping open.

"Look, you little cunt," he told her. "I'm going to town, and if you say anything to the old lady, I'll kill you. You got it?" Henry was whispering but scary.

Becky nodded and then pulled Henry on top of her. He knew the girl liked fucking, so he'd comply. A couple of minutes later, he'd cum, not worried about what the girl wanted. She tried flirting with him, wanting more. He pulled her tiny tit toward his mouth and bit the nipple. She shrieked, and he covered her mouth.

"Shut up!" he seethed. "The old bitch will hear you. I'll be back in a little while."

Henry put on another dead man Mooney shirt and left for town. He was thinking about the receptionist back at the hotel and decided he would stop there before going to the hardware store. If a male clerk had taken her place for the day, Henry was also open to fucking a man. He liked both.

The café door was propped open, and sure enough, the busty young blonde named Lee was on duty that day. Henry was already standing in the doorway when he saw Lee was already talking with another woman at the counter. It was a lady cop, the one whose picture he'd seen in the Nocona News. This could be real trouble.

Henry needed all the manly charm he could muster, as it was too late to turn around and leave. The two women had seen him. His slim body looked smart in clothes, and his hair was full.

"Hi," he addressed Lee. "It's great to see you again."

The blonde smiled at Henry. Sarah was instantly curious. "Who is this stranger?" she wanted to know.

Henry looked at Sarah and nodded.

"Ma'am," he offered, tipping his head toward Sarah. "My name's Hank."

"Hello," Sarah said, choosing to acknowledge him with slight apprehension. Ever-conscientious, Sarah would find out more about this newcomer.

"I've never seen you before," she said, searching his face.

"Oh, well, I'm here for a day or two while I decide where I'm settling," Henry explained. "This town seems friendly," he said and glanced at the receptionist. "We met a while back."

Henry imagined the blonde was anxious to get him back in bed.

"That's good. Where are you coming from?" Sarah asked, determined to sound friendly and non-threatening to keep the man talking.

"From Arkansas. Hot Springs," Henry lied.

"That's a nice place. Why are you moving to?" Sarah kept up the friendly interrogation.

"Well, if you really want to know," Henry explained, "I gotta mean ex-wife back there. I decided to take my girl and settle in Texas."

"You have legal custody of your daughter?" Sarah raised an eyebrow.

Henry did not hesitate. "Yeah, she's sixteen. She wanted to come with me. My ex is a drunk and beat my girl a lot. She was ready to move." Growing uncomfortable with the law lady, he changed the subject. "I'm real hungry and thought I'd get a meal. You wanna join me?"

He smiled at Sarah.

Caught off-guard by an odd liking for this stranger, Sarah decided eating with him would cause too much gossip. Sarah Sears had a reputation to guard and secrets to keep. Zach was her only confidant, and somehow she trusted the man-child with her life.

"No, but thank you," Sarah said, exchanging a friendly smile with Henry.

The receptionist was annoyed by now. She did not intend to lose her new lover, especially to an old lady cop. "Come on, Hank," she said. "Let's get you something to eat."

Henry nodded again at Sarah and followed the girl to one of the empty booths. Henry planned to eat, fuck, and then plan on how he'd get this law lady alone. The stuff he'd do to that cop made him have a bigger than usual hard-on. His animal instincts were in overdrive.

Sarah's instincts were also on alert warning her against danger. A single man younger than eighty who was not a homosexual in Nocona, Texas, was intriguing. Going against her gut to steer clear of him, she found herself wanting instead to get to know more about this man.

***

Sarah's newfound independence severely angered Pete Sears. But leaving her and his beloved Olivia was not an option. Besides, who else would he ever get in this tiny town? No, he'd just put up with his uppity wife until he couldn't take it anymore. He knew he might explode on her at any time, but she now had a fucking gun and the right to use it.

"Shit. I'm in a shitload of trouble if I punish the bitch," Pete told himself one day waiting for Sarah to get home and fix him some dinner. "How'd I let this happen?" He was mad at himself. "Well maybe she'll get fired, and then I'm gonna be the man I used to be. My old lady needs to pay for what she's doing to me."

A few minutes later, Sarah opened the front door.

"Hello," she yelled up the stairs. "You up there, Pete?" Not waiting for an answer, Sarah called out, "Olivia, are you upstairs?"

Walking downstairs and into the kitchen, Pete answered. "She's not here. She's over at the church again."

Sarah had gained the upper hand in the Sears household. She wasn't sure what God would want her to do, but she did know she hated this weak monster. For now, she would continue to lessen her interactions with him.

"I'll have dinner ready in a little bit," she said, reaching for a skillet and opening a drawer of cooking utensils.

"How about us going to the Dairy Hut instead?" Pete suggested and actually grinned at Sarah. She almost dropped the spatula in her hand. Eating out was very rare in their house. She felt her stomach twinge. Was he leaving her? That was not fathomable. He needed her money, the stability of a good wife, and his daughter. The son of a bitch wasn't about to leave. But asking if she wanted to eat out was unusual.

"Okay," Sarah said slowly and put the spatula back in the drawer. "Let's go."

The Nocona Dairy Hut was situated on the busiest intersection in the town. Virtually any car turning off the state highway and headed downtown had to pass in front of or beside the café. Sarah and Pete sat in a front booth. Anytime the couple sat opposite each other this way, Sarah's thoughts went back to their honeymoon and the food he smashed in her face. Years later, Sarah still despised this memory and the humility he forced on her.

People rarely saw the Sears together in public. Plus, her new job caused a little stir wherever she went into town, and they soon noticed other couples were staring at them.

"What are the assholes staring at?" Pete mumbled.

"Nothing, just eat," Sarah answered. She was looking out

the glass and away from her husband when she spotted an old blue car slowly pass by. This time she had a good look at the driver, and she swore to herself it was the Arkansas man behind the wheel!

As Sarah turned down the bedcovers alone later that evening, the stranger she'd met earlier entered her thoughts. "Maybe it's a coincidence, but I'm gonna find him tomorrow and get more information," she decided. Her hormones stirred faintly before she fell asleep, but Sarah rested fitfully. Pete spent the night the same way he spent most nights: masturbating to porn. He couldn't get an erection since Sarah had gained so much control of his mind. He'd only enjoyed sex for his ability to dominate, and now that was gone.

Meanwhile, Henry drove the streets of Nocona on the way back to the Mooney place, thirsty for the excitement that only rape and murder could satisfy. But this time, he was focused on only one woman: the plain but pretty law woman. Henry was determined to dominate this woman, demean her, and control her. He fantasized that night about fucking her hard and making her suck him. A pretty lady cop, it couldn't get better than that.

He awoke the next morning to the sound of Old Lady Mooney's voice.

"Get up!" she was yelling through the locked door of his room. "I don't appreciate you locking the door."

Henry despised the old woman more every day.

"The sun's up, and you're not," she complained. "If you're gonna work for me, you work when the sun's up."

"Yes, ma'am," Henry answered. "Sorry 'bout that, Mrs. Mooney!"

She grunted and walked toward the kitchen.

After Henry got dressed, he sat down for breakfast with his employer.

"I'm going to head back to town to pick up a new rake and hoe for the yard," he said. "I'll need to drive your truck."

"Always something," the old lady growled. "Didn't you just go into town yesterday?"

Becky walked in just then and pulled out a chair at the table.

"Becky, let's you and me can some beans from the garden today," Mrs. Mooney said sweetly.

"Ain't never canned before, but I'll try," Becky answered just as sweetly back.

"Yes, you will. And you'll do just fine."

The old lady liked having the girl to keep her company.

Henry ate his fried eggs and bacon, ignoring the women. Then he hurried out the door armed with an excuse to meet up with Sarah Sears. He knew getting too close was dangerous, but Henry Lee Lucas thrived on danger.

***

The sheriff's office ran efficiently under Sarah's watchful eye. Ruby and Zach completed the endless state-required paperwork on time and with little drama. Most infractions involved an abusive husband, a drunk, or a traffic offender. As such, people continued to be comfortably safe and were mostly concerned with petty thefts and the occasional fight, which was usually contained within the offending family. Sheriff Will seemed pleased and only checked in with her from time to time for updates. He had his eye on a promotion and was more focused these days on state level politics since nothing of consequence ever happened in Nocona.

Small town entertainment was reserved for fall high school football games, winter basketball, and hot summer nights of baseball. Henry liked baseball, the only game he played as a kid. He could see baseball diamond lights from Mrs. Mooney's house and decided he'd like to watch a few innings before heading back with the old lady's yard tools he'd picked up in town and thrown into the truck bed.

He parked Mooney's rusted-out truck on a side street and watched the teams play from a safe distance. The young boys on the field reminded him of his youth, a time when he lived in terror of his father and was ignored by his mother. Henry was the worst outcome of the family sins.

Sarah's route home led her by the baseball fields. Having only a daughter and a mostly reclusive husband, Sarah hadn't been to a baseball game since childhood. Slowing the patrol car as she neared the lights, she decided to take advantage of the gathering and search for some more leads among the townspeople.

Always vigilant to his surroundings, Henry saw Sarah's car approaching in his side mirror. He prepared his psyche to make a friend of the law lady. He rolled down his window and waved at her as she passed.

Sarah saw Henry.

"Howdy," Henry offered.

"Hello. What brings you out here?" Sarah said, surprised to see him and feeling flush. Henry knew she had purposefully sought him out.

"Nice night, ain't it?" he asked.

"Yes, nice night," Sarah agreed.

The Little League parents were yelling and clapping loudly nearby, paying no attention to the unlikely duo attempting to bond. They were two lonely misfits, survivors of unseemly acts that had disrupted their potential to live normal lives.

"Wanna sit in the truck with me and watch a little ball?" Henry inquired, making his move. Sarah Sears knew better to get in a stranger's vehicle but was strangely drawn to his offer.

"Okay, but I gotta go home in just a few minutes."

"Sure," Henry said and grinned.

"Looks like you're still liking our little town, Hank," Sarah said to prod the conversation.

"Yep, it's looking better all the time." Henry smiled at Sarah again. She felt a little uncomfortable with his answer. The open windows allowed the hot and muggy air to enter, and both Sarah and Henry were sweating.

"How about let's drive through the Dairy Hut and get a cold drink? I'll bring you right back," he assured her.

Sarah fought her instincts but nodded okay. Henry knew the law lady would be his. He'd won over another one.

Henry joked with the drive-thru lady at the Dairy Hut and ordered. "Two Coke floats, ma'am," he said politely.

Sarah watched Henry and thought how nice he seemed. With their drinks in hand, Henry pulled the truck into an empty space in the parking lot. He shut down the engine and turned toward Sarah.

"What is a pretty law lady like you doing in a truck with a stranger?" He was smiling, his eyes piercing through Sarah's soul. "Ain't you married?" Henry was doing all the talking. Sarah looked half-frightened and half-embarrassed.

"How *did* I allow myself to get in this position?" she wondered. This was the only man Sarah Sears had ever been alone with other than her husband and Zach. She was confused by her own actions.

"Yes, I'm married," she said quietly.

"Why ain't you at home by now?" Henry pressed her further.

Sarah looked down speechless.

"Bad deal, huh?" Henry inquired, concern in his voice.

Sarah again slightly nodded, not looking Henry in the eye.

"He beat you? Slap you around? Cuss you out?" Henry asked, probing her for information he could use.

Tears welled in Sarah's eyes.

Henry knew he'd opened a floodgate. He was pleased with himself. Vulnerable women were his specialty at any age. "Such easy prey," he thought. But he liked this woman. She wasn't a slut or a bitch, just in the wrong place at the wrong time with the wrong man.

Henry reached for her face, lifted it up toward him, and slightly kissed Sarah on the cheek. She cursed herself for wanting more from this man. Maybe just to hold her and let her cry on his shoulder.

Henry decided to nurture this encounter and play with his prey until he grew weary. Without a word, he started the engine and drove back toward the game.

Sarah sat silent—disappointed in herself, but helpless to resist. She knew if this man stayed any length of time in Nocona, Texas, she'd see him again, but she admitted her desire only to herself.

Henry pulled up beside the patrol car and reached across Sarah to open her door. He brushed her breast, and she caught her breath. He brought out a sexual desire she felt had left her body. Yes, she wanted to know more about this Arkansas traveler.

"Well, you best be getting home. Good night," Henry said and touched her hand.

"Good night," she said and walked as if in a trance back to her car.

Under a strange and exciting spell, Sarah couldn't sleep that night. She thought of this stranger, knowing she would ultimately succumb to him if he chose her. Sarah touched her breast and remembered his forearm brushing against it. She did not know it then, but Sarah was about to make love to a killing animal, a demented soul of Satan.

Henry laughed out loud, driving the three miles back to Mrs. Mooney's. Pulling in the graveled drive, Henry was surprised when the headlights revealed Becky sitting in a tiny tree swing. She was mad.

"You're always going to town, and I never get to go.

I stayed here all day with that old woman and peeled vegetables," she moaned.

"Come here, little girl," Henry said, not wanting Becky's mood to spoil everything. Becky slid in the truck beside Henry, and he backed out of the driveway.

Mrs. Mooney was looking out the front window and watched Becky slide into the front seat of her truck, leaning a bit too close to Henry.

"That doesn't look like daddy-daughter to me," the old woman mused under her breath. "Bastard," she said, thinking of poor Becky. "I may have to get rid of him and finish her raising myself. Bastard!"

Henry drove about a mile away, pulled over to the side of the dirt road, and decided to butt fuck his little blabbermouth to keep her on track.

"Roll over on your stomach, little girl. Ever had a butt fuck?" Henry asked.

"It hurts, Henry," Becky whimpered.

"Shut up, cunt. You're Henry's slave tonight."

Becky knew this wouldn't be the last time she was a sex slave.

Henry was slightly irritated. He didn't want to keep being with Becky like this to keep her quiet. But he didn't want to kill her either. "Damn, this is a problem!" he told himself.

"A few more days, little one," Henry assured her. "We will rob the old bitch and skip town. Be patient with me and keep your mouth shut. Can you do that for your daddy?"

They both laughed at this ridiculous ruse.

***

Zach was working when Sarah opened the door. No Ruby.

"Hey, Sarah, Mrs. Grimes called and wants to come by and talk to you. I told her it would be okay this morning. Is that okay?"

"Sure," Sarah said and wondered why Alice Grimes would want to talk to her. Alice's daughter, Amber, and Olivia were friends. Both girls volunteered at the church with Reverend Thomas. Sarah hoped the mom hadn't caught the teenagers doing drugs.

Alice arrived a few minutes later and asked Sarah to close the door to her office. She was uncomfortable, and Sarah could tell some bad news was about to come out of the woman's mouth.

"What's wrong, Alice?" Sarah asked.

Tears were slowly running down Alice's cheeks when she looked at Sarah and said, "I think my daughter's been raped."

"What? Who?" Sarah asked, sounding incredulous.

"I don't know. She won't tell me. But she's pregnant."

Alice sobbed. In a small Texas town, rape is terrible. But pregnancy is much worse. This would have to be handled quietly, or the entire Grimes family would be shunned.

"How can I help?" Sarah asked. "Are you sure it was rape?"

Alice looked hurt by the question, and Sarah was immediately sorry she'd asked.

"I'll help any way I can," Sarah followed up, hoping to smooth things over with the woman.

Alice stood up, her hurt turning into rage. "Amber is sixteen!" she screamed. "Of course, it was rape!"

Alice was becoming hysterical. Sarah was relieved that Ruby had gone to a doctor's appointment. Ruby loved scandal, and teenage pregnancy was great fodder. Zach, however, would keep quiet and do whatever he could to help resolve this matter.

"Alice, if you get any information out of Amber, let me know. I will be discreet and see if I can find out any information from Olivia or anyone else about who might have done this," Sarah said.

"You don't do anything! No one can find out. Promise me!" Alice responded firmly.

Sarah agreed, and Alice gathered up her keys and handbag and left crying. Zach looked up and immediately felt sorry for the woman.

"If it's rape, I'll have to kill the asshole," Sarah thought as she watched Alice walk to her car.

God wanted her to rid the world of sinners. Rapists were the worst. God and Sarah would not abide by animalistic behavior. This is why God gave her this job. Sarah was convinced of this. She planned to go to the high school tomorrow and talk to some of Amber's teachers.

***

Old Lady Mooney silently seethed against Henry the

next morning. After last night, she was convinced he was raping his own daughter. That explained why Becky was so reserved when she came home. Mrs. Mooney struggled with her choices. Should she call the police? Or shut her mouth and tell the no-good drifter to move on? Or just shoot him dead?

Mrs. Mooney's family was poor, but they were not criminals. Even though her children had escaped poverty and Nocona, Texas, and although she rarely saw her grandchildren, she was sure they were never abused.

The old lady didn't like men much, but she did have an affinity for young girls like Becky.

"Mrs. Mooney," Henry called out. "Are you in there?" She was sitting on the threadbare couch after breakfast, watching the morning news shows.

"What is it?" she barked at Henry.

Savvy of people's moods, Henry knew his time at the Mooney house was growing short.

"Ma'am," he began, "I could use a few dollars. My car's nearly empty on gas and, although I appreciate the clothes you gave me, I need to buy some that fit me better." Henry was planning on wooing Sarah and needed to make a better presentation.

"I don't have any cash," Mrs. Mooney replied. "But my social security check should be in the mail today or tomorrow. I don't like much about the government, but they are on time most of the time." Without meaning to, the old woman had made a fatal casual remark.

Henry's sinister mind was racing. Old Lady Mooney was

a recluse, so who would know if he killed her and then ran, taking her cash with him? But what about that law lady? Raping a sheriff's deputy was too enticing. Henry even liked the idea of maybe not having to force her; she seemed to like him.

"Yes, ma'am," he responded. "You think I could get a little pay when you cash your government check?"

"We'll see," the old woman grunted, still weighing her options with Becky's perverted father.

***

Henry planned to catch Sarah when she was in town. He often drove by her office to watch her and had even followed Sarah to her home more than once. But he hesitated to go to the door, as that could expose him a little too much. He felt sure Sarah Sears was blinded to his charms, but other people might be saner.

He drove once more by the sheriff's parking lot, but her car was not there. "She must be roaming around this place looking for criminals," Henry thought and drove on, watching for her. He spied the patrol car in the high school parking lot. Henry liked high school girls. They were so dumb and trusting, and Henry had tortured and killed several in his 40-plus years.

Sarah was walking toward her car when she noticed Henry pulling up beside her, this time in his sedan.

"Hey madam," he greeted her. "How about a drive to the river? I ain't never been."

Sarah grew up near Red River, and she knew little good ever came from the muddy waters. She winced, remembering being raped there by the two thugs she'd killed in Oklahoma.

"Okay," she said warily. "But I can just let you take a look there, and then I have to get back. I have to catch a rapist."

"What?" Henry said, his nerves on high alert. "A rapist?"

"Well, one of the high school girls got pregnant," Sarah told him, feeling oddly at ease entrusting him with this information. "And her mother insists it was rape. She says there's no way her baby girl would want to have sex with anyone, and someone must have forced her."

Henry laughed and joked, "Don't young girls fuck in Nocona, Texas?"

Sarah frowned on Henry's crude language, and he changed directions fast.

"Just a short drive and back," he promised her. And Sarah got in the passenger seat.

Lots of mischief happened on the Red River banks: all night beer busts, drugs, and sex—mostly unprotected and sometimes forced. No highway reached the water's edge, just muddy roads with tree overgrowth hanging overhead. Farmers liked to plant watermelons along the sandy fields near the water, and several pecan orchards provided the little Texas river towns with plenty of pecan pies at Thanksgiving and Christmas.

When the narrow country lane ended and the sand started, Henry shut the motor off. He turned to look at Sarah. She was intimidated but stimulated.

"Tell me about yourself, Sarah Sears. How did you get

here?" Henry wanted to know.

Sarah had never once told a man anything about herself. Pete knew all he wanted to know when they got married and had hardly said a kind word in decades. No other man dared to communicate with her and most likely didn't want to, Sarah presumed.

Sarah began telling Henry about growing up in rural Texas and how she'd gone to community college before she married. She told him about her daughter. Even though Olivia was foul-tempered like her dad, she'd brought Sarah the only joy she'd known until recently. She explained how much she loved her job. Sarah kept some information to herself. The killings were to rid the community of sinners, and only God and Zach knew Sarah was doing God's work.

She, in turn, asked about Henry. He took sinister pleasure in spinning his life's lies. A jilted husband with a drunken, drug-addicted wife, he'd decided to rescue his daughter and flee to Texas. He wasn't sure where he'd settle. "But I like where I am at this minute," he told Sarah, and she smiled back.

Henry reached over to take her hand, and she pulled it back gently.

"You scared of me?" he asked.

"No," she said. "But I've never been with any man but Pete."

"Son of a bitch," he murmured loud enough for Sarah to be aware of his concern. "What are you gonna do about him beating you?" he asked, remembering what Sarah had told him the other night.

"I don't know," Sarah answered. "God says you can have only one husband, and I'm afraid I picked the wrong one."

Henry reached across the seat and kissed Sarah on the lips. She didn't stop him and put her hand in his. He started kissing her on her neck and chest.

She was breathing rapidly and didn't resist his lips and wandering hands. He unbuttoned her uniform and kissed her breasts, softly at first and then harder. She was quivering. He started unbuttoning her pants. Her holster was in place, and Henry gently unbuckled the leather, laying the gun on the floorboard.

He was sliding her pants down and pushing her panties to the side as his fingers entered her vagina. The other hand rubbed her nipples. Sarah was overwhelmed with his desire, and her own was raging. She couldn't believe she was letting a stranger make love to her in a car on the Red River not far from the site where she was abducted earlier in the year.

Henry thrust his penis inside Sarah, and she let out a little sound.

"It's okay, Sarah," he told her. "God wants you happy. I can make you happy."

A killer in a killer, they heaved together. Sarah Sears was fucking a raging maniac.

"That SOB better never touch you again!" Henry said after they finished. He was firm, making himself out to be Sarah's savior. "You are special, and I will take care of you."

Henry knew sheltered women like Sarah often mistook sex for love, and he was saying all the right words. Henry had a willing fuck buddy, and he decided to let her live a while longer. This was Henry's mistake.

7

Like a wayward teenager, Sarah was embarrassed that she had given her body to Henry, a man she hardly knew. What was happening? Guilt overwhelmed her, and she began to cry. Henry hated nothing more than a crying woman.

His psyche was growing weary. Maybe rape and murder suited Henry Lee Lucas much better than wooing some God-fearing female. Patience was not Henry's asset; rage and demonic acts seemed more his forte'.

Henry started the car and backed the tires through the muddy bottom land adjacent to the river. "I bet this river has a lot of secrets," Henry muttered as much to himself as Sarah.

She nodded, remembering her rape last year.

Sarah silently vowed to stay away from the wet clay banks of the river from now on and focus instead on whoever raped Amber. This was her job, not having afternoon sex with a stranger. Praying for forgiveness was her first priority, and Sarah hoped God would listen to someone who had strayed from her husband and from her savior. Sarah Sears wanted

God's graces desperately.

The demented duo drove in silence, each entertaining their own thoughts. When they got back to where she had parked at the high school, Sarah bounded from Henry's car, making sure to make no future commitments. Henry smiled and drove away, pleased with his performance. Henry fancied himself as a puppet master, taking what he wanted when he wanted it.

Shaming and berating herself, Sarah hurried to her office, hoping for solitude. She closed the door to be alone. With little regard for Sarah's privacy, Zach entered and laid a fax on Sarah's desk. It had a grainy picture of a criminal, underscored by the message, "Please keep a look out for this accused killer, Henry Lee Lucas. White male, five-foot-ten inches to six feet in height, thin frame. Dirty blonde hair that may be colored now. Perhaps traveling with a teenaged white female accomplice."

Sarah's breathing stopped. Staring at the blurry photo, Sarah saw the man who had kissed her passionately only a few hours earlier. A stranger who stirred Sarah's sexuality. "Surely this is not Hank," she whispered to herself. She willed her eyes to see someone else. Had she, Sarah Sears, had sex with a killer? She instinctively knew it was true.

Sarah felt faint. She excused herself and vomited in the bathroom toilet. Then she took off her uniform pants. With paper towels and soap, Sarah dug inside her vagina, trying to scrape away any semen left inside her. She must cleanse herself of any traces of that man. She vomited again from the pain she was inflicting on herself and the disgust of succumbing to a possible killer.

Sarah was ashamed and remorseful. The only way to get even was to catch and kill her brief lover, never letting anyone but God know she had been duped. Sarah had to think of something. She must talk to her only true friend and protector, God.

***

Henry slowly drove out to the Mooney place, thinking tomorrow might be the time to kill the old lady, get the cash she had from her government check, and head west. And the cop lady he just fucked? "Better kill her too," he thought. She seemed pretty clever and might decide to try to do her job: finding and arresting Henry Lee Lucas.

Henry preferred to hate his prey, pretending they needed for him to kill them. This state of mind was easy to maintain regarding the old lady; he sensed her growing dislike for him since he'd turned out to be an unskilled handyman. But the lady cop...she was kind and loving, attributes that confused Henry. Too bad she was already in Henry's web. It was a case of wrong place, wrong time for the cop lady. She must be dealt with, and Henry acknowledged to himself that he would have to kill her.

Other than the dim light shining through the old lady's bedroom, darkness consumed the night when Henry let himself in at the Mooney place. Henry cursed to himself, "Where the hell is the girl?"

Becky Toole was an obstinate little bitch, just like her

uncle. Henry briefly thought of Ottis, locked up somewhere in Florida and probably cursing the guards and God. Henry knew Ottis was pure Satan, but he was also Henry's friend and had easily accommodated Henry's most morbid sexual acts.

Startling Henry, Becky stepped into his room on the porch.

"I'm not staying here another minute," she said. "That old woman is making me iron clothes now. I hate her."

Shut up," Henry hissed. "Tomorrow we will leave, but we need some money."

"Tomorrow the old lady is supposed to get some," Becky whispered. "I heard her mention her check was coming."

"That's when we leave then," Henry said. "Now shut up and go to bed." Becky made a crumpled face at Henry and stuck her tongue out at him. He declined to slap her but had the urge to do so.

"I can't fuck this little bitch enough to keep her quiet," he thought. "She's dangerous."

Henry laid across the bed and had a conversation aloud with himself.

"If I kill the old woman, I guess I'll throw her body in the river."

"Shit, that don't work cause the water is low. She'd wash up in a day or two."

Henry considered the old garage but knew the police would check for her body there. He remembered seeing an old iron pot-bellied stove in the ruble behind the barn.

"I can cut her up and stick her in there. I'll burn her body to ashes and then throw on some water to cool them off."

Henry was happy with his plan.

***

Sarah prayed on the way home that night. At times, she felt she didn't understand God. Why would he allow her to sin in such a heinous way? But Sarah never questioned God's plan for her.

Pete Sears was growing more reclusive, spending all his waking hours in his office. Rarely nowadays did Sarah rile his temper but instead was ignored. Pete would sometimes try to engage Olivia but got little response.

Sarah and Olivia had always had a distant relationship throughout Olivia's childhood, but Sarah sensed that thawing lately. She suspected Olivia respected her more now than when she was a compliant wife accepting her husband's abuse. Children's eyes see the truth, and Sarah had been growing stronger ever since she started working for the county.

Olivia was home alone in her bedroom that night, the music loud, and the door locked. Her childhood long gone, she was dressed in short black leather skirts and thigh-high boots when she came to the dinner table later. Pete didn't like the daughter she had become.

Never shirking her wifely duties, as promised, Sarah prepared the nightly dinner, and the Sears ate in silence. Sometimes Pete would look at Sarah, shaking his head, not uttering a word.

Sarah's mind chose to craft its own reality that night, accepting only that the man in the police flyer was not the same man who had made love to Sarah. She would inspect the picture again, the knot in her stomach telling her head the truth.

Around 7:30, Sarah left fried eggs and bacon for Pete on her way to the office. She was never late for work, preferring to be with her office family, Zach and Ruby. Life offered little to Sarah, but she was grateful that God had provided her a meaningful job.

Zach was at his usual post, drinking a large Slurpee. Ruby was on her way to a funeral in a neighboring town. Funerals provided ample gossip networks for weeks afterward. Ruby never missed one.

"Good morning, Zach," Sarah said.

"Hey, what's up?" Zach said, happy to see Sarah. "Think you oughta look for Amber's rapist today? Or maybe that killer man on the handout yesterday? God, this place is gettin' busy." Zach seemed happy about the activity.

"I feel kinda sick," Sarah confessed. "I think I'll stay around the office this morning."

Zach looked at Sarah, a little surprised that she didn't have the enthusiasm she typically had when a criminal was on the loose.

Sarah's heart pounded as she eyed Henry's photo again. Gazing at pure evil is difficult. Her hatred of criminals caused her to kill, but she felt God cleansed her soul after every murder. She wasn't sure how God felt about her having sexual intercourse with a killer. She must go to God's house and pray. Sarah Sears was no longer pure in her heart. Henry Lee Lucas had soiled her forever, and only God could remove the stain.

***

Sarah sat in her patrol car, crying uncontrollably. Having driven across town to her church, hoping to pray her sins away, she was deterred by a couple of skinny white guys painting the steeple and the doorway of the chapel.

Sarah saw this interruption as a sign, believing God was ignoring her desperation. Still, she made her way inside and settled on a cushioned pew alone.

Choosing to remain with a husband who abused her and a daughter who resented her, she now had a lover who was the devil's son. Sarah had little hope. The Colt .45 pistol suddenly weighed heavy on her hip. The cold steel could serve as an instrument of salvation only after God forgave her.

Sarah began to pray, "Dear Lord, I humbly ask your forgiveness of my sins. I have sinned, Jesus, and for that I ask that I be forgiven. I want to be with you in Heaven. Thank you, Jesus, and God. Amen."

After she was sure she was forgiven, she went back to the car. Once this was over, Sarah Sears would seriously consider ending this hell on earth and shooting herself with her sheriff's department revolver. She again touched the steel resting in her leather holster. Sarah jolted as a blue vehicle honked and pulled in beside her.

It was Henry.

"Hey, pretty cop lady. What are you doin'? How about meeting up after your work and having some fun?" he teased. "I thought about you all last night. Just laying there wishing I could touch you, kiss your breasts, and take off those policeman's pants." Henry was smiling.

Sarah looked at Henry, stunned that this accused killer would talk to her in this overly-familiar manner. Had she lost her mind, allowing him to make love to her? She felt her life was over, but maybe she should do one last righteous deed. Maybe God wanted her to kill Henry Lee Lucas.

She forced a smile back at Henry and said, "I'm swamped today. I have to go home right after work."

Lucas was immediately suspicious. This cop lady was not the same as she was yesterday. Henry wondered if she knew who he was. If she did, he'd have to kill her. He looked at Sarah, squinted his eyes in the hot sun, and said, "Well, that's no good. Maybe tomorrow."

Backing his car out of the church driveway, Henry noticed the men painting the steeple. "What a waste of time," he thought. "Who cares if the cross is bright white?" God was never on Henry's mind.

Her heart pounding, Sarah had to clear her mind and devise a plan. She wanted to know more about Henry and his victims. Did he just kill once? Was it many times? Were his victims men and women? Any blacks? Children? She had to know what made him kill or satisfy herself with the knowledge that he was simply just a suspect.

Sarah knew how lazy law enforcement officers could

be, and they might have just conveniently tagged Henry because he was a drifter. He would not be the first person to be convicted because he was poor and disenfranchised from society.

Sarah determined to find out more about this man before she either arrested or simply killed him in revenge. Her mind would guide her actions. She needed time to think and a good distraction. The best way for her to focus was to find Amber's rapist. That case was cut and dried. Sarah would kill the asshole.

***

Cautiously driving toward the old river bridge that she swore she'd never visit again, Sarah felt dread, fear, and strange exhilaration. She'd agreed to meet with Henry again—and might still succumb to his advances, allowing herself to have sex with this man.

Throughout her married life, Sarah had read hundreds of women's magazines featuring stories about affairs. They usually told of women finding men other than their husbands attractive, even at times fucking them. But she never considered herself as a willing partner to such sin. "It happened only once," she told herself. "And maybe again today."

Sarah believed God would forgive her one more time for allowing sex with this man, as much as God had forgiven her the murders she had committed. Sarah was, after all, an imperfect human. She was helpless because God had chosen her to rid the world of rapists, child molesters, and brutalists.

Sarah had a strong sense of fate and intended to further befriend Henry by spending some time alone with him. If he indeed were a killer, God would implore Sarah to kill him. She was resigned to this plan.

"Hey, gorgeous cop lady," Henry said when she got out of her car and sat beside him on the hood of his Chevy. "Come here and give me some lovin'." Henry invoked faint rage mixed with sexuality within Sarah. She hated how he demanded her to comply with his wishes, yet she felt strangely attracted to his commands.

"Hi," she said meekly.

"I brought some whiskey," Henry announced.

"Oh no, I don't drink," Sarah answered.

"Okay, suit yourself." Henry looked surprised but slightly delighted. This woman was so different than the cheap whores and unwilling victims Henry usually fucked. He liked Sarah Sears' aged innocence.

Henry suddenly pushed Sarah against the hood of his car, embracing her and running his hand down her khaki blouse. She had her gun holstered to her side. Henry reached for it, and Sarah flinched.

"What's wrong, my little sweetheart?" Henry cooed. "I'd never hurt you. I like you. Hell, I think I love you." He was inflicting all his charm.

Sarah laid her pistol on the top of the car, allowing Henry to open her top. Pulling her breasts out of her bra, he began to run his hands over her nipples. Sarah's vagina was pulsating.

"Stop," she was telling herself, but not to Henry.

He pulled her pants down and ran his hand over her crotch before suddenly holding her wrists together. She began to struggle to free herself, but he started wrapping rope tightly around her arms.

Henry was laughing, holding her arms above her head before forcing himself inside her.

After a few quick, hard thrusts, Henry came in Sarah. She was excited yet disgusted. "This must stop," she was praying quietly. "I've lost my mind." Sarah now knew Henry was capable of anything. She saw the wildness in his eyes and sensed his pleasure in controlling another person. Henry was the accused killer in the picture at her office.

Sarah was more frightened of what might happen after Henry released her. He might want to kill his victim. She needed to escape, but she had to remain calm.

Henry suggested they build a fire on the red clay riverbank. While Sarah redressed, he zipped his trousers and walked toward some fallen tree limbs to gather wood. Sarah wondered if he might break her neck with the sticks.

Instead, he returned and piled several pieces on top of each other. Gathering some dried leaves and grass, he lit the stack with his cigarette lighter. The banks of the Red River were lonely and isolated, except for the murderous pair. Henry waved for Sarah to sit beside him on a log. She declined. As he turned his back toward the fledgling blaze, Sarah retrieved her pistol.

"Think you may need that?" Henry asked, pointing to the gun when she joined him at the fire and holstered her weapon.

"No, I'm just used to it being there," Sarah mumbled.

"What's your old man like when he's not beating you?" Henry asked her.

"I really don't know," she replied. "Mostly quiet and preoccupied."

"Does he still fuck you?"

"No, never," she answered. Where was Henry going with his line of questions?

"You want him killed?" Henry asked and touched her shoulder. Sarah was shocked, but a faint smile betrayed her lips. She'd prayed for Pete Sears to die hundreds of times. God would take him when the time was right. She could not ignore her mind asking if maybe Henry was the man God sent for the job.

"Why do you ask that?" Sarah looked at Henry.

"Well, I figure you'd be better off with him dead. I could kill the asshole, and you'd be rid of him. Think about it, and let me know. I feel like I owe you something. You've been so good to Henry."

Sarah feared this man. "I'd better get home," she said and looked toward the road. Walking toward her patrol car, she suddenly turned and said, "I'll let you know about my husband, and thanks for the offer." Henry was lighting up a cigarette. He nodded.

Sarah pointed the car toward the narrow country road. What a strange and unlikely pair they were: two killers. One a God-loving woman, and the other a killer for kicks. Sarah Sears needed to clear her head.

Pulling in the driveway, Sarah spied Olivia and a boy sitting in an unfamiliar car outside her home. She pulled up beside the vehicle.

"Hi, honey," Sarah waved.

Olivia looked at her blankly, and the boy looked the other way. Sarah so wished her daughter was her friend.

The front door opened as Sarah stepped on the porch. "Get in here, you bitch!" Pete demanded.

"What is it?" Sarah asked, feigning normalcy. As she turned to Pete, he threw a punch, glancing off her mouth. Her lip burst and blood ran down her chin. Sarah tried to sidestep him and push him back away from her body.

"You bitch. Don't you lie to me. Have you been meeting up with some man?"

"What are you talking about?" Sarah cried.

"I knew it! Let a bitch get out of the house, and they become the town whore!" Pete was red-faced and ran toward Sarah, grabbing her hair. Her pistol bounced against her hip. She could kill him now.

Pete pushed her on the couch and grabbed an old ashtray. Sarah thought he might bash her head in, but instead, he threw it at her, barely missing her face. The front door suddenly opened, and Olivia entered, looking at the two of them. Their daughter said nothing and went upstairs.

Someone must have seen her with Henry and told Pete. Sarah Sears had no one on her side except for her pistol and Henry Lucas.

Pete charged outside and started up his old pick-up. Sarah wondered if he'd try to find the man she was with. If he did, Sarah knew Pete would be the one to lose. Pete Sears was mean and hot-tempered, but Henry was a professional. Pete would die if he confronted him.

Sarah bathed her lip in ice water and washed her face. She fried some bacon and made three bacon and tomato sandwiches. This and some potato chips and pickles would be enough for dinner, along with some packaged fried pies she'd saved in the pantry. Everything was on the table in case Pete or Olivia needed dinner. Sarah was somewhat a creature of habit, always making sure the Sears family didn't go hungry.

Locking herself inside her bedroom later that evening, she knew her night would be spent suffering. Thoughts of what her future held overwhelmed her. She prayed, asking God if Henry Lee Lucas was the Messiah sent by God to rid Sarah of her abuser. Sarah knew God moved in mysterious ways. If Henry killed Pete, Sarah could have a new life. Henry would be pinned with the murder, and no witnesses would ever suspect her involvement. If Henry tried to implicate her, she'd simply testify against the killer. Sarah could rid herself of both men this way. Sarah finally fell into a fitful sleep.

***

Henry pushed open the front door of the Mooney shack. The old lady was waiting and tore into him. "You ain't doin' no work around here. So after tonight, I want you and the girl outta here. She's eating and bitching all the time, gettin' on my nerves."

Henry ignored her and headed for his bed. He wasn't in the mood for either of these cunts, Becky or the old bitch. Henry might just kill both of them tonight.

The small bedroom door was open, and he spotted the teenager on her stomach with headphones on.

"Where you been all day?" she asked.

Henry gave her a cold stare.

Becky had grown up with heartless killers, and her gut told her to shut up. She rolled over and didn't make a sound. Henry laid down on her left side, motionless. He was ready to kill, but he hoped it wouldn't be the girl.

When the morning light came through the thin curtains, Henry smelled bacon. Mrs. Mooney seemed in a better mood.

"I got my money in the mail yesterday," she said. "Could you drive me into Nocona today so I can cash my government check? I need to get a few groceries."

"Sure," Henry agreed. He knew the old lady would never suspect this would be her last trip to the little town, unless she were traveling in the trunk of his car. He'd wait until she had the cash. Old Lady Mooney would never bitch anyone out again after today.

Henry waited while the woman cleaned up after breakfast. She never bathed but used a wash rag to clean her body parts. He could see her sagging breasts and bulbous stomach from his seat because she'd left her bedroom door open slightly.

"Why would she do that?" he thought. Surely the

old woman didn't think that he, Henry Lee Lucas, was a desperate man. Henry thought of himself as irresistible. The cop lady had proven that. And what should he do with Sarah? He liked her, but he also knew staying around Nocona, Texas, after killing the old woman would get him caught.

His only option was to be on the move. He'd stuff the old broad's bones in that stove, burn them, and go back to see Sarah one more time. Henry would keep his word to the cop lady. If she wanted her bastard husband dead, he'd take care of that also.

He also wanted to make sure Sarah never told anyone about their sexual encounters, but he felt certain she wouldn't. Sarah Sears didn't want to lose her job or be thought of as a small-town slut. "She'd keep her mouth shut," he convinced himself.

After these killings, Henry and Becky would head toward Wichita Falls or maybe Oklahoma. He wasn't sure at the moment.

8

Sarah Sears had to make a decision today. What would she do with Henry Lee Lucas? In her gut, Sarah knew Henry was the killer pictured on the flyer. In tiny Nocona, Texas, any stranger attracted the town criers. "Who's the stranger?" everyone would soon be wanting to know if he stayed around much longer. Henry wasn't the type to cower in dark corners.

Staring in the mirror at her home, Sarah dabbed antiseptic on her face, tending to Pete Sears' blows to her body and her pride. The thought of seeing him bleeding on cold concrete, perhaps in the garage downstairs, at once delighted Sarah and repulsed her.

Olivia's father was the only man Sarah had ever known as a husband, but not as a lover. Henry Lee Lucas' semen was now a part of Sarah's physicality.

Sarah prayed, "Dear God, why did you let me be seduced by a killer?" She immediately admitted that maybe God permitted it so that she would recognize another killer because she was a killer.

***

Mooney never deposited her government check; she only believed in cash. Her hard life had prepared her to be wary of thieves and con artists, and she believed banks were part of a government scam for old people. She'd take her money in twenty dollar bills, stick them in a small cloth coin purse, and put it in the left side of her brassiere. This was Mooney's safe place, as nothing could slip out of the generous holster.

Henry drove to town feeling agitated and delighted. He'd get a fix today, not from alcohol or drugs, but from making an old woman see her God. Today was Mrs. Mooney's last day on this earth, and he would play God today—just the way Henry liked it.

The old, black iron stove where he planned to dispose of her body sat on some piles of dirt among some junk at the back of the Mooney place. The old lady once told him the beds were once for worm farming, something that turned out to be a hoax set by traveling salesmen who got the old lady to invest in their scheme. When she quit giving money to the worm farmers, she left the beds to dry up.

Becky didn't need to see this murder, Henry concluded. He'd act alone. He planned to lure the old women to the worm beds, knife her, steal the cash, and cut her up into pieces small enough to fit in the old stove. Smoke from a small fire would not arouse suspicion from any passersby.

"Okay, I'm ready," the old woman sneered at Henry, interrupting his thoughts. "I'm gettin' too old to make these trips into town," she continued. "But a person's got to eat. I'd better stop by and get some milk and stuff after the bank. When are you and the girl going on? I don't have anything left for you to do." She sensed Henry's anger.

Never one to fear much of anything, Mrs. Mooney did not like this man. She wanted him out of her house. The girl had to go with him.

"I'm leaving later today," Henry answered. He didn't look at the woman and lit up a cigarette. The two backed out on Highway 82 in Henry's car for the three-mile ride to the bank. Pretty soon, Henry would have some cash and be on the road again. But leaving the cop lady behind made him strangely sad. He liked playing with the emotions of an innocent person like her. Henry had slept with mostly prostitutes and drug addicts in his life. This woman was different; she was pure.

He decided to do her a favor and kill Sarah's husband before he left. Henry knew where Sarah's house was located because he'd followed her throughout his time in Nocona. He thought the best way to kill Pete Sears was to do it fast and straightforward. He'd knock on Pete's door and stab him repeatedly when he answered.

"Hell, this is will be a good deed for Sarah," Henry thought. It was Henry's way of paying her back for her companionship and trust. He felt good about murdering Pete Sears.

***

"Good morning," Zach greeted Sarah. "How's it going?"

"Okay," Sarah said and tried to hide her face from him. She didn't like to upset Zach with any of her problems. She knew he suffered from acute anxiety, and anything that happened to Sarah could drive him over the edge.

"You don't look okay to me," Zach replied and studied her red cheek. "He hit you again."

Sarah nodded.

"I still think we could kill the son of a bitch."

Sarah looked away.

Just then Ruby came in the office carrying her lunch box and a single carnation. "What's with the flower?" Zach questioned Ruby.

"Oh, I stopped for a fried pie and coffee at the store," Ruby said. "That crazy clerk was all chipper and handed me this. I felt like I had to take it. Now it'll need water."

Ruby sighed. She was anxious to get on the phone. Nocona always has something new for Ruby to hear about each morning.

Sarah's mind was on fire and made it impossible to relax at her desk. She was staring at the handbill that blared Henry Lee Lucas as a suspected killer. Frustrated, she walked out to see Zach and told him she would be back soon. He was suspicious that Sarah knew something he didn't.

Sarah spotted Henry's car parked at the curb in front of First National Bank. "Dear God," Sarah muttered, "please don't let him be a bank robber too."

She had no choice but to arrest her casual lover. Guilt overwhelmed her, and Sarah was angry at herself and Henry. Other than Zach, Sarah Sears had never known a good man. Henry had turned out to be just another bastard.

Sarah continued praying as she walked up to Henry's car window, her right hand close to her pistol. Henry was sitting alone in the driver's seat, waiting on Mrs. Mooney.

"Hey, cop lady! Wanna fuck today?" he said a little too loudly, giving her a cheesy grin.

Embarrassed, Sarah managed to smile politely and reply, "No, I have work to do, but how about after work?"

Henry was surprised that this unlikely lover wanted more sex. But Henry had always known his sex appeal. Women were so dumb and weak. Concerned that Mrs. Mooney would come out of the bank any moment, Henry tried to get rid of Sarah. "Hey, I gotta go too. Where do you wanna meet?"

"River bridge?" she suggested.

He nodded and said, "See you around 5:00." He had a lot of work to do today, sawing up an old carcass before showering up and getting ready for rough sex with a cop. Henry liked how his plans were shaping up for the last few hours of his life in Nocona, Texas.

Mrs. Mooney had stuffed the $20 bills in her bra once she cashed her check, and then she returned to the car.

"Stop by the Piggly Wiggly," she commanded Henry. "I need milk and a few TV dinners." Henry nodded again. This old lady needed nothing but a miracle, and today wasn't the day for her to have one.

The Piggly Wiggly grocery store was on the way to the Mooney house. As Henry approached, he gunned the accelerator and drove past it.

"What are you doing?" Mrs. Mooney challenged him. "You dim wit, there's the store!" she said and pointed as they drove down the street.

Henry just smirked at her, saying nothing.

"Where you goin', you asshole?" Mrs. Mooney was angry.

"I'm not going anywhere, you old bitch. You're the one that's going! To your grave!" Henry said.

The old woman tried to grab the wheel, and Henry swung his right fist into her skull. Mrs. Mooney passed out. He was careful not to speed. A highway patrolman was always a danger for Henry.

Pulling into Mooney's driveway and opening the passenger door, Henry pulled out the old lady's limp body. She slumped on the ground, her head bleeding from his blow to her temple. She was moaning and awake now. Becky ran out the door and screamed, "What the hell?"

"Shut up," Henry demanded her. "Get a blanket right now off the bed."

"What happened?" the girl asked, surprised.

"I said now!" Henry yelled.

Becky grabbed the plaid wool quilt on the old woman's chair. "Here," she said as she pitched it to Henry.

He looked at Becky and said, "Help me wrap her up."

Becky recalled the conversation she'd had with Henry

earlier. "We need her money, and we have to kill her to get it," he had said.

Becky Toole knew murder and knew money. Money always won! Mooney would have to die.

They rolled the quilt around the old lady's body as she moaned and begged for her life. Henry took off his undershirt and stuffed the corner of it in her mouth to smother her. She didn't last long, as her body was already traumatized by the hard blow to the head. Mrs. Mooney shook for a few seconds, gagged, and then stopped moving. Henry figured she died either choking on her own vomit or her windpipe had collapsed.

"Help me carry her out back," he instructed Becky. Once they were outside, he motioned toward the pot-bellied stove.

"I may be able to get her in there without cutting her up, but I'm not sure," Henry said. "Go get me that hacksaw in the old barn."

Becky did as she was told, no talking back or asking questions. She knew Henry had work to do.

***

Sarah prayed all afternoon that God would lead her to his way, the right and just way. She was confident she'd arrest Henry that day and lock him in the jail until the federal authorities took him. Sarah Sears saw not only her chance for God's redemption but also her opportunity to prove her heroic qualities. She would become a local hero, keeping her mouth shut about any relationship she'd had with the killer.

Sarah would try never to think of Henry Lee Lucas again. God had plans for Sarah, and the late afternoon would bring justice to everyone concerned.

Her gun holster held a loaded .45, and she placed a 12-gauge shotgun beside her driver's seat. The clock ticked slowly in her office as she waited for the appointed time. Meanwhile, Zach brought in another fax showing a headshot of a teenage girl along with the picture of Henry. The headline blasted, "WANTED for MURDER."

Sarah sat, stunned. Might Henry have a youthful accomplice? What if the girl was still with him? If so, Sarah would never leave the car when she met up with Henry. She would just wave goodbye to him and keep driving. Two killers could overwhelm her. The change of plans irritated Sarah. She chastised herself once more for ever allowing this man to enter her mind or her body.

Five o'clock struck, and Sarah fingered her pistol as she picked up her worn leather handbag. "See you tomorrow, Zach."

"Stay away from that bastard you live with! He needs to die!" Zach told her firmly.

Sarah nodded and exited the office door. Ruby was already backing out of the office driveway. She never missed square dancing evenings at the VFW Hall.

***

"You stay outside, close to that fire," Henry warned Becky as she sat near the stove on a rickety chair.

"Those damned stray dogs might pull out some of the bones," he said. Becky pouted and argued, "But I don't want to babysit a corpse."

Henry snapped, "Shut up and do as I say! Tomorrow we'll head on up the road."

"Where you goin'?" Becky whined.

"I told you to shut up, or I'll beat the shit out of you!" Henry yelled.

Becky knew she'd pushed the limit. Mrs. Mooney's burning flesh now mingled with old ashes and made a putrid smell.

"If anybody comes up here, say the old lady is gone, and you're burning a dead cat," Henry told her.

He walked around the front of the house where he'd parked and started the car. Today he'd have to tie up loose ends. He'd fuck the cop lady one more time and then strangle her. He liked her, so he couldn't bring himself to shoot her.

Just then, a white sedan pulled in the driveway. A heavy, middle-aged brunette climbed out the driver's seat, waving at Henry. She carried two brown paper sacks. "Hi, there!" she called. "Is Mrs. Mooney at home? I brought her some tomatoes."

Henry looked puzzled, but he quickly decided to put on a good act. "No, she went to the grocery store."

The lady looked surprised. "How? She doesn't drive."

"Oh," Henry reacted. "I dropped her off. I have to go back and get her in a few minutes."

The woman was curious but not overly inquisitive. "I'm Della. Who are you?"

"I am her nephew. My daughter is out back," Henry replied, desperate to show a little Lucas charm.

"Funny, Mrs. Mooney never mentioned having a nephew," the lady mused and squinted in the sunlight.

"Yeah, I never got to know my aunt very well," he added. Lies came easily to Henry.

"Well," the lady belabored, "I guess you can just leave the tomatoes in Mrs. Mooney's kitchen. She loves my fresh tomatoes."

Henry needed to get going right away to meet Sarah on time. The tomato gardener wanted to chat. Henry was growing more desperate. "I'm sorry, ma'am, I need to go get my aunt," he finally said. At least fifteen minutes or more had passed, and the woman showed no signs of starting her car and leaving.

She was growing more interested in Henry and continued asking him questions. "Where you from?" she persisted.

"Oh, Florida," Henry answered without making eye contact. "I really gotta go, ma'am."

"Well, I'm just surprised Mrs. Mooney didn't tell me she had company. I usually take her to the Piggly Wiggly when I bring over the tomatoes. She gives me five dollars." The woman seemed disappointed to miss payday.

Henry was clearly agitated by now. "I'm happy to pay you, but I have to go!" He tried to be calm. "Maybe I should just strangle this bitch and get this over with," he thought briefly. Chatter was not Henry's strength unless it advantaged him.

Taking her sunglasses out of her handbag and placing them on her face, she finally relented. "No matter," she said. "Just tell Mrs. Mooney I'll see her next week. I'll call her in the meantime." She got back in the driver's seat, started the car, and rolled down the window.

"Thanks, ma'am," Henry called, holding up the bags of tomatoes. "Aunt Rose said she may go on a little trip next week with us. I'm not sure."

"Well, that beats all!" the lady exclaimed. "Mrs. Mooney never goes anywhere but to Nocona."

Henry hoped to follow the nosy lady out of the driveway. Sarah would already be at the river bottom waiting now.

***

Sarah waited at the bridge until 5:15, looking for a flying cloud of dust as Henry approached in his car. For the next fifteen minutes, she saw no sign of him and finally decided things around Nocona must have become too hot for Henry. He and the girl had probably escaped. Sarah wanted to go home and determine her next steps because she couldn't think straight.

Meanwhile, Henry cursed the brunette visitor and the highway at the same time as he made his way to the river. The Mooney place was on the west side of town, thirty minutes from the muddy sands of the Red River. Henry wanted to speed but had to use his customary restraint when driving.

He finally drove over the river bank, hoping to spy the cop car, but it was very late now and Sarah was nowhere in sight.

"What the hell?" Henry asked. Maybe she didn't come. Perhaps Sarah was on to him. Or maybe she'd already left.

"Dammit!" Henry yelled. He was pissed off, whatever the situation turned out to be.

Thinking of Mooney's body, Becky's insolent behavior, and the danger lurking in overstaying one place, Henry decided it was time to leave Montague County. He'd do one last deed, just because he'd promised: kill Pete Sears and let the cop lady live. Henry felt good about his decision.

***

Meanwhile, Olivia barely made it to the Sears' front porch without passing out. Holding a bloody towel in her hands, she was bleeding badly through her vagina. Pale and weak, she tried to yell for her father to open the door. Pete found his wounded daughter unconscious on the front step. Panicked, he scooped her up in his arms and carried her to the couch. Dousing a cloth in cold water, he bathed her face, imploring his daughter to wake up.

"Olivia, what happened? Are you okay?" He shook her shoulders gently.

Pete Sears loved his daughter and would kill anyone who harmed her. "Honey, what happened to you?"

Olivia whimpered, "Daddy, will you hate me if I tell you?"

"Of course not, baby, I'm here for you," Pete said.

Just then Sarah walked to the front door, wondering why

it was left open just before she saw a smear of what appeared to be blood on the porch step. She could see Olivia on the couch, Pete crouched over her. Seeing a bloody towel, Sarah suspected a gunshot wound, but why Olivia?

Henry entered her thoughts.

"Olivia, Pete. What's going on?" Sarah cried.

Pete glanced at Sarah and back at his daughter. "Olivia," he pleaded, "tell us what happened."

Sarah was not sure where the blood had come from, but Olivia's bleeding appeared to have stopped. She quickly grabbed a clean towel from the kitchen just in case and brought Olivia a glass of water.

Pete stayed by his girl's side, waiting for an explanation.

"I had an abortion." Olivia barely spoke the words, tears running down her face.

"An abortion," Pete repeated.

Olivia was crying uncontrollably now.

"Who was the father? And who did this abortion?" Pete insisted, his anger boiling. Who would do this to his baby?

Olivia hesitated, then she whimpered, "Reverend Thomas."

"Reverend Thomas did the abortion?" Sarah asked, flabbergasted. "Why him?"

"Because he is the father, okay?" Olivia cried out defiantly.

"What?" Sarah said and locked eyes with her husband. Reverend Thomas had raped their daughter.

"Did he rape you?" Pete demanded answers.

"No, I had sex with him for two years!" Olivia screamed,

crying harder. Pete and Sarah waited for Olivia to calm down before one of them asked, "Why with him?"

"He gives a lot of us money, drugs, and some booze," Olivia explained matter-of-factly. "It's easy, just fuck him occasionally. But I got pregnant, and that made him mad."

Her parents sat in shock as Olivia explained that the priest had performed abortions for other girls.

"Usually, he says, he does a good job," Olivia added. "Mine was fucked up, and I couldn't stop bleeding. I panicked and left."

Pete Sears was in shock and began pacing. "How did you get here?" he demanded.

A knock at the door interrupted the inquisition.

"Who the hell?" Pete said and hurried toward the door. Sarah looked out the window and recognized Henry's car in the yard.

"No!" Sarah yelled at Pete. "Let me get it."

But Pete had already opened the door to find Henry standing there with a knife.

"Hi, gorgeous," Henry said, looking over Pete's shoulder. "I told you I'd kill your old man."

At that moment, Henry stabbed at Pete's stomach. Pete stepped back, but Henry had severely wounded him.

"Stop!" Sarah yelled and pulled her gun, pointing it at Henry. "Enough, or I'll kill you!"

"Well," Henry sneered. "You've changed your mind. Gettin' all lovey-dovey, are you?" But Henry suspected Sarah was serious. She would pull the trigger if Henry made any attempt to harm her family any further.

"Okay, cop lady. I'm leaving unless you shoot me in the back, and I don't think you will."

Pete was on the floor, clutching his stomach and bleeding profusely. Olivia was screaming as Henry ran to his car and fled.

Sarah jammed one of Olivia's fresh towels on Pete's wound and helped him to her car. She went back for Olivia, who could stand up by now. Olivia and Sarah worked together to get Pete in the backseat. He almost passed out many times. Sarah raced to the hospital, using her two-way radio to alert the doctors of a knife wound and a teen suffering a botched abortion. The Sears family was in peril.

Within minutes, the hospital staff prepped Pete for surgery. The bleeding had to subside for him to live. Betty Connor, Nocona's only R.N., took Olivia to the doctor next, nodding for Sarah to stay in the waiting area. But Sarah ran to Olivia's side. Nurse Betty was insistent and told Sarah, "We'll take care of your daughter."

***

A killer's mind is a strange enigma. Henry was a cold soul who'd never loved anything that lived, but he felt an odd betrayal committed by Sarah Sears. He had promised to kill her abuser, thinking he was doing a favor for the woman. Sarah might feel indebted to him, maybe even caring for him because of his largesse toward her.

Instead, she had sided with her husband. This duplicity infuriated Henry. "Figures," he thought. "You can never trust a bitch. They'll always turn against you." He briefly toyed with the idea of killing Sarah just to make sure she knew she'd fucked over the wrong person, but he knew his time in Montague County was short. He'd better get going while he could.

Wheeling in Mrs. Mooney's drive, he noticed a little bit of smoke still rising from the stove a hundred yards toward the back of the property. He surmised Becky had done a good job of keeping the animals away from the cooked flesh while he was gone. Becky propped open the screen door of the home with her hand, and Henry noticed she was drinking a Diet Coke.

"What's up? Where you been?" she questioned Henry.

"Get your stuff. We are leaving now," he demanded. Becky was happy to leave this place; she loved new adventures.

***

Nocona had three doctors, all general practitioners. They treated colds, delivered babies, and sewed up wounds. Although rare occurrences, they could handle the occasional emergency. A stabbing and a botched abortion were manageable if there was no widespread infection. All three doctors had been summoned, and all determined that Olivia and Pete would be okay, just traumatized for different reasons.

Sarah Sears had a lot to deal with herself. What story would she tell her law enforcement cronies? Why was Henry at her house? The county sheriff would be calling soon to get information, and Sarah's story had to be rock solid. She had no lingering fantasies about the murderer. She wanted to kill Henry and see him die at her hands. God would want this.

And then there was Olivia, poor Olivia. Sarah needed to find out whose baby had been murdered and why Olivia would allow herself to be butchered in such a manner. Olivia was sedated for the night, but after she awoke, Sarah would get a name. She could not allow herself to believe Reverend Thomas was the perpetrator. Whoever did this to Olivia Sears would be punished. Sarah would make sure this person never touched her daughter again.

Meanwhile, Henry planned to travel to Amarillo, Texas, and go on to Colorado from there. He could hide out in the Rocky Mountains until all this blew over. Henry hated mountains but knew they'd provide ample cover. After staying in Wichita Falls for the night, he could be in the Texas Panhandle by the next day.

Becky threw her suitcase and a brown paper bag in the car.

"What's in the bag?" Henry asked.

"Old Lady Mooney's stuff like shampoo, conditioner, and stuff I might use," she replied. Becky Toole enjoyed being a thief. They both laughed.

Henry pulled out on Highway 82 and headed west. It was late in the day, and the sunlight streamed through the windshield. Henry realized he was tired and hoped he'd get to rest in Wichita Falls. He wanted to sleep.

Becky was spraying some of Mrs. Mooney's cheap

perfume on her neck. Two of society's worst were on the run again.

***

Both Pete and Olivia slept through the evening in their respective hospital beds. Sarah stayed all night on the waiting room couch, afraid Henry might try to kill again if she went home alone. She was weary and agitated, but Sarah prayed throughout the night, asking God to make her clear-eyed and determined. By the morning, she knew she'd find Henry and kill him, and then she'd deal with Olivia's abuser.

Pete was groggy from medication when he awoke to see Sarah standing next to his bed. He asked her what had happened to him.

She explained that a serial killer had tried to stab him to death.

"Why me?" Pete asked, confused.

"Because he wanted to kill me," Sarah said, "but it was you who opened the front door." Sarah sounded very plausible.

"Why you then?" Pete was still perplexed.

"Because I was about to catch him," Sarah soothed, once again sounding very convincing.

"Wow, I was in the wrong place at the wrong time then, huh?" Pete joked. "But I'm glad he didn't kill you or me."

Sarah was pleased Pete had shown her some kindness.

"You're gonna be all right, just sore," she told her husband. "The doctors did a good job."

"Am I supposed to be hungry?" Pete asked his wife. Sarah smiled and buzzed the nurse.

"Why isn't Olivia here with you?" Pete asked before the nurse arrived. He was always concerned about his daughter.

"Do you remember when she came home last night before you went to the front door?" Sarah inquired.

"Not really..." Pete's voice trailed off, and he looked in Sarah's eyes.

Sarah frowned and continued, "She was bleeding..."

"Why?" Pete questioned.

"Because she'd had a botched abortion."

"What?" Pete was upset and curious. "An abortion? I don't understand."

Sarah realized that Pete did not remember any of the details from the previous evening and decided to wait to tell him about Olivia's confession that it was Reverend Thomas.

"I don't understand either," Sarah offered. "But I'm going to find out the story when she wakes up."

"Is she okay?" Pete sounded concerned.

"Yes," Sarah assured him.

Nurse Betty entered the room with a tray of soft breakfast food for Pete and helped him rearrange his pillows.

Sarah left and went to check on her daughter. Olivia was awake but not communicating with the nurses who were asking about her pain level.

"Good morning, honey," Sarah said brightly. "Are you hurting anywhere?"

"No," Olivia snapped at her mom. "Just let me sleep."

"Okay, in a minute," Sarah said kindly as a nurse's aide

walked in, holding a tray of food.

"Would you like some breakfast?" the aide asked.

"No," Olivia snapped again. Sarah waved the young girl out of the room.

Sarah spoke more firmly this time. "Olivia, I want to know who the father is." Assuming Olivia had been delirious with pain when she accused Reverend Thomas, Sarah wanted some real answers. "You said Reverend Thomas was the father and that he'd performed your abortion. Now I'm ready for you to tell me the truth."

Olivia raised herself up on one elbow, looked Sarah in the eye, and said, "The father was Reverend Thomas. He fucked me for two years or more. And for that, I got drugs, alcohol, and whatever else I wanted. When I got pregnant, he did the abortion. I never thought you'd find out. Now I'm fucked!" She threw her head back onto the pillow.

Olivia explained that he'd done this to other girls. Some were her friends, and some had left town already. "I don't know how many years he's fucked girls, but a long time," Olivia added. "He'd get good stuff off the street to trade us for sexual favors. Sometimes he wanted me to suck him, and sometimes he wanted to stick it in me. Sorry, Mommy, you don't have a saint for a little girl."

Olivia was hateful to Sarah. Then she softened a tiny bit. "Will you tell Daddy? I just can't."

Olivia seemed remorseful. When she broke down crying, Sarah saw in Olivia a flash of the little girl she had read nightly stories to and tucked in safely. There was no longer the hardened edge that a perverted priest had brought to her only daughter. Olivia needed her mother's help, and Sarah would remove Olivia's danger. She would kill the reverend. This man would no longer prey on the town's young girls and women. God wanted this sinner dead. Sarah would obey God.

***

Henry successfully averted the lazy patrolmen in the scruffy town of Wichita Falls. He stayed in a motel on the banks of the Wichita River, the perfect place if he had to escape through the back of the building and slide down to the dry weed-infested riverbed. Henry could hide in the brush, leaving Becky to fend for herself before he headed to the Rocky Mountains to disappear.

He slept through the night with no interruptions. Becky dressed in her short skirt and low cut blouse, spraying on more of Rose Mooney's cheap perfume.

Henry wasn't aroused. "Stop spraying that cheap shit on your tits," he growled. "It gives me a headache."

Becky pouted.

When he went downstairs to check out, he slid a wad of dollars at the motel receptionist. The woman taking the money was chatty. "Where you headin'?" she inquired.

Henry hated women who asked questions but answered her anyway. "Toward Amarillo," he mumbled.

"Oh, not this morning you're not," the clerk said. She was pious.

"Why not?" Henry asked.

"The freeway's shut down," she said, counting the bills. "There's a six-car pileup right out of Vernon, people killed on both sides of the road. Since it's only two lanes there, they won't let you around it. It's been all over the news. Just happened 'bout an hour ago. Two eighteen-wheelers hit head-on, doin' about 80. Both cars behind the rigs hit' em, and cars behind them ran into the backs of those cars. My God, there must be a thousand cops and patrolmen there! Might as well have some breakfast and stay in Wichita Falls a while. No reason to sit on a highway."

Henry nodded. She was right. Clearly agitated but glad the woman warned him, Henry did not want or need a bunch of cops breathing around him. He'd get some breakfast and then watch the television in his room, checking on the progress of the accident.

***

Nurse Betty entered Olivia's room and announced she could go home later that day when she was ready. Sarah smiled, and even Olivia seemed relieved.

"Thank you," Sarah whispered to the nurse. Nurse Betty frowned at her, wanting to lecture Olivia about having an abortion but decided to hold her tongue.

Country nurses had seen and treated most everything, but botched abortions carried with them lots of unanswered questions and likely poor judgment. The nurse left the room disgusted.

Sarah stroked her daughter's hair, choosing not to

mention her decision about Reverend Thomas. She asked Olivia, "Honey, will you promise me one thing?"

Olivia looked apprehensive.

"Will you stay away from Reverend Thomas for a few weeks? I want you to heal and get your head on straight."

Olivia nodded, "yes." Sarah knew she'd have him dead within days.

"That's my girl," Sarah beamed and went to check on Pete.

He was sitting up in the bed, his tray empty. He reached his hand out toward Sarah, something he'd rarely ever done. "Thank you for saving my life. I can never thank you enough."

Sarah answered, looking directly at him, "You are my husband, and what God joins together, let no man put asunder." It was the first tender moment between Sarah and Pete Sears, wife and husband, in their whole lives.

"I'm taking Olivia home today," Sarah continued. "The nurse has released her. No infection and the bleeding had stopped. You and I can discuss what to do about her when you come home." Pete seemed relieved that Sarah was making the decisions. He was not the control freak he'd been for more than twenty years.

"Okay," he agreed, laying back on his pillow. This scrape with death had profoundly changed Pete Sears. He was no longer at war with his wife.

Sarah took Olivia home that afternoon and got her settled into her room to rest.

***

Zach answered the sheriff department's phone. "Where have you been? I've been worried sick," he chastised Sarah.

"I've got a lot to tell you, Zach," she said, "and I'm going to need your help." Zach was intrigued. He liked working with Sarah, especially on crimes of any kind.

"When are you back in the office?" he asked. Zach was excited to get the scoop.

"Let Ruby go home. I want to talk to you with no one there."

"You got it, boss," Zach said. He always complied with Sarah in all things.

Sarah tiptoed into Olivia's room at home, leaving a note on her dresser. It read, "I'll be back shortly, and I love you! Love, Mom."

Zach had a pot of coffee ready for Sarah. He knew she loved her coffee with vanilla-flavored creamer. Sarah sat at her desk, and Zach pulled up a chair. He could hardly wait for Sarah to put him in the game. Sarah looked stern and resolved.

"Zach," she said, "there are two people God wants us to get rid of, and the earth will be a better place." She proceeded to explain Reverend Thomas' role in repeatedly raping her daughter in exchange for drugs and alcohol.

Zach was secretly happy that the reverend turned out to be a sinner. This minister had often called out Zach for being a "fag" and predicted Zach would burn in Hell for his sexual preference. Zach hated all religion and especially Thomas. He would love to help kill the self-righteous bastard.

The weekend was approaching, and Sarah hoped never to hear this man deliver a sermon again to any believers. She planned to kill the reverend on Saturday. Pete would be home from the hospital by then, and Olivia would still be bedridden. The day before the Lord's Day was the best day to rid her community of a scourge of a man and a fraud of God's word.

"Can you help me kill him on Saturday?" Sarah questioned Zach.

"You bet," Zach answered quickly. "What's the plan?"

"I'll call him and make an appointment asking him to meet me alone," Sarah began. "I will be a little flirty on the phone. He has come on to me in the past. I plan to come near his body, as though I want to confess some sin to him. When I get close enough, I'm going to reach for a tissue in my purse, and instead, I'll grab a sharp knife and stab him in the throat. I have just the blade to do it." Sarah thought of what was under her mattress at home.

"Do you need me to help you dispose of the body?" Zach asked.

"No," Sarah answered deliberately. "I want all of Nocona to know what this man did and make it clear that some distraught parent couldn't stand the thought of his molesting another child. I want to castrate him and hang him on the cross at the altar."

Zach sat spellbound.

"Can you fake handwriting and tell the community why

he was killed this way? Make it short but powerful."

"Yes, but who's number two?" Zach was scintillated.

"Henry Lee Lucas," Sarah said firmly.

"Hey now," Zach replied, sitting back against his chair. "That guy is really mean. Maybe it would be better to let some other county take on that killer. He's probably not in Montague County anyway. What's got you so worked up?"

"He tried to kill Pete," she said.

"What?" Zach asked and looked at Sarah, surprised. Why would Henry Lee Lucas even know Pete Sears?

Sarah wove her story to fit her actions. She told Zach how she had approached the killer in town and tried to apprehend him, but he got away. Unbeknownst to her, Lucas then followed Sarah to her house. She figured he wanted to kill her, in case she suspected him of the murders.

"Pete answered the door," she continued, explaining to Zach how Henry stabbed her husband and drove away before Sarah could stop him.

"I have to find him. He might come back to kill my family or me," she added. "Zach, God has anointed me to kill this stranger."

Zach never fell for Sarah's God talk, but he was in on helping get rid of Henry Lee Lucas. "How can I help?" he responded eagerly.

"I'm not sure yet," Sarah answered, "but I will probably need you to be involved some way."

"I'm your man," Zach said, always a willing team member.

"It's getting late, and I need to stop by the hospital and check on Pete. Tomorrow I'll set up the appointment for

Reverend Thomas on Saturday. I don't have to tell you not to say anything to Ruby. Our secret and our bond."

Zach shook his head and smiled at his friend. He now realized how lucky he was to have Sarah Sears in his life.

***

Pete Sears had time to reflect on his life. He was beginning to feel grateful for his family, especially Sarah, who had been a faithful and dutiful wife. He vowed to be kinder to her and to treat her with respect. No wonder Olivia disrespected her mother so much in the past, he concluded. He would speak to his daughter about this and hopefully rectify her relationship with her mom.

Feeling a renewed sense of gratitude, Pete determined to change his behavior permanently. He would show his daughter and more so his wife how much he appreciated them. Pete suddenly felt shame for his repeated and hateful abuse of this woman who had been devoted to him for decades. His heart dreaded the realization that he might have already lost whatever love Sarah could have felt for him in their early years. Pete would do everything he could to make up for the lost time between the two.

Sarah pushed open the hospital room's door. Pete's eyes lit up when he saw her, but the surprise on Sarah's face moved him. What had he done to his family through his thoughtlessness and cruelty?

Sarah regained her composure and asked, "How are you feeling?"

Pete had actually been thinking about how an animal felt when he'd stabbed it in the gut on one of his many hunting trips. "A little sore," he confided.

"Well, you get to go home tomorrow," Sarah informed her husband.

"That will be great," Pete said, seemingly happy about the news.

"Is there anything special you'd like to eat when we get home?" Sarah inquired.

"Nope, whatever you cook, I'll love!" he said.

Sarah was once again startled by Pete's new attitude. What had happened to her surly and mean-spirited man? She'd been hurt so often that she questioned if it would be a matter of time before he turned on her. But, she decided, she'd keep up the cheerful demeanor until such time.

They talked for a while and then Sarah told him she'd see him tomorrow. "Have your traveling clothes on," she said.

"Sarah," Pete called out to her as she opened the door to leave.

"Thank you for everything you've done for me and for being my wife." Pete looked remorseful. Sarah walked over and touched his arm.

"You're welcome," she told him.

***

Henry was enjoying his coffee, watching Becky rifling in her whipped cream and strawberry pancakes at a small diner. He often toyed with ditching Becky, as she cost him extra money. And sex with her wasn't exciting after so many times. But the kid knew too much and would likely be incarcerated if he left her somewhere. Police might rape her and beat her until she sang like a bird. If not, she'd turn to prostitution and some pimp would abuse her, he surmised. Henry had a soft spot for her.

He paid the check, and he and Becky went back to the Wichita Falls motel. Henry went by the office to check on the interstate closure. The clerk informed him it was still a problem but was getting better. There were six fatalities, she informed him.

Henry was rightfully wary of cops, and the highway patrol was particularly a problem. They loved to arrest anyone who did not look like a West Texas farmer or a churchgoing, faded beauty with too much makeup.

"I think we'll stay here again tonight and take off tomorrow morning. If you have the room, that is," Henry said.

The clerk was happy to have a paying customer, and this man had a certain charm.

"That's great. Where you headed after Amarillo?" The clerk was more than a little curious.

"Not sure," Henry answered. "Got some relatives in Grand Junction, Colorado. Might go there."

The clerk nodded and said, "That's a long drive, I bet."

"Oh, it's okay," Henry replied, ready to disconnect from this woman.

"See you in the morning."

He walked into the motel room and yelled, "Becky

unpack your shit. We're staying here again tonight."

Becky didn't complain. At least she wasn't at Mrs. Mooney's house, tending to a fire of flesh.

***

"Hi Reverend," Sarah sounded chirpy but a little needy. She had stopped by the church to talk with the pastor.

"Hello, Sarah," he greeted her, welcoming her into his office. "What can I do for you?"

The reverend had heard Olivia was in the hospital. When he called the front desk at the hospital, Nurse Betty had confided in him that it was a botched abortion. Reverend Thomas was concerned Olivia might have told her mother the details of their relationship. The man of God needed to know what he was dealing with, so he proceeded cautiously.

"How is Olivia? I heard she was in the hospital," he said, concern in his voice.

Sarah despised this charlatan more than words, but she maintained her composure.

"I think she's going to be all right," she replied. "She told us her girlfriend helped her self-abort. She almost bled to death."

"Do you know the young man who fathered the child?" the reverend asked sheepishly, trying to cover his anxiety.

"No," Sarah said, resolute. "Maybe someday she'll tell us, but not now."

The reverend was relieved by this news and asked, "Well, how can I help, Sarah?"

Sarah explained how the ordeal with Olivia had tested her faith. "I need you to pray with me," she concluded. "Would you do that, Reverend?"

"Of course, when is a good time for us to schedule an appointment?" he asked.

"Is tomorrow okay? I really need you," she begged.

The reverend grew slightly aroused. He'd always wanted to fuck Sarah Sears. Maybe tomorrow he'd get a chance? "Yes, tomorrow is good," he said.

"I can come by at 2:00 if that is okay. Just you and me, right?"

"Yes, Sarah, come to my office tomorrow at 2:00. But Sarah you know there will be three here with us."

Sarah was disappointed that another person might join them until the reverend explained that the third person would be God himself.

"Yes," Sarah agreed, smiling contentedly. "God will want to be there."

***

Sarah and Zach laid out the plan for Reverend Thomas' demise. Sarah would meet him at 2:00 and be sure the murder took place by 2:30. Zach would be waiting in the men's restroom at the church and enter Reverend Thomas' office only after 2:30.

They planned to carry the reverend's body to the baptismal pool where Sarah wanted to castrate the holy man. If possible, she even wanted to tie him somehow to the wooden cross behind the altar, leaving the body in full view so the congregation could see the reverend as a fallen man of God. He was someone who deserved retribution and punishment for what he did to the town and his flock. In her dark fantasy, Sarah envisioned his spilled blood covering his priestly white robe.

Zach already had the note prepared to explain the reverend's evil deeds. One of Zach's secret skills was forging handwriting. He copied the script of a former inmate whose personal belongings had been left with the sheriff's office after the man had a massive stroke while incarcerated in the Montague County jail. No one would ever check a dead man's handwriting.

Sarah and Zach planned to leave the note by the reverend's body as his confession. Sarah took quiet delight imagining this flawed sinner paying for his sins against her daughter and countless other girls and women. God would smile down on Sarah for this just deed.

***

Pete looked anxiously at the nurse taking his vital signs in preparation for discharging him from the hospital Friday morning.

"Looks like you're fine, Mr. Sears. How about you going home?" asked Nurse Betty.

Pete nodded. "Will my wife be here to get me?"

"Yes, she's driving the car up to the entrance to meet us. I told her yesterday you were healing quickly, and you'd be just as well off at your house. Besides, we might need your bed. You never know around here," Nurse Betty joked.

Sarah waited downstairs for the nurse to bring Pete to the front of the hospital. She thought about how she longed for normalcy, even if it involved spending time with her abuser. However, Pete had been different the day before. Like a cowed dog, Sarah didn't trust her judgement. She needed to steel her emotions for her husband.

Sarah saw Pete and the young nurse's aide making their way to the car. She was pushing him in a wheelchair. Pete's bulky bandages showed under his loosely hanging shirt. Seeing his wife, he smiled.

"You ready?" Sarah called.

"I'm ready to go home. I can't wait to be home with my family," Pete said.

Sarah got Pete and Oliva settled in by Friday afternoon, and they both slept through the evening and into the next day. Saturday morning brought sunlight and hope to the Sears household. Sarah was pleased that her husband continued showing uncharacteristic kindness. Olivia seemed surprised by her father's turnabout, but she welcomed his new demeanor. Sarah made a hearty breakfast and announced that both patients should remain in bed today. They appeared compliant and eagerly ate the food Sarah delivered to them on trays in front of the television downstairs.

As Sarah prepared to see Reverend Thomas, she put on fresh make-up, the birthday perfume Zach bought for her last year, and a blouse she usually rejected because the bust was a little snug. Sarah evoked a strange sex appeal to men who liked compliant and willing women. Being young and married had previously necessitated her behavior and looks to some degree: never too sexy, but never homely and plain. Pete had dictated everything, from her dress to her hygiene.

Meanwhile, Zach was particularly chipper as he got dressed that morning. He hated the reverend and wanted to touch his pasty skin after the warm blood had seeped out of his body.

Sarah told Pete and Olivia that she had to go grocery shopping and also stop by the office, accounting for the hours she would be gone. At 1:55 pm, she parked at the church and headed inside for her appointment. Sarah's footsteps on the old wooden floors sounded ominous as she made her way to the reverend's office. She was nervous, yet determined to carry out God's desire for her to avenge and protect her daughter.

"Hello, Sarah," Reverend Thomas said and appeared delighted to have Sarah in his presence. "Sit right here by me. Can I get you anything to drink?"

"No, thank you," she said. Sarah sat down across from him and tried to force tears but was unsuccessful. She wanted the reverend to think she was distraught and could easily be taken advantage of.

"Now, how can your reverend help you?" he asked.

Sarah leaned toward him and Reverend Thomas, in turn, leaned toward Sarah.

"May I have a hug?" Sarah asked, her voice barely audible. "I think I just need a hug."

Reverend Thomas patted his knees and said, "Sometimes, all it takes is a little affection, and I certainly have affection for you." Sarah despised this man even more.

She smiled, leaning forward to show her ample bust. Reverend Thomas was beginning to breathe faster. Sarah thought about how she never wanted to hear his breath again.

The reverend reached toward Sarah's blouse, eyeing her breasts. His hand was moving toward her right nipple when Sarah pulled back just enough to tantalize him.

"Excuse me, sir. I need to get a tissue from my purse," she feigned.

Reverend Thomas grunted, a bit irritated and afraid Sarah would back out of their sexual encounter.

Sarah reached in her purse, simultaneously pulling out the knife and plunging it into his throat. The pastor gurgled and reached toward her, grasping at her. Sarah stood up and stepped out of reach, laughing at him. The struggling Reverend Thomas got to his feet, blood spurting on his white robe and surrounding furniture and books. He was wobbly and looked ready to collapse at any moment.

Arms extended toward Sarah, the reverend fell against his desk and knocked over a small Jesus figurine.

"Pray, you bastard," Sarah hissed. "You are not a man of God. You're a hypocrite and a sinner. God directed me to kill you and make the world a better place. Die, you scum!"

Sarah was calm as the church office grew quiet. She knew from previous experience that after a few gurgles and forced breaths, the body's heart and brain die and the quiet takes over. Sarah stepped outside the office and called for Zach, who was hiding in the men's room as planned.

"You ready?" he asked Sarah when he saw her. He was anxious.

"Yes," Sarah affirmed. "The deed is done."

Zach entered the reverend's office and surveyed the scene. "Not bad, county investigator. You deserve a promotion," he joked.

"Wear these gloves so we won't leave fingerprints," Sarah said, pulling two plastic sets of gloves out of her purse.

Sarah was ready to finish the job.

An old blanket Zach had stuffed in his bag worked perfectly to wrap the body while carrying it to the baptismal pool. Sarah had brought three sharp kitchen knives.

"I want his dick," she told Zach, who seemed disappointed. "You can cut off his balls."

"What should we do with them?" Zach asked. He often lacked creativity and looked to Sarah for instructions.

"Let's feed them to the wild dogs around town," she suggested.

Sarah and Zach began sawing the scrotum. Blood was plentiful and began covering their gloves.

"Shit, this is messy," Zach complained. He had a high sensitivity to cleanliness.

"Just keep going," Sarah insisted, impatient in case someone should saunter in and catch them with the body.

***

On Saturday morning, Henry packed up and paid the remaining bill to a young man who had taken the clerk's place from the day before. "Where you off to, mister?" he asked politely.

Henry was getting weary of all the questions these West Texas people asked.

"I'm headed to Amarillo. I heard it's nice there," he forced himself to say.

"Not as nice as here," the clerk persisted. "It's dusty and ugly. Here, at least we have some tall, green trees and the riverbed."

"Well, I guess that's good," Henry said and walked back to the room to get Becky. She was eating a candy bar left over from last night. "Let's go, little one," Henry called out.

Becky smiled. Sometimes she liked Henry, but other times she wanted to kill him.

***

Reverend Thomas' robe was now crimson from the blood spattered around his crotch after Sarah and Zach finished their handiwork.

"Let's get him on that altar," Sarah said. "I want the entire congregation to see him for what he really was. Satan's bastard!"

Zach began rolling his body in the same bloody blanket.

Sarah hoisted one end and Zach the other. They crossed the immaculate church floor and dragged his body past the pews, finally stopping at the tall, wooden cross that had been erected on the altar a few years ago. Nothing was as gorgeous and poignant as the cross on Easter. This spring the Reverend Thomas wouldn't be at church to pick out a new young and defenseless girl to prey on.

Hoisting the body up to the beams was difficult. Finally, Zach laid the cross on its side and began to tie the body to it with some rope he'd brought.

The county cops proved a formidable team, finally hanging the lifeless church leader on the cross. They steadied it with two large wooden tables pushed together on each side. Blood stains were apparent in the body's groin area. The reverend's arms hung limp beside his wounds, his chin resting on his chest. Zach placed the forged letter on a table directly in front of the corpse while Sarah deposited the knives and other evidence into a cheap plastic bag.

Relieved, Sarah hugged Zach. "I love you like a son," she told him.

"I love you like my grandmother," he quipped before adding, "I meant...a sister!"

According to their rehearsed script, Sarah left the church first. She calmly got in her car and went home. Zach was to wait until sundown to leave. He would stay close enough to the altar to see if anybody entered the church. If someone did come in, they had discussed that Zach should run out the back and hide in the woods.

He had walked to the church, so no one could report

seeing his motorcycle there. As far as others knew, he had no reason to kill Reverend Thomas, nor did Sarah. He was her family pastor. Besides, a small woman like her could never hoist such a big man on a cross and certainly neither could a skinny boy like Zach.

Sarah would attend Sunday school the next morning, as usual. There she would hear the reaction to the horrific death of the town's prominent pastor. There would be girls and women in the congregation he'd probably molested, but it was doubtful if they'd ever come forward with the truth. Small towns are unforgiving to women for many trespasses, but sexual acts (regardless of whose fault it was) almost always caused the woman to be scorned. Fairness never entered the equation.

9

On 7:00 am Sunday morning Sarah's pager buzzed. A pang of fear entered her body when she realized no one had called her yet to report the murder. Was she already a suspect? Guilt and panic tried to creep into Sarah's psyche when she looked at the number. It was her boss, the Montague County Sheriff. Having had little sleep during the night, Sarah felt edgy and nervous. She called him back immediately.

"Well, Sarah, it seems there's been a big crime in our little town last night," Will said.

"What?" Sarah asked, sounding shocked.

"Someone killed the Methodist minister and goddamn castrated him," the sheriff said, disgust in his voice.

"Reverend Thomas?" Sarah questioned again. "Why would they castrate him?"

"Hell if I know, but you'd better get down there and see what kind of fucking mess we have on our hands," he ordered. "I'll be there shortly."

"Yes, sir," Sarah agreed. "Do you know who found him?"

"A poor old lady. It was her turn to bring refreshments

early for the congregation," he explained. "They say she's about to have a nervous breakdown. See if you can calm her down. You're better at that than me. You know to retrieve any evidence you can find, yeah?"

"Yes, sir, I will," Sarah said and hung up, realizing she was pretty much safe now. The only thing she might have to deal with is if anybody saw her go into the church on Saturday afternoon. Maybe she would have to plant some evidence. The only thing she knew for sure was that she better go to the crime scene right now.

She slipped downstairs to tell Pete where she was going. Pete Sears was not stupid, so she would need to be careful as she concocted her story. "Pete," she said, "if you feel pretty good, may I bring you some cereal and milk? You should rest while I go to church."

"Why are you taking your gun?" he asked, eyeing Sarah's holster.

"There's been a murder at the church, and I need to investigate," Sarah said.

"Who got killed?"

"The reverend," Sarah said, trying to be matter-of-fact.

Pete still had no memory of the night he was attacked, including any details about the reverend and his involvement with their daughter. But something about Sarah's demeanor this morning made him briefly wonder if his wife was involved, but it was beyond his comprehension that she could kill anybody. She probably met some unsavory characters through her job, but she'd never hire a hitman.

"Sarah," Pete said firmly and looked directly into his

wife's eyes, attempting to read her face. "Did you have anything to do with his murder?"

Sarah Sears had always been truthful to a fault with her husband, and she believed what had happened yesterday was God's way. She had to chance it that Pete could keep her secret. As mean as he'd been during their twenty-odd years together, she still trusted her husband. But now was not the time.

"Pete, when I come home, we need to talk," she told him.

Pete instinctively knew at that moment his wife was involved, but he could not imagine why or how. He felt no sorrow for the minister, but he did fear for his wife. Pete Sears realized that he wanted to protect her and their family. This he would do.

***

Sarah saw Zach's motorcycle in the office parking lot on the way to church.

"What are you doing here on a Sunday?" she asked him when she walked in and saw him organizing files.

"I'm working on my alibi," he said and chuckled, a little too cocky. "I've been here working all weekend. The town is already abuzz about the murder!" he added.

"Zach, now's the time to keep our mouths shut," Sarah told him. "Promise me that forever this is our special secret."

Zach knew if he slipped up, he could lose his only friend. "You got it, Sarah, to my grave!"

"Thank you, son. Or maybe nephew. Either way, I love

you!" she bantered with him and left for the church.

Sarah pulled slowly into the church parking lot and gasped when she saw the ambulance blocking the entrance to the front door.

She profoundly believed that God had selected her to perform his retribution, but she wondered if perhaps she had been sloppy. Or maybe Zach made a mistake and left fingerprints. Someone could have noticed either one of them leaving the crime scene the day before.

Stepping out of her police car, Sarah hurried to the men carrying a gurney to the ambulance. She had a clear view of a white sheet wrapped around a corpse.

"What happened?" Sarah demanded to know.

"Someone butchered Reverend Thomas," answered Larry Stout, the most talkative of the paramedics.

"They castrated him!" Larry added. He was bewildered. The other medics were quiet in their disbelief.

The congregation was beginning to assemble in the churchyard, adding to the overwhelming stress of the situation. Whispers, shrieks, and cries emanated from the crowd. Old women were hugging each other as men shook their heads. The adults were attempting to keep the children away from the scene. There was an occasional outcry. Pastors were leaders of the community, not murder victims.

Sarah observed the crowd but tried to stay close to the ambulance workers. She didn't want to interact with the worshipers.

Sheriff Will pulled his vehicle onto the black tar surface of the parking lot, swinging open his car door. Sarah eyed him walking toward her and the crowd. He spied her and nodded as she approached him, Sarah trying to appear shocked yet in control.

"Sarah, have you investigated inside the church?"

"No, sir, I just got here," she offered.

"Well, let's go in there," he said briskly.

Sarah was sordidly aware of her demeanor. She played her part well, displaying anger, resolve, and shock. "This is how a country investigator should act in the face of a community," she reminded herself.

Sarah knew from her studies that one's mind plays games with reality when it has earlier deviated from normal behavior. She saw her church in a detached, unfamiliar way, as though through a stranger's eyes. The familiar building now had an ominous look with its large, wood-carved angels placed on each side of the blood-soaked altar. The holy men appeared to be staring directly at Sarah.

She shook her head and looked away.

There was already a stench. The scene shocked Sarah, even though she was its maker.

"Hard to believe anyone would be so brutal and demented," Will offered his thoughts as he looked around.

"Sarah, control yourself!" she commanded quietly. "God was your partner in this deed, and God may need you again. You and God have overcome another Satan worshiper. The preacher was a direct emissary of the devil. You did the right thing!"

Sheriff Will interrupted her silent conversation and said, "Sarah, take care of the evidence here if you find any.

This is disgusting. The press will be calling, so I'm going to the office. Call me if you find anything interesting."

The sheriff walked away, his head lowered.

Sarah saw the ambulance leave the churchyard. She looked at it through a distant lens, half-smirking. "Goodbye, Satan. God and I won again!" she told herself.

Sarah scoured the scene, making sure there was nothing to point to her or Zach. They were a capable team. She never worried that Zach might fold under pressure. Zach had long planned his retribution for those who had bullied him and would not consider burning his able accomplice. He hated any person with the power to discriminate against and intimidate him. Reverend Thomas certainly demonstrated this type of control.

The local cops arrived next, sirens blaring. The crowd was now overcome with emotion, and gawkers tried to get close to the scene. Every person wanted to remember the details of all that happened and would likely share them with neighbors and friends for years to come. A castrated pastor was an enticing story, one that would live on for decades. Curiosity and gossip would overtake the little town.

Sarah knew she'd need to be a good actor to maintain her innocence. Her natural shyness and reticence to engage with others would play in her favor. As long as the sheriff allowed her to conduct the investigation, she'd remain on solid ground.

Satisfied she'd covered her tracks, Sarah approached the senior church deacon named Mr. Dearing and said, "The paramedics took the body to the coroner's office, and I need to file a report. Are you getting a cleanup crew for the blood and mess?"

Sarah was injecting reality into the unbelievable scene, and the deacon just stared at her. Again, Sarah secretly prayed she could maintain her calm.

"What?" Mr. Dearing asked and looked at Sarah blankly. He seemed in a trance, trying to escape the situation.

"Mr. Dearing, you will need to get the church secured and cleaned up," Sarah ordered. Just then, the two Nocona police officers approached Sarah and the deacon.

"Boy," Bill Dean, the older of the two cops, said. "Somebody really hated the preacher. I've never even seen a deer butchered this bad!"

Sarah nodded and walked toward the door to leave. Deacon Dearing continued talking with the police. She needed to get away from this place; her psyche was beginning to control her actions.

Later in the day, Sarah went to the hospital morgue where the body was being held until an autopsy could be performed. "I need to speak with the attending doctor herc," Sarah told Nurse Betty who happened to be working the floor that day.

"Go ahead. He's in his office," she replied.

Sarah went down the hallway and knocked on the office door.

"Come in," the doctor called, and Sarah could see he was taking notes.

"I'm Sarah Sears, county investigator in charge of this crime. Do you have any comments?"

The doctor looked up at her and frowned. "Whoever did this was an amateur. They used a common kitchen knife. I even think it was a woman."

Sarah felt a shiver. "Why do you say that, doctor?"

"Because men usually use knives that kill big animals and cut cleaner than these wounds," he explained. "These were like a small kitchen serrated knife that a lady would use to cut up a steak or pork chop."

"I see. Anything else?" Sarah was trying to remain calm. This doctor could be a problem.

"Nope, just a horrendous crime, " he said. "Why would anyone want to kill the good reverend?"

"Doc, I wish I knew," Sarah said and turned to leave before adding, "May I come back if I need to?"

The doctor nodded.

When she got back to her office, she checked in with her boss.

"Anything interesting yet?" he asked. "You know Sarah, we could both get big promotions and raises if this murder is solved."

"Nothing yet. I will stay on it," Sarah assured him.

"Keep me informed."

"I will," she again promised her supervisor.

***

About mid-afternoon that Sunday, Pete had moved to the living room couch to watch sports. When Sarah finally got home, he peered at her strangely, as if he'd never seen her before.

"What's Olivia doing?" Sarah asked to deflect Pete's curious gaze.

"She's pretty upset," Pete said. "People have been calling the house about the reverend's death all day."

Pete stared at Sarah inquisitively. "Can we talk now?" he asked.

"Yes," Sarah said and sat down beside her husband.

Pete gestured for Sarah's hand. The change in Pete Sears was astonishing to Sarah. All she'd ever known from her husband was hateful remarks and blows from his fist. Intimidation and hurt were his hallmarks.

Once again, Sarah put her trust in God. If God had spoken to Pete, then Sarah must believe in her husband, she told herself. She remembered her bible and the wisdom of God. "What God joins together, no man must put asunder." Sarah had relied on this truth for twenty years.

Sarah sat down next to Pete. She needed to tell him what had happened, beginning with Henry Lee Lucas. She wasn't sure if she'd leave out the sex, but she would detail her interactions with the killer.

"Pete, a lot of things have happened. Please listen to me before you say or do anything, okay?" she began. Her old fears regarding her husband crept into Sarah's mind, and she hoped God would remain with Pete while she told her horrific story.

Like many married couples, the years had familiarized the two people. Although sorrow and pain had gripped the Sears household for decades, Pete was now a changed man.

He had feared death just a few days before and knew little about God. But Pete now chose to believe Sarah's God had given him another chance. So he decided he would remain quiet and show his wife patience, the best he knew how.

"Pete, I need to tell you about the man who tried to kill you. I believe he is a serial killer, and he found out where we lived," Sarah said.

"But why us?" Pete asked, curious as to why a stranger would target his family.

Sarah reminded him she'd been on the killer's trail. She continued her story, leaving out her brief sexual encounters with Henry. Pete Sears was now a kinder, gentler man, but his wife having sex with a depraved killer would be too much for him to bear. Sarah would never tell anyone of her demented tryst with the felon. Only she and God would know. If Henry tried singing to the authorities, she'd refute his story, assured no one would ever suspect her, the dedicated police lady. She'd just paint Henry as a crazy man, which she suspected would be totally accurate.

Sarah took a breath and spun more of her tale. "I was driving by the baseball field last week and saw a strange car. We had received a crime sheet at the office showing Lucas' picture. No one knew he was in town. I stopped to get a closer look at the car, and I was sure it was him driving. But he pulled away before I could arrest him."

Pete seemed to be following so far.

Sarah continued, "Anyway, I drove to the office, and he followed me. I was scared. He drove right on my back bumper, trying to intimidate me, and he did! I pulled in, and he just sat in his car staring at me. I hurried into the building and told Zach to send out a notice to the other counties letting them know we'd seen Lucas in Nocona. The next time I saw this man, he was on our porch."

Sarah paused before she lied, "He probably was after me instead. I'm so sorry, Pete. This was not right. You took the knife he intended for me."

Pete didn't move. It was evident to Sarah that he believed every word. She had never lied to Pete before. Her heart was beating rapidly, but she knew her husband would never suspect his wife of infidelity. Sarah reached toward Pete and squeezed his hand.

"Where do you think he is now?" Pete asked.

"I'm not sure," Sarah answered, trying to think fast. "I bet he's left town since he stabbed you. He knows the police will be looking for him."

Sarah knew this also wasn't true. Her office hadn't sent notices about Lucas to anyone. She planned to find him and kill him herself. God's world would be safer if the devil's demon was destroyed. Sarah was sure God needed her help.

Pete seemed drained and laid back on his pillows.

"Pete, there's something else I need to tell you," she said.

Sarah knew she needed to confess to killing Reverend Thomas. She assumed Olivia was hysterical by now and wouldn't keep the secret about her pregnancy for long, even though she'd trusted her mother to tell Pete in due time.

Sarah would never tell Olivia that she had murdered the reverend, but she felt she could tell Pete. She trusted her gut and her prayers because God was telling her to include Pete on her murder. After all, Henry had to pay for his sins one way or another. If she hadn't done it, Pete would have killed him for what he did to Olivia.

"Pete, you know Olivia went to the hospital because she was hemorrhaging from the abortion," she began.

Pete was staring at Sarah, hatred in his eyes.

Sarah worried about what he would do.

"Pete, it was Reverend Thomas."

"What are you talking about? Are you crazy?" Pete was close to shouting, shaking violently.

Sarah continued. "Reverend Thomas was giving our daughter drugs in return for sexual favors. He raped our daughter, along with others. If they got pregnant, he performed the abortions."

"Stop," Pete shouted at Sarah. "Nooooo!"

Her husband's voice bellowed like the calves she'd seen castrated in feedlots. He was like a wounded animal. His eyes glassed over and he tried to stand but fell back on the sofa, defeated. His only daughter molested by a preacher and then butchered like a cow.

"I'll kill him," he yelled out.

"Shhhh," Sarah whispered, pointing toward Olivia's door upstairs. "I already have," she said bluntly.

"What?" he stammered. "You did what?"

"I killed the reverend Saturday in his office."

Once again, Sarah was calm and resolute.

Dumbfounded, Pete could no longer speak. He stared at his wife, realizing his earlier fears were valid. She was a murderer.

"Pete, I knew you'd kill him if you got the chance," Sarah told him. "And I didn't want blood on your hands. I'm the one who investigated his death, Pete. I believe the community will think it was Henry Lee Lucas who did this."

Pete could not look away from this woman, someone he'd lived with for two decades. A meek, shy, insecure woman who never fought back when her husband abused her. He wondered what had snapped inside her. Was the need to protect their child so great that Sarah could kill someone? Someone she had considered a godly man? Had he never really known Sarah Sears?

"How did you kill him?" Pete wanted to know. Again, Sarah quieted Pete, putting her finger gently over his lips.

"I stabbed him. I made an appointment with him, went to his office, reached to hug him, and killed him with my sharpest, longest kitchen knife. Don't worry. I cleaned it and put it back in our kitchen."

Vomit welled in Pete's throat.

"Pete, I also castrated him," Sarah admitted.

Pete began to throw up on the white cotton pillowcase. Sarah went to the kitchen and brought back a cold towel, rubbing his face. He was bent forward but straightened up when Sarah touched him.

"I need to go up and see my daughter," he demanded.

"Not now, Pete."

"Does she know about you and him?"

"No, and I'm not going to tell her," Sarah said firmly. "I'd like you to keep our secret."

"What if someone finds out?" Pete asked. He was scared.

"They won't. I can handle that part," Sarah told him. Pete knew his wife was a capable woman.

"Can I trust you as my husband and in front of God?" Sarah was trying to read Pete as she asked the question. He hesitated, thinking of his mortality, again reaffirming to himself that God had saved him from a murderer for a reason.

Pete instinctively knew his wife did what she thought best for her family. This mother could not bear the thought of a robed monster molesting children, including friends of their daughter. The picture in her mind of her own minister forcing her only child to commit sick acts against her will was far too much for Sarah Sears. His wife had to do something. For this, he could and he would forgive her.

Pete reached for Sarah's hand. "I don't want to know any more. Is our daughter going to be okay?"

"Yes," Sarah answered and breathed a sigh of relief. "Except I believe she may be hooked on the drugs he provided her. I'm not sure, but I suspect that."

Sarah sounded very sad, and Pete now wept softly.

***

They sat in silence, motionless, until they heard loud noises from Olivia's room that sounded like someone sobbing.

"Olivia, are you okay?" Sarah called as she went upstairs to check on her.

"I didn't want him dead!" the girl moaned.

Olivia was becoming frantic. "Why did someone have

to kill him?" she screamed.

"Reverend Thomas was a child molester, honey," Sarah reasoned. "Anyone who hurts a child hurts God. To send him to hell was God's way. This was the work of God!"

"You're crazy, you bitch! I hate you! Get out!" the girl screamed. "Get out!"

Sarah tried to comfort her child, attempting a hug. She pushed Sarah away and repeated, "I said, get out!"

Sarah stood her ground. "Olivia, he hurt you," she said softly. "And I suspect he raped your friend Amber too."

"Where will I get my shit now?" Olivia seethed. Sarah suddenly realized her daughter was a drug addict, panicked by the thought of losing her source. Sarah needed to talk to Pete about what to do now, so she left their daughter's room, and Olivia slammed the door behind her.

Sarah walked down the stairs, tears clouding her eyes. She would help her daughter overcome her demons. With Reverend Thomas gone, Sarah would have to oversee Olivia getting clean. She knew her task would be difficult, but with God's help, they would both survive.

Minutes went by with the only sound in the Sears household coming from the small clock on the shabby mantle. It had been a wedding present from friends of Sarah's parents. She always loved the familiar ticking.

"Pete," Sarah began, "we need to take care of Olivia and get her off drugs. And I need to find Henry Lee Lucas. I need to do both right away." Sarah knew this was God's will.

Silence fell on the couple once again. Pete saw Sarah as an equal now. She was no longer his servant but a partner, a determined policewoman. He knew he could not talk her out of tracking down a killer who'd almost killed him. So as a husband and a partner, he vowed that he must help his wife. Pete Sears would be the killer and Sarah, the accomplice.

***

With an approximate population of 105,000 people, Wichita Falls, Texas, is about 50 miles west of tiny Nocona. Another 50 miles west is the 12,000-person town of Vernon, Texas. Either of these western communities dwarfed Sarah's hometown. Residents of Nocona can drive south to the Dallas Fort Worth area in about the same time as going west. Any Noconan who moves to these larger Red River locales will rarely see his former Nocona friends except to visit family on Christmas holidays and Easter Sunday.

Sarah's Aunt Sadie was her mother's half-sister who moved to the Vernon area many decades ago with her now deceased husband to work on a West Texas ranch. Childless, Sadie remained in her country home when her Ralph died of emphysema. She would occasionally write Sarah's mother, always asking for Sarah or her sister to visit.

"Be sure to come and stay awhile," she'd typically add to the letter's postscript.

The Nocona clan often discussed going to Vernon but only once could Sarah remember driving the three hours to Sadie's house. A family disagreement had ensued about how far the ranch really was with Sarah's father complaining, "I don't know, but it was a hell of a drive!"

Sarah liked her distant aunt and had always hoped to go again to see her, yet never got the chance after becoming Mrs. Sears.

Aunt Sadie had recently sent a short note that successfully reached Sarah, although it was addressed using Sarah's maiden name. Sarah suspected her aunt might be suffering from slight dementia. But overall, the letter was sweet and inviting.

Considering how to get Olivia away from her "druggy" addicted friends, Aunt Sadie's ranch popped into Sarah's mind. Although Sarah hated to admit it, Olivia was often a bitchy, spoiled brat. But she could be sweet when she wanted to be. Sarah wanted to get her daughter away from Nocona and protect her from as much hateful gossip and bad influence as she could manage. Sarah considered if perhaps Olivia could finish her school year in this rural environment in Wilbarger County, Texas.

Her aunt would love having the company, and Olivia would be forced to be drug-free under Aunt Sadie's watchful eye. Sarah never considered she might be naive about the availability of controlled substances even in Vernon, but anything would be better than Nocona for Olivia.

Pete would need to be consulted before she contacted her relative. Sarah needed his approval and support. Sarah and Pete were partners on the Reverend Thomas situation, and now would be partners on his daughter's recovery too.

Olivia was headstrong and would likely throw a huge fit when they proposed the plan. Spending a few months in a lonely house miles from nowhere without adequate television reception would not suit the teen. Sarah needed to act quickly while Olivia was recovering from her injuries.

Still in shock, Pete appeared to listen to Sarah's suggestion, but hardly communicated a response. Pete was typically quick to make decisions, and Sarah had never overridden anything he dictated. However, Pete was weak and preoccupied.

"Whatever you think," he said at last. "But you tell her." Pete never liked conflict with his baby girl.

"I will, but Pete, I need you to stand behind me on this. Olivia will have a hissy! If you feel like making the trip, I think we should take her tomorrow. I can call Aunt Sadie right now. She's always home."

Pete glanced at his wife, nodding his head. She worried Pete was sliding back in his shell.

But Pete was busy silently plotting Henry Lee Lucas' death.

***

Pete Sears had grown up with guns of all kinds in his home and in the homes of his friends. When he won a marksmanship award in military basic training school, he was quite proud and his old man complimented him. Decades later, Pete could still hit a buck's neck hundreds of yards from a deer stand. Shooting accuracy came easily to Pete.

Sarah dreaded confrontation also but knew this was the best for her daughter. She felt certain God had guided Aunt Sadie to write that letter when she did. A sign from God was not to be ignored.

"Olivia, open the door. We need to talk," Sarah told her daughter after talking to Pete.

"Go away!" the girl shouted.

"Olivia, you must open the door! Your dad and I need to tell you something."

Her daughter's curiosity made her unlock the deadbolt. Sarah entered. "Where's Daddy?" Olivia asked.

"He is resting, as should you," Sarah scolded.

"Is that what you wanted to tell me?"

"No," Sarah said, trying to force a smile. "I want you to go to Vernon, Texas, and stay with my aunt for a while."

"What the hell?" Olivia screeched. "Where is Vernon?"

"Two or three hours west of here. And don't curse."

Olivia was furious, raising her voice and screaming, "You're crazier than I thought. I'm not leaving. All my friends are here!"

"No, Olivia, that's what you're doing," Sarah said firmly. "You're going away for a while. Get out the clothes you'd like to take, and include enough for school."

"Go fuck yourself!" The wild child was livid.

Sarah had a plan for Olivia. Nurse Betty had given Sarah five or six sleeping pills in case Pete couldn't rest. A soft drink would be just fine to dissolve one for her daughter that night. Olivia would be so groggy by morning they'd have no trouble loading her into the car for the trip to Vernon.

"Hello, Aunt Sadie?" Sarah said into the phone receiver. After a short conversation, all was agreed. They would leave in the morning.

***

The bedside clock buzzed, awaking Sarah at 5:30 to give her plenty of time to pack a few of Olivia's clothes and get Pete situated in the car. Sarah would drive to Vernon and deposit Olivia to stay with Aunt Sadie. If Olivia tried to run away, Sarah would have her admitted to the girls home in Dallas. At least this would serve as Sarah's threat to her daughter.

Sarah would have to share Olivia's past with Aunt Sadie and make sure the older woman could manage her daughter a few months. Sarah had work to do. She had a killer to kill.

Pete was awake on the sofa when Sarah descended the stairs. "You're awake," Sarah said, startled.

"Yes, I'm going to load some stuff in the car."

"What do you need to take?" Sarah asked, "I can do it. You probably shouldn't lift anything. You need to take it easy. I'm driving us to Vernon."

Sarah surprised herself with her new-found confidence and control.

"You get Olivia," Pete insisted. "I know what I need to do, and I can manage it, really."

Sarah was curious about what her husband could possibly be taking to West Texas. She had made sandwiches the night before and filled the cooler with drinks. She switched on the coffee pot and got the thermos ready for the trip, praying the sleeping pill was keeping Olivia asleep while she readied the car.

Pete opened the door to the closet in his office upstairs

and saw several boxes of shotgun shells and several sleeves of 30-06 rifle shells. He stuffed the rounds in his travel bag and got out two guns. Pete kept his weapons in pristine working order, not for use against humans but for deer and bird hunting.

Still weak from surgery, he carried the shell bag downstairs first. The metal weighed several pounds. With Sarah still in the kitchen, he threw the bag in the car's trunk.

Each gun mandated a trip up and down the stairs, but Pete was finally packed and ready. He and Sarah would find the killer's trail. Stopping off in Vernon might be a good start. Every day Pete was getting stronger, and when they found Henry, this expert marksman would kill him from several hundred yards away. Lucas would never have a chance to return fire. Pete was confident just one shot would send Lucas to his grave.

Upstairs, Olivia was barely coherent. Sarah threw a blanket around her daughter's shoulders and helped her down the stairs. She knew Olivia would be difficult if she were lucid, but the sleeping pill had worked its magic, and the girl was groggily compliant.

Sarah laid her in the backseat of the car and wrapped the blanket around her. Olivia fell back asleep.

"Pete, are you ready?" she called.

Her husband lightly slammed the screen door and headed to the car. He was casually dressed and wearing a light jacket covering his bandages. Sarah opened the trunk to put in two suitcases, immediately spying the two powerful guns. Why would her husband want those?

Pete saw Sarah's surprised look when she saw the rifles. He looked her straight in the eyes.

"Pete, why do you have these guns in the trunk?" she inquired.

"I'm going hunting," he said dryly.

Sarah's mind took her to their traumatic honeymoon and the dead antelope shot from the highway.

"What in the world will you hunt?" Sarah asked, hesitantly.

Pete answered slowly and deliberately, "Henry Lee Lucas."

Sarah gasped. "How? I don't understand."

"Oh, yes you do, Mrs. Sears, police lady," Pete seethed, a familiar roughness to his voice. "You know about killin' and so do I. Together, we're gonna catch the monster, and I'm gonna take him out. One clean shot to the heart and he'll never stab or kill anyone else. I must do it. He might hurt you or our family."

"Pete, I'm scared," Sarah whimpered.

"No need," he responded. "We've both killed before. I'm still a good shot. You just ain't been keeping up with your husband." Pete smiled. "Think you can find Henry?"

"I think so," Sarah nodded.

"Well, then let's get Olivia to your aunt Sadie's."

Sarah backed out of the driveway in her state-issued patrol car. She'd call Zach later and check in. Zach and her boss would need to know she was on Henry Lee's trail. The sheriff might not like that, as he probably wanted her to be working on the reverend's murder. She would try to evade him so that she and her husband could take the law into their capable Sears hands. Sarah's mind was controlling her thoughts, issuing her the satisfaction of seeing Henry Lee Lucas bleeding from her husband's rifle. She, Pete, and God would have their retribution. It was God's way.

10

Sarah had a suspicion that Henry was again on the run. However, she was unsure which road he took from Nocona. Returning to Florida would be too risky, so Oklahoma or somewhere out west was more likely.

Pete was silent but pleasant on the drive. Approaching Wichita Falls, Sarah planned to stop for gas and to make a phone call to her office. Avoiding Ruby's gossipy interrogations, she would speak only to Zach about the reason for her call. He could then assuage the sheriff, deflecting his questions and intentions.

Reverend Thomas' murder would be the topic of conversation in that county for months, maybe years. Sarah smiled to herself, knowing that this evil, corrupt church leader could try to get in Heaven, but the truth was that Sarah's God sent the preacher to a burning hole called "Hell."

"Hi, what's goin' on?" Sarah asked Zach on the other end of the phone.

"Oh shit," Zach said, sounding nervous and excited. "Guess what?"

Sarah was a little perturbed that he didn't get straight to the point. "What is it, Zach?" she insisted. Her heart was beating rapidly.

"Old Lady Mooney's bones were found stuffed in a pot-bellied stove in her backyard! The city cop found them yesterday afternoon. Everybody's saying that drifter Lucas killed her and Reverend Thomas. Ain't that great?"

"Zach, don't say that. Forget anything you know about the reverend and focus on how I'm going to catch Henry Lee Lucas. Does anyone know if he's left town?"

"He's nowhere to be found," Zach reported. "When will you be in the office?"

"Zach, listen carefully and follow my instructions," Sarah said. She explained she was taking Olivia to Vernon, Texas, that morning to stay with her aunt while she searched for Lucas.

"Will you be back this afternoon?" Zach asked, worried. He needed Sarah with him, there was so much going on in town with two murders.

"I said to listen carefully," Sarah was firm. "I'm not coming back until I have either captured or killed Henry Lee Lucas. God is telling me I must rid the earth of Satan's son."

"But Sarah, what if the sheriff comes here and asks me lots of questions?" Zach pleaded.

"Zach, you're very smart. You know nothing about anything except I called in and am taking Olivia to Vernon. You're not sure when I'm getting back, but you told me about Mrs. Mooney. Tell the sheriff I'll call back later today."

Zach paused.

"Nothing else, you understand?" Sarah said. "Don't be too talkative about the reverend's murder. You and I both know that too much talking is bad anytime and especially now. Soon everything will be back to normal—just you and me taking care of each other and our little town. God will be pleased with both of us."

In the past, Zach didn't trust God or anyone else. But Sarah was always right, so he was beginning to think maybe there was a God. If so, Zach hoped he had the same God as Sarah. She seemed to talk to hers a lot.

"Okay, Sarah," Zach whispered, away from Ruby's prying. "I got your back. Be careful."

"One more thing," Sarah added. "Try to find out anything you can about Mrs. Mooney's murder and which way Lucas is running. Oklahoma or to the west?"

She had spent a lot of the drive that morning thinking about Henry's profile. Criminals like to return to the scene of their crimes, but he was hardhearted and stone cold. He would not let his sense of murderous satisfaction get him caught. Like a wolf, he would move on from his prey, she assumed. The dead had no benefit to Henry. Money and sex were his primary goals in life, and seeing his victim's dried blood didn't excite him in any way.

Sarah was also sure he'd killed Mooney, but why? Did the old lady find out who he was and what he'd done? Or did he want something from her? Questions flooded Sarah's mind. Did the woman have money stashed somewhere? Regardless of where Lucas was headed, Sarah and God wanted him in Hell. She could put him there.

Sarah started to hang up the phone with Zach.

"Okay," she said. "I'll talk to you later this afternoon. Be calm and smart, partner." Sarah knew how to control Zach. He was so pleased that Sarah depended on him this way. He would keep his mouth shut and help his friend.

"Hey, Sarah, hold on a minute," he said. "A fax is printing out." Sarah was disturbed by how often Zach would try to keep her on the phone.

"Okay, but just a minute. I've got to go," Sarah explained. She could see her car from the payphone outside the gritty convenience store. Oil field workers were coming and going with their hands full of drinks and donuts on their way to the surrounding oil patches. It was hard for her to hear, as the wind was blowing and the dirty trucks kept pulling up near her.

Olivia had awakened and was looking over the backseat toward Pete. Sarah was anxious to return to the car. Olivia had to be out of Nocona, but she wasn't going to like it. Sarah needed to be firm with her daughter.

"Got it," Zach said and began reading the fax into the phone line. "This is from the sheriff's office in Wichita County. It says a highway patrol spotted a car like Lucas' blue Chevy on Highway 287 headed north toward Amarillo. It looked like two people in the car. The officer was on the other side of the divided four-lane and couldn't get across to pursue him."

Sarah wondered if the patrolman just didn't want to tangle with the killer.

"Got it, Zach! Good work!" Sarah hung up.

Olivia was getting out of Sarah's car, still woozy from the sleeping pill her mother gave her the night before. Sarah ran toward her.

"Olivia, what are you doing? Get back in the car."

"No, bitch," Olivia slurred. "I'm not going to a hellhole. I'm going home."

Sarah reached for her arm, and Olivia jerked away. She instinctively pushed Olivia toward the backseat door. Olivia was screaming at her, but Sarah had to get control. She slapped Olivia hard on her face and pushed her inside at the same time.

Olivia, stunned, began crying. "I hate you," she hurled the words toward Sarah.

"Someday you won't," Sarah responded and started the car. "But for now, go ahead and hate me. You're going to Vernon!"

***

Aunt Sadie lived about eight miles west of Vernon, closer to a small town named Crowell. Sadie was well known in town, often attending church and buying gasoline there. A solid Southern cook, her fried chicken, white gravy, and whipped potatoes were ready for the Sears family. She had made up some pie crust with extra sugar and opened a can of cherries for a cherry cobbler. Sadie liked cooking and missed eating with Ralph.

She had stripped the single bed in her tiny guest room,

washing all the covers and adding a vase of wildflowers on the 1940s-antique dresser. Having a teenager would be a challenge, but she looked forward to the company.

Sarah had never driven her state car very far after the Oklahoma trip where she got rid of the two thugs that raped her. This was her second longest trip, and it gave her a strange kind of pleasure showing other drivers a woman could be a law officer. She was careful to drive the speed limit, although a state trooper was unlikely to pull over his comrade.

Pete had not said a word since Sarah had pushed and slapped his daughter. He was mentally struggling to accept his now powerful and take-charge spouse. Although he was grateful she'd saved his life and felt fortunate to be alive, Pete was perplexed about the future of his family. Not a deep thinker when it came to emotional issues, he decided to let his fears subside. He could and would deal with whatever came in the future. For now, he would regain his manhood and kill that son-of-a-bitch, Henry Lee Lucas.

Olivia interrupted his thoughts by letting out a scream. "I'm bleeding again." Blood had stained her nightgown and the pallet Sarah had put in the backseat. "Help me!"

Sarah quickly pulled the car to the side of the highway. She grabbed Olivia, this time as a caring and scared parent. The girl looked pale and frightened.

"Mom, I can't go to some fucking country hick place while I'm bleeding to death. Take me home!"

Sarah was busy mopping up the blood with a towel she kept in the trunk, and Pete wrapped his arms around his daughter. He looked at his wife and said firmly, "Sarah, our daughter needs to stay with us. She is still sick." Sarah shook her head, agreeing to her husband's command.

"I'll call Aunt Sadie," she said. They were only a few miles away from the hospital in Vernon.

For the next ten minutes, the family was utterly silent. Sarah questioned God's motives. How could her family be in such a dire situation? A daughter in physical and emotional peril? A wounded husband? And a wife willingly having had sex with a killer? What would happen to this Texas family?

Sarah never questioned her murderous deeds—these were acts demanded by God. She believed God talked directly to her, so there was no reason to question it. But everything else was in doubt.

After making a short phone call informing Aunt Sadie that the Sears family would no longer be visiting her, Sarah felt relieved that Olivia's bleeding had stopped. Timidly, she asked Pete if they could head on toward Amarillo, now only a few hours away. She explained that the fax delivered to her office affirmed that Henry was headed that way.

Pete was as determined as his wife. "Let's go," he nodded toward the west.

The stretch of lonely highway across West Texas made the drive more ominous for Sarah. While Olivia and Pete slept, Sarah's mind pulled back again to their honeymoon. The trauma of Pete's abuse, the shock of skinning an antelope, and the disappointment of a scarred marriage haunted Sarah's psyche. She began to pray.

"God," she began, "if killing this murderer is not

something you want me to do, give me a sign. I need your guidance and comfort now."

God said nothing in return as Sarah drove.

***

The Big Tex motel was ripe for all kinds of crimes. It was situated on a creek bed in the poor part of Amarillo on the south side. People with little to lose liked the message displayed on the motel's sign: "We rent for an hour, a day, or a lifetime."

The night clerk at the Big Tex eyed Sarah's uniform and especially her gun.

"Are you a lady cop? Where you from?" she asked.

This woman seemed a little too inquisitive.

"My family is with me. They are both sick, and we need a room. I've come upstate to hunt a criminal. Have you seen a strange man and maybe a girl together in a blue car?"

"Lady, the only strange thing I've seen is you," she snorted. "A lady cop dragging her family with her on a hunt." The Big Tex clerks rarely divulged who might or might not be staying there. "Make sure you don't use too much hot water in the shower," she noted. "The building works off old heaters, and they don't give too much hot water."

"Yes, ma'am, and thank you," Sarah added. She was going to put Pete and Olivia to bed, and then she'd drive to every motel and café parking lot in this city to find Henry's car. It was probably a wild goose chase, since he'd probably stolen another one by now. But she had to start somewhere.

It was standard procedure for anyone from another county sheriff's department to check in with the local office, but not Sarah. She believed God wanted her to kill Henry herself, not help someone else do it. The Amarillo sheriff's department was probably already alerted to his possible existence in their city. She didn't want to be called back to Montague County. So she would go this alone.

About 250,000 people called this desolate outpost home. They had a reputation for being friendly and hard working. Sarah hoped Henry was not spending the night among these nice folks.

***

"Henry Lee, I'm hungry. Can we go eat? I want some strawberry pancakes," Becky whined.

"Goddammit, shut up, bitch," he replied. Henry was growing weary of this teenager. He hated most, if not all, women, and she was no different. "Her whining is so damn irritating," he told himself. "Her pussy isn't worth her bitching."

"I said, I'm hungry!" Becky was persistent.

Henry was getting madder and barked, "Did you hear me, bitch? I said, shut up. I need to think."

Fiddling with the old television inside a room at the Big Tex motel, he was looking to hear any news about him. His savvy, reasonably intelligent mind had kept Henry out of jail thus far, and he needed to scheme his future steps.

"You never do anything I want," Becky's shrill nag hit the

wrong nerve. Henry rushed to the bed and backhanded her across her face, her nose now bleeding as she cried. Henry's emotions hit a high. He'd had enough, he promised himself. This immature bitch was going to die. He needed to go this part alone.

Henry jumped on Becky, ramming his dick up her crotch.

"Stop!" she yelled for the first time ever. But Henry continued to thrust in her vagina while putting his hands around her neck. She began fighting back, arousing Henry even more. The harder he thrust, the tighter he gripped her throat. She was gasping for her last breath when Henry ejaculated. Nothing excited Henry Lee Lucas more than necrophilia—a dead woman full of Henry's semen.

Becky Toole had stayed too long in a demon's den. She now paid the ultimate price: being raped and strangled in a cheap Amarillo, Texas, motel room.

Henry zipped his pants, grabbed his old leather knapsack, and slipped out the door. It was time to move on. The lazy motel clerk wouldn't check on the room until tomorrow afternoon, giving him time to head to the Colorado mountains.

***

Exhausted, Sarah gave up the search at midnight. She needed rest and was anxious to check on Olivia and Pete back at the Big Tex. She was frustrated with no sign of Lucas' car.

Sarah would check in with Zach tomorrow morning.

She knew she was likely in hot water with her boss for leaving town, but God was her partner now. She felt confident he would help her find the killer.

Watching late night television, Pete was waiting on Sarah in the room.

"Where've you been?" he asked, agitated yet relieved she was okay. Olivia was fast asleep in the bed next to him.

"Checking out hotel and restaurant parking lots. I hoped to see his car. I would know it if I saw it," she explained.

Pete suspected that Sarah knew Lucas more personally than she let on. There was no reason for him to think that, beyond a husband's suspicions. "Any luck?" he asked.

"Nope, but tomorrow's another day," Sarah said and slipped in bed beside Pete, the first time in decades she wasn't scared of him.

***

As a precaution, Henry decided to stay in town and begin his Colorado journey in the morning. Becky's body would start to rot, and he couldn't stand the smell of death, even after killing so many people. He had paid for the night at the Big Tex, but he decided he'd just sleep in the old blue car, parking overnight in a safe place out of sight like the driveway of an empty house for sale.

The local Amarillo police knew many of the motel night clerks because most crimes were committed after sundown. Prostitution, sex crimes, drugs, alcohol, petty thefts—most of these perpetrators stayed in shabby motels. They were the dens of sin. Early the next morning, Ben Stewart, a ten-year veteran cop, pulled in the Big Tex motel. He carried the precinct rap sheet showing Lucas' face, announcing him as a suspected murderer in Nocona, Texas, with possible other crimes in other states.

"Hey, Jo Ann, how's everything going?" Ben greeted the motel clerk on duty.

"Okay," she said and nodded, taking a slow drag off her Camel straight cigarette. "What's up, Ben? You want some coffee? There's a little chill in the air."

"Nope," Ben replied. "I gotta go to the rest of the motels in town. Here's a flyer. Seen this guy? He's a bad one."

Jo Ann turned ashen while staring at Henry Lee's face.

"Ben," she whispered. "He's here."

Ben looked alarmed. "You're sure?"

"Yep, came in last night. I think there was a woman in his car."

"Holy shit, which room?" Ben asked. He was nervous. Ten years arresting two-bit petty criminals hadn't prepared him for a hardened criminal, a serial killer. "I'm calling for back up."

Jo Ann looked out the office blinds. His car is gone. "Maybe he left. I'm not sure." Although Jo Ann's shift was about to end, she felt compelled to find out if the guy she met was Henry Lee Lucas.

Ben was feeling equally brave and curious. He joined the police force after he got laid off from the PPG plant a few years ago. Being a cop seemed pretty easy here, and he basked in the awe and respect that wearing a badge and a gun brought him.

Tracking down serial killers and checking motels for criminals, however, was something left for the FBI and the sheriff's office. Ben was expected to give traffic tickets and watch for shoplifters in the mall. But he did have pride, so he'd muster up the bravado to do his job here.

"I'd better go check the room," Ben said. "Can you go with me?"

When they opened Lucas' room, the room was dark and had a slight stench.

Ben hung behind Jo Ann with his gun out of the holster. An affable cop, he was not one to lead a charge of any kind.

Jo Ann knocked on the open door and asked, "Hello, anyone in there?" No sound.

She knocked again. The same.

She turned on a light. The shape of a woman's body was slumped on the bad.

"Shit, probably a meth overdose," Jo Ann said. She was disgusted with the tragedy drugs brought her community. "Wake up, girl!"

Henry never left a victim breathing. He was proud of the fact that he completed his mission 100% of the time. Becky was dead and beginning to decompose.

"Jo Ann, don't touch her," Ben ordered. "I need to call the department. An investigator needs to handle it from here."

"Damn," Jo Ann sighed and felt sorry for the girl. This would cut short the guests staying at the Big Tex for the day. Cop cars always scared away the type of people who stayed there. Jo Ann and the other clerks were paid a small bonus if the motel stayed full. So there would be no bonus this week.

***

Sarah hardly slept, feeling the daunting presence of Henry somewhere nearby. Despite her protests, her vagina quivered with the thought of him on top of her. She felt faint and sick at her stomach.

She got up, made her way to the bathroom, and placed a wet cloth on her forehead. Remembering how she'd sinned with a killer, a thrust of vomit entered her throat.

"Pete, I need to check in with Zach," she said to her husband after she dressed. "I'd better call the office."

Olivia awoke and went to the bathroom to clean up. She was feeling better, and Pete was healing well. Sarah thought she could leave them again this morning while she searched for Henry.

"I'm going with you wherever you're going. We are going to kill him together," Pete said, adamant that he would kill this bastard, not his wife.

"Kill who?" Olivia asked, walking out of the bathroom. She had overheard their conversation, but she was not part of the plan to kill Henry Lee Lucas. "Don't tell me either of you is going to kill somebody," she said, thinking of Reverend Thomas, her drug supplier. Olivia might have been suffering from drug withdrawal had she not been given pain killers for her abortion.

Sarah decided to tell Olivia why they were in Amarillo.

Olivia was startled by this information. What had her mother become? A hunter of murderers?

"Well, I'm going wherever you guys are going," the girl announced. "I'm not staying here in this ratty place." Nothing, it seemed, had changed the bossy teen's attitude after all.

Sarah informed Pete and Olivia to stay put at the motel while she quickly stopped by the sheriff's department to use the phone and let her boss know she was on the job.

Harold Stein was the officer on duty in Amarillo. He was busy faxing a notice of the Big Tex motel's murder when Sarah walked in.

"Howdy," Harold said, surprised to see a short, middle-aged woman wearing a sheriff's uniform, a gun on her side. "What can I do for you, ma'am?"

Sarah explained she was the investigator in charge of finding the killer, Henry Lee Lucas. Harold frowned and pushed the faxed copy toward Sarah. "You think this murder at the Big Tex has anything to do with your man?"

Harold had worked in law enforcement for three decades. Nothing shocked him. He guessed the latest victim was a drugged-out prostitute who visited the wrong sleazy motel room.

Reading the fax, Sarah turned pale. Instinctively, she knew this was Henry's work. This was probably the girl he had with him in Nocona.

"May I borrow your phone?" she asked. "I need to call my office in Montague County."

"You bet, little lady. Anytime." Harold Stein was a good

man but exhibited the typical Texan's male chauvinism. As he addressed Sarah, he made sure she kept that pistol in her holster.

"Hell, I bet she's never even fired a gun," he thought. "A lady sheriff, huh. This damn women's lib thing has gotten way out of hand." He excused himself to the office kitchen to pour himself some coffee while she made her phone call.

Zach answered the phone, just as Sarah hoped. She didn't have the patience for Ruby's relentless gossip.

"Zach, I'm in Amarillo. There was a murder here last night. I think Henry Lee Lucas has his fingers are all over it."

"What are you planning to do, Sarah?" he asked. Before she could answer, Zach continued, "I talked with the sheriff yesterday. He needs you back here. They are all talking about Reverend Thomas. There are tons of wreaths, flowers, and notes hanging on the fence around the church. The Lions Club, the women's club, and all the churches are having prayer breakfasts. I even heard a tent revival is on its way to the county."

"Do they still think Lucas did the murder?" Sarah asked.

"I think so," he replied. "But a lot of people don't know who Lucas is. Ruby's been gossiping with every old woman in the county. Rumors are crazy. Some even say the reverend had a gay lover who killed him. Wouldn't you know the assholes always blame us 'fags'!"

Straight white men hatred was always present in Zach's soul.

"Okay, Zach, just stay calm," Sarah instructed. "Tell the sheriff I'm on Lucas' trail and that we will find the reverend's killer. He will be proud of me."

"Sarah, be safe!" her partner said.

"Zach, just stay quiet. I'll talk to you tomorrow. Never forget we're partners and need to take care of each other."

She hung up just as Harold walked back to his desk. There was no reason for Harold to be jealous of this woman. She probably filled a quota, he reminded himself. Harold didn't like the liberal government and hoped to retire next year. His menial office duty was fine for him until then because it kept him out of danger.

"Lady, good luck. You might go over to the Big Tex and take a look around," Harold suggested.

"Thanks for the advice," Sarah placated him. "That's a good idea."

Harold liked this strange woman.

***

Jo Ann's shift was way past time, but she stayed on with the daytime clerk, a twenty-something student who passed the time studying when she wasn't renting rooms at the Big Tex. Jo Ann didn't want the girl to panic and quit with all the commotion going on. Then she'd have to work two shifts until they found someone. She told the girl to take care of the office while Jo Ann mingled with the city cops.

Traffic had virtually stopped in front of the motel, and rubberneckers were getting out to see what happened. The cops were stern, demanding the onlookers keep going. The ambulance arrived and prepared the body to be transported to the morgue.

Sarah placed a small siren on the top of her Montague County car and pulled into the motel parking lot. A city cop approached. "Ma'am," he said. "What are you doing in that car?"

Sarah smiled and pulled out her badge. He frowned and let her drive through the crowd. She stopped by the room where Pete and Olivia were staying and told them what had happened overnight at the motel. She instructed Pete to keep Olivia inside and not to go out for any reason.

Pete watched his wife work the policemen from the window of the motel room. Now that he paid more attention to his spouse, he was amazed at her efficiency. Maybe she was always a "take charge" person, but he still wouldn't allow himself to give her credit.

Pete Sears had suffered his whole life with bouts of anger. His dysfunctional, no-good family upbringing made it worse, and the war had sealed his attitude. Pete had poor self-worth and refused to let anyone penetrate his weaknesses. He knew he was ready to rid himself of his demons, but only after he killed the killer. He would get his retribution, just as his wife had done with Reverend Thomas.

One more killing and the Sears family would be whole again. Pete would make up for the twenty years he'd wasted. He needed his family more than ever.

"Why are we still here?" Olivia asked. She had a slight fever and was weak from her blood loss.

"I don't know. Just rest, honey. There's some cookies in that sack on the floor by the bed," he said. "Eat a few to tide you over while your mother is talking to the police."

Characteristically, Pete had always been kind to his only daughter. "Your mother will be through in a few more minutes."

"I don't get it," Olivia complained. "She must think she's Annie Oakley with that gun strapped on her. What a fake."

"Olivia, I want you to be nicer to your mother," he scolded. "She has taken care of both of us."

Olivia was startled to hear her father say a kind word about her mother. "What is going on in this family?" she again thought to herself.

***

"Hello, ma'am," Sarah nodded toward Jo Ann at the motel reception desk. "May I ask you a few questions?"

Jo Ann was still amused at a lady was wearing a sheriff's uniform. "That's okay, but where are you from again?"

"I'm Sarah Sears, the Montague County sheriff department investigator assigned to this case."

Jo Ann puffed on her cigarette, staring at Sarah. "Why a cop from somewhere called Montague County?"

"I'm on the case of a killer named Henry Lee Lucas," she said. "He murdered an old lady in Nocona, Texas."

The paramedic wheeled Becky's body beside Sarah and Jo Ann, lifting the corpse into the ambulance. Jo Ann shook her head. "I saw this girl yesterday in his car, and now she's dead."

"Whose car?" Sarah asked, sniffing a lead.

"I already told Officer Ben all this, but there was a man with her in a blue car. They stayed in that room. When I looked out this morning at daylight, the car was gone. I thought they'd both left during the night. I was sure glad I got his money upfront."

"What did the man look like?" Sarah questioned. Jo Ann let out the smoke from her lungs, precipitating a crackly cough.

"Pretty good looking, slim, medium height, about 40 years old I guess."

"Did he say anything to you as to where he had been or was going?"

Jo Ann nodded, sucking in tobacco again. "Asked me the road to the state line. Said he and his daughter were moving to the Colorado mountains. I knew better. He just wanted an easy fuck, and the girl probably needed the money. Oh, well, that what the Big Tex is good at. A quick piece of pussy and ten dollars for the room."

Jo Ann stared at Sarah to get her reaction. Sarah didn't move.

"But he paid twenty-five for the room overnight," Jo Ann continued. "I figured the girl would do him several times for that much. But none of my business."

Sarah realized Henry Lee Lucas was fucking the girl, then her, then the girl. She felt ill and excused herself after thanking the woman for her time.

"You bet," Jo Ann said. "And good luck finding him. Stay safe. No need to let the fucker kill another woman."

Sarah choked back the vomit as she went to Pete's

room. "I think he must have left town last night or early this morning, heading toward Dumas and probably on to Colorado," she told him. "You feeling okay?"

"Yes, Pete nodded. "Let's get him! Olivia, get your stuff. It's time to go."

Olivia was asleep again. Pete and Sarah loaded her into the backseat. She would track the monster down, Sarah reminded herself, and God would help her kill the scum.

Quickly pulling into a filthy convenience store, Sarah practically ran inside to buy three chocolate donuts, two large cartons of chocolate milk, and two coffees for her and Pete. Olivia never complained if chocolate was on the menu. Sarah's insides were trembling, as she had a foreboding she would see Henry again soon.

After breakfast, both Pete and Olivia fell asleep. Sarah suspected the trauma was taking its toll on her passengers. She felt guilty forcing them to go through the misery of tracking down a criminal. But certain God was guiding her, she told herself she'd never let anything happen to any of the Sears family again.

Driving north on the desolate highway between Amarillo and Dumas, Texas, Sarah briefly allowed herself to wallow in her own pity. Had she waited longer to marry, finished her education, or maybe even left small-town Texas, she wondered what she could have become. Daydreaming, she was startled when she thought she saw a highway patrol car up the road. But it had no lights on.

Slowing down as her sheriff's vehicle approached the black and white car, she noticed the officer slumped over the wheel. She veered off the two-lane road and backed up, waking Pete.

"What's going on?" Pete sounded concerned.

"Something's wrong!" Sarah was alarmed. "The officer in that car looks hurt or dead."

Sarah jumped out, pistol drawn, and approached the car. Pete also opened his door and climbed out slowly, gritting his teeth with pain.

Sarah slowly looked inside the front seat and saw a bullet wound in the officer's temple. Blood was running almost black through the congealed areas. Racing back to her car, she yelled at Pete, "He's dead. Get in, I need to call the Amarillo police. Dumas is not too far ahead."

Gunning the accelerator, Sarah knew Lucas was the perpetrator.

***

West Texas storms are also serial killers. They can destroy many lives and properties in brief moments. Dusty raindrops from a storm began to spatter on Sarah's windshield. The wind was picking up from the west, the most common direction of the deadliest twisters.

She continued to speed up the narrow lane toward the next civilization. Sarah's nerves were beginning to fray. Where was Lucas? She was getting desperate. Henry was a killing machine.

The wind was blowing harder now, making the rain a weapon of destruction. Sarah could hardly see through the windshield, but she didn't want to stop looking for Lucas before he killed again.

A slow freight train was parked on the highway overpass ahead. The engineer must have worried about the west Texas weather, Sarah concluded. Lightning was a danger for boxcars, often causing fires.

Sarah could see two cars parked under the concrete barrier, one on her side of the road and the other several hundred feet away on the other side. Lightning was striking nearby, and the wind was whipping the car to the side. She had to stop. Texas women like Sarah know how to shelter for a tornado: get out of your vehicle and get in a ditch. Glass windows are daggers in a windstorm.

Sarah pulled up behind one of the parked vehicles. Through the rain and blinding wind, she could see the car was blue, and a man was sitting behind the wheel. She instantly recognized Henry Lee Lucas. God had led her to him.

"Pete, it's him!" Sarah was scared and rattled. "I'm getting out, and I'll shoot him through the glass," Sarah told her husband, thinking it was raining too hard for Henry to identify her vehicle.

"Stop!" Pete begged his wife. "He could have his gun pulled. Don't, Sarah. I can kill him with my rifle." He was already reaching over the backseat to the floor underneath Olivia, who was waking up with all the noise.

"Olivia, hand me that rifle!" Pete demanded.

The dusty wind and rain together made a muddy paste covering the windshield. Every nerve ending in Sarah's body was on edge. She was breathing rapidly, praying to her God.

"Guide and protect me, Lord. I'm here because of you, to do your work!"

The passenger door of Sarah's car opened suddenly. Henry grabbed at Pete Sears. Sarah's husband was overtaken and instantly became a killer's hostage.

"Drop the gun, Sarah," Henry said. "You know I'll kill him and maybe take the girl just for fun, you ungrateful bitch. Maybe I'll just kill all of you."

Sarah knew to do what he said. This man lived to kill, and Pete was easy prey.

Henry reached inside the patrol car, grabbing Sarah's gun. "Get out, all of you!" he ordered. The wind was closing in, shaking the car side to side. "Get out!" Henry repeated as he stuck a knife next to Pete's neck and pulled Sarah toward him.

Henry yelled at Olivia, "You too, little cunt!"

The teen wouldn't budge. Olivia Sears would not obey this madman. Men had hurt her and her mother enough, she decided, and this monster would not control her.

With Sarah and Pete lying on the ground, Henry pointed the gun toward Olivia and threatened, "I'll kill you now!"

Darkness was approaching, and the storm clouds had completely covered the sun. The wind whipped the car, and rain pelted their bodies. Henry reached over the backseat, grabbing Olivia's neck. The car lurched sideways when the wind hit it broadside.

Henry fell back, his knife falling on the front floorboard.

Pete stood up and grabbed the knife. He flailed toward

Henry's body, stabbing him in the thigh as Henry yelped in pain.

Pete called to his wife, "Run, Sarah! Run toward the fence!"

Lucas regained his balance and aimed his gun toward Pete. Sarah was running through the mud toward a wire fence, baseball-sized hail pelting her, when she heard the shot. Turning to look at the massacre, she spotted Pete's body on the pavement.

Henry was coming after her, brandishing a gun and a knife. Sarah pulled the barbed wire fence apart and fell through the opening. He was getting close enough for a clean shot. Sarah knew that without God, she would die on a deserted stretch of highway, a tornado carrying her to Heaven.

Henry was cursing during the chase. He looked like a madman, his body being manipulated and contorted by the wind. He climbed through the fence and was just taking aim at Sarah when she heard a shot rip through the wind.

She ran a few more steps and realized she was not hit. Turning around, dreading the sight of the killer still coming toward her, she saw Henry Lee Lucas' body in the grass and mud. Hesitant to approach him, she was aware he had his weapons and was still dangerous. Henry's body didn't move. Wet sand covered his bloody shirt, and his back was oozing dark stains.

Sarah could make out his knife, but no gun.

Had her husband killed her lover? Sarah wondered. Was there another killer in the Sears family? Sarah kicked the knife out of the dead man's hand. She picked it up and staggered toward the car. How hurt was Pete, and was her daughter okay?

Her husband was still on the cement, but he was moaning. He was alive!

Olivia, blood on her dress, stood holding her dad's deer rifle, her body shaking. She dropped the gun and ran toward her mother.

"Is he dead?" Olivia cried..

"Olivia, did you shoot him?" Sarah asked.

"Yes, I'm not letting anyone hurt you or Daddy. Is he dead?"

***

ONE MONTH LATER

The Sears family arrived a few minutes late, sliding in the last pew of their home church in Nocona. Pete was sitting nearest the aisle. The young preacher, yet unaware of any sins committed by his parishioners, smiled toward the back of the church. Having a full house was his dream fulfilled.

For that moment, in that tiny town, Sarah Sears was at peace. At peace with her sins that God had forgiven. At peace with her husband, who no longer abused her. And at peace with her only child, who had lost her hate and learned to love.

The Texas sun burst through the stained-glass panes

behind the altar. Pete reached for Sarah's hand. A red-headed cardinal seated on the pecan tree limb outside the window chirped happily. Sarah felt that through this beautiful bird, God was sending her a message.

The church pianist stroked the keys, and the worshipers immediately stood. Sarah smiled as she easily recognized her favorite hymn, *How Great Thou Art*.

"Thank you, God, for allowing me to do your will," Sarah prayed silently. God was present this Sunday morning in Nocona, Texas, and for now, all was well.